Rave Reviews for Austin S. Camacho's
THE TROUBLESHOOTER

The author of this tale of derring-do unfolds the story line at the pace of an action movie. He also uses cinematic tricks to establish characters quickly. The technique is reminiscent of Tom Wolfe's Bonfire of the Vanities, with quick shifts from one locale to another.

John Goodspeed,
the Easton Star Democrat

This very enjoyable novel features tight writing plenty of action and intriguing characters. Some reviewers have mistakenly compared this author with Tom Clancy. A better comparison might be made between Hannibal Jones to the "Lucas Davenport" character of the Prey series by John Sandford. This author and his three mystery novels to date are well worth the read and worthy of a place on your bookshelf.

Kevin Tipple,
The Readers Room

Without a doubt, THE TROUBLESHOOTER is one of the most exciting and entertaining pieces of literature I have read in an extremely long time. Mr. Camacho's characters are gritty, realistic, and fascinating. The heart-pounding climax at the end of the novel will keep you reading late into the night!

Angela Etheridge,
Romance Reader's Connection

To Gwenn,
It was great to meet you!

THE TROUBLESHOOTER

by

Austin S. Camacho

Austin S. Camacho

Cover design by Cathi A. Wong

Published by:

Intrigue Publishing
7707 Shadowcreek Terrace
Springfield, VA 22153 USA
Telephone: 703-455-9062

Printed in the United States of America
Published April 2004

THE TROUBLESHOOTER

-1-

MONDAY

Raul thought he had seen it all before. The white Volvo 850 GLT slid precisely over to the curb. The thin guy getting out had honey colored skin, but not from the sun. He had on wraparound dark glasses. Black suede jacket. Sharp creased black slacks. Black driving gloves. And Raul knew that smile. A pimp, a high roller, or maybe one of those high class con men. It all fit, except for the walk.

He walked like a cop.

"I need to see Adolfo." The black guy, barely six feet tall, had to look up into Raul's eyes. Raul didn't wear shoulder pads under his gray suit coat, but his body made it look like he did. When he pulled himself to his full height, the other man was lost entirely in his shadow.

"Who the hell are you?"

"Jones," the newcomer replied. "Hannibal Jones. Got a message for Adolfo."

"Adolfo ain't seeing nobody today." Raul was stone faced, the very model of the professional tough guy. He was pleased with his image.

"He'll see me." The black guy started past. Raul laid a hand on his shoulder, covering it completely. He figured he could toss this guy all the way to the gutter with one arm.

Jones did not so much pull or toss Raul as simply fold under him. The bigger man rolled forward, landing hard and awkwardly, face up on the cement. By the time he lifted his head, Jones was jogging down the four steps to the door.

Hannibal stepped into the small office, staring through a haze of acrid cigar smoke. He smiled as he walked toward the desk at the back, past two more fullback types sitting on either side of the room. Both guards drew pistols and aimed at his back, but Jones kept his eyes on the short, round man at the rear desk.

"No guns, please, Adolfo, I just want to talk."

"Well, before the boys break something you might need, just who the hell are you?" Adolfo Espino tapped ash from his cigar. "I ain't seen you on the force, and I don't know you from the street."

Jones perched a hip on Espino's desk. "Look, I ain't a cop, I'm just here to help somebody avoid some trouble." He ran a gloved hand back through short, dark brown hair that was more wavy than kinky. "One of your customers wants to renegotiate his loan contract."

"Uh-huh." Espino's swivel chair creaked as he leaned back grinning. "Eddy. Nicky. Throw this asshole out."

The one called Eddy grabbed Hannibal's left arm with both hands, while his partner took the back of Hannibal's collar. Hannibal glanced left. Poor guy, he thought. He's had his nose broken too many times already.

"Hey, can't we talk about this?" Hannibal's training fed responses to this situation directly to his limbs without the need for conscious thought. His right fist snapped around, smashing Eddy's already flat nose. Hannibal's left arm swung around and forward, dragging Eddy with it. As Eddy's head crashed down into the desk, Hannibal's right foot lashed back at an angle, dislocating Nicky's right knee. The big man howled. Before Nicky hit the floor, Hannibal had Espino out of his chair by his collar.

"Now, let's chat a bit before the rest of your friends show up." Hannibal breathed directly into Espino's face and pressed the muzzle of his pistol into the right side of Espino's neck. He figured Espino would recognize the cold steel tube for what it was.

"Ray Santiago," Hannibal continued in a smooth, quiet voice. "Know him? He only owes you a grand. You hold the paper on some gambling debts."

"Yeah. Yeah I know him," Espino said, but Hannibal could see in his eyes that he had no idea who Ray Santiago was.

"Well, he's hit on hard times and he can't pay you all at once. So, tell you what. He'll go two hundred a week starting Friday, and an extra two bills at the end. Okay?"

Fear gave way to shock on Espino's face. Then the door slammed open. Hannibal glanced quickly over his shoulder. Three newcomers held automatics trained on him. Espino waved his hands to stop them where they stood.

"Put me down," Espino said slowly, staring into Hannibal's nearly opaque lenses. "Put me down and this don't have to get messy."

Hannibal paused just long enough to show he had to think about it, then slowly lowered Espino into his chair. Espino got comfortable before reaching into a desk drawer for a new cigar. It was a show of calm and control not lost on Hannibal.

"Put the guns up and close that door," Espino barked to his guards. As they did, Hannibal slid his own pistol into a shoulder holster under his right arm.

"Now, let me get this straight." Espino watched closely as Hannibal shoved his hands into his jacket pockets. "You're not trying to get this guy out of his debt, just arrange a payment schedule?"

"It would have been so simple if you had a listed phone number," Hannibal said, smiling into Espino's face with impossibly white teeth. He pointedly ignored the men behind him. "Mr. Santiago knows he owes the money. He just don't want your goon squad busting up his furniture while he's trying to pay you back. Or his face for that matter."

The loan shark could not help chuckling. "Well, boy, you got more balls than brains, that's for sure. How do I know he'll pay?"

"Because, my man," Hannibal leaned forward, pulled Espino's desk drawer open and plucked out a cigar. "I'll bring you your money personally, every Friday, without fail, until it's all paid up." He pulled a very small Swiss Army knife from his pocket and used its scissors to clip the end off his cigar. "Got a match?"

Espino signaled to one of his men, who tossed Hannibal a disposable lighter. "So, what happens if you don't show up?" he asked.

"Then you come talk to me," Hannibal said, pulling a leather case from an inside jacket pocket. "I'm a bit easier to find than you are." From the case Hannibal flipped a card onto the desk. Espino picked it up. The card bore Hannibal's name and the word "Troubleshooter" in big letters. Below that, an address in Alexandria, Virginia and a telephone number were listed.

"Hannibal Jones, eh? And you're not in from outside the Beltway," Espino said. "Funny I don't know you. Must be new in town."

"Not really. I've just been keeping a low profile." Hannibal held his smile, but his eyes prodded Espino's for an answer. After a brief silence Espino sighed, snorted and actually smiled back.

"Well, you're one crazy son of a bitch, but since you asked so nice, we'll try it your way."

"Cool." Hannibal drew on his cigar, tasting the sweet smoke before blowing out a long stream over Espino's head. "Do me a favor, huh? Let your doorman know I'm coming Friday so we don't go through this nonsense again."

-2-

Hannibal liked Cindy Santiago's home. She had lent character to her small, two-bedroom brick row house on the edge of Old Town Alexandria with subtle, if feminine decorating touches. Lacy cloths covered tables at each end of a big chintz sofa. Porcelain and crystal figurines crowded shadow boxes, the mantle and nearly every other surface in the room. Victorian artwork was carefully spaced on the walls, preventing a cluttered look, yet filling the house with flowers. He even caught a faint hint of the scent of wildflowers, probably provided by bowls of that strange confetti-looking stuff his mother had called potpourri.

He had removed his Oakley sunglasses when she answered the door. His hazel eyes held her attention for a moment, but she had let him in with a smile. After directing him to the couch she went to get her father.

When they returned they stopped in the living room doorway for a moment, giving Hannibal a brief chance to examine them side by side. Ray Santiago was short and bulky, while his daughter was tall and svelte, but that was hardly the only difference. He was almost bald, but she had carefully trimmed deep brown hair, hanging three or four inches below shoulder length. Her face glowed with anticipation of tomorrow, while her father's scowling visage implied a dread of what the next day would bring.

Of course, she was beautiful. Her Latin heritage showed in her high cheekbones, dark eyes and broad smile. She had a high, narrow waist, and he thought her form just a little top heavy. Ray, on the other hand, looked like what he was: an aging Cuban workman, wearing a lifetime of struggle on his face and starting to thicken around the middle.

"Cynthia..." Hannibal began.

"Cindy, please."

"Okay, Cindy. Could I please have a moment or two with your father? We have some..."

"Of course," she replied. "Man stuff. Go right ahead. I'll get coffee." She headed toward the kitchen, her hose swishing against her business suit's rust colored skirt. Her melodic humming supplied background music. Ray sat in the overstuffed chair at the far end of the couch. His dour face struck a stark counterpoint to the bright Latin tune Cindy hummed.

"What did he say, Hannibal?"

"He said you could pay in installments," Hannibal told him. "Two hundred a week for six weeks. No violence and no threats to your daughter."

Ray heaved a short-lived sigh, but then reality brought him up short.

"I thank you for all your help, Hannibal, but where will that leave me?" Ray asked. "Since I got fired from the cab company I haven't made a dime. I don't even know how I'll pay you. As it is, living here with... "

He stopped when Cindy returned carrying a silver server set. She placed the tray gently on her Queen Anne coffee table, then poured and prepared cups for three. While the men lifted their cups, Cindy picked up a remote control and switched on the large screen television on the entertainment center opposite her sofa.

"I don't mean to be rude," she said with an embarrassed smile, "but I really can't stand to miss the evening news. So, did you guys make any progress with, um, whatever it is you're working on?" Hannibal guessed she knew nothing about her father's problem. It was no surprise that Ray wouldn't want to share his problems with her.

"In fact, I was just about to ask your father for some help." He lifted the tiny cup, swallowing half its contents. "My business is growing, and I need a good courier who could double as a chauffeur. What do you say, Ray? Help a guy out?"

"You know, Papa, when I joined Nieswand and Balor right out of law school, it was a smaller firm." Cindy sat beside Hannibal, speaking to him directly now. "Three years ago their business law practice was all about small, new businesses. Just in time they plugged into the Internet startups that were still happening back then, and business in that area really exploded. Business law just happens to be my specialty. The firm has grown enormously, and I've grown right along with it." She turned back to her father. "If Mister Jones' investigative firm is moving up..."

"I'm afraid I can't offer much to start out," Hannibal told Ray. "How about three hundred a week?"

"It'll certainly help, Papa," Cindy put in. "Especially with your love of the ponies."

Hannibal leaned back into puffy cushions, suppressing a smile. "Yes, I believe that's what originally brought your father and me together."

Like most men, his eyes were easily drawn by beauty or disaster. In an effort to keep from staring at Cindy Santiago he looked at the glowing screen across the room, which momentarily arrested his attention. The show she was watching showed firemen battling a fierce blaze in a set of close set brick buildings. Then he remembered that Cindy was a self-confessed news junkie. He wasn't watching a drama, but what appeared to be live footage. He slowly sat forward as recognition pulled him nearer the television.

"I don't see how I can say no to such a generous offer," Ray said. "When do you want me to start?"

"Right now!" Hannibal snapped, bouncing to his feet. "That's my apartment complex burning down!"

-3-

Ray pulled Hannibal's Volvo as near the fire trucks as he could, while a policeman tried to wave him away. Hannibal popped the passenger door and dived out of his car before it had quite stopped. Behind him, Ray pulled away, looking for someplace to park. The parking lot was cordoned off, fire trucks parked at odd angles cutting off all access. Hannibal marveled at the night air's clarity, the soft summer breeze carrying none of the thick smoke he saw rising straight up from his building. The shouts of emergency personnel completely overrode the roaring of the blaze. He did not think of cash, credit cards or furniture as he ran for the door. His mind was on his papers, his records, and his computer disk files, which are the heart and soul of any investigator's business. He needed to save those records, and that one photograph.

"Hold it man." A firefighter's hand clamped on his shoulder so hard it turned him around. "You nuts? You can't go in there."

"Look, I..." Hannibal reached for his wallet before he remembered he no longer carried the kind of ID that would guarantee him access through police lines. "Look, there's stuff in there I got to get. I won't get myself killed, I promise."

While he talked, he was backing slowly away. When he turned he fell into a dead run, dodging around two men wrestling with a high power hose, finally throwing himself through his building's outer door.

Inside, he tried to ignore the smell of burning plastic and wires. Stark shadows gave the hall a haunted house look, lighted only by dancing flames. Darkness dominated the end toward his apartment. No fire had reached that area yet. He figured he could reach his rooms, gather an armload of valuable papers and disks, and escape before he was in any real danger.

"Mommy?" That one word, spoken in a little girl voice, so out of place, rooted his feet to the spot. It came from behind him, back there, toward the wall of heat.

Well, so what? He was no firefighter, or policeman, or rescue worker.

His mind flashed a quick message about his hand made Italian shoes, his suede jacket. But he shrugged and turned around.

After ten steps toward the fire, he was bathed in sweat. Facing a wall of dense smoke he called out "Where are you honey?"

"I want my Mommy," the little girl's voice replied. Despite the crackling flames, it was enough for him to locate the door. His eyes had begun to burn, and the stench of paint peeling back with the flames stung his nose. Still, hurrying could prove fatal for him and his target. After pulling off his jacket, he pressed his hands against the apartment door. Warm, but not hot. Sending up a silent prayer, he tried the door, giving thanks when the knob turned.

Acrid smoke belched out as he pushed the door inward. He dropped to his knees, gagging. With tearing eyes he stared around, searching for the other person in the apartment.

"Come on out, honey," he called between hacking coughs. A gray cloud hung a foot off the floor. He lay flat on the thin carpet to get a breath.

"I want my mommy," the plaintive voice insisted. "Where's Mommy?"

Probably arguing with a policeman, he thought crazily, being told it was too dangerous to reenter a burning building.

But he had a directional fix now, and crept across the carpet toward the girl. The place was set up like his apartment, so she would have to be in the smaller bedroom.

At the doorsill he scanned the room. The furniture was all pink and white, with a desk and chairs in miniature. Beneath the dust ruffle around the bed's edge he spotted two blue orbs, not an inch apart. In them he could see the girl was far too terrified to come out on her own.

A wall nearby cracked like a gunshot, and the fire's roar suddenly seemed closer. Hannibal dashed on hands and knees across the room. His right arm stabbed under the bed, his hand wrapping completely around a thin arm. With one quick yank he had the girl out and in his lap.

"Well, hi," Hannibal said with the brightest voice he could field. He wrapped his jacket around the girl's narrow shoulders. She was five or six years old, he guessed, with blonde hair trimmed above shoulder length and teeth a little too big for her mouth. "What's your name, honey?"

Something broke behind her eyes and the girl began screaming, a new scream with each breath. Still, she did not struggle, which he greatly appreciated as he wriggled his arms under her and pushed himself into a low crouch. He had seen soldiers low crawl this way with a rifle cradled in their arms the way he was holding the girl now.

He dashed blindly through the living room. He was on his feet when he left the apartment, hugging he child to his chest. The hallway was a tube of even thicker smoke, completely filled, but he did not need to see. His right side felt as if he was standing beside an open oven door. He simply trotted away from the heat, following a mental picture of his building to estimate the distance to the outer door. After bumping his shoulder against a wall twice, he seemed to almost fall sideways, then down three steps to the walk.

His eyes burned terribly, he was wracked with coughing spasms and his arms were getting tired. He staggered on for a dozen steps, afraid to stop for fear of falling. Then a high piercing wail of "My baby!" penetrated his ears, and the girl's weight was lifted from him. Two pairs of strong hands grabbed his arms and lowered him into a seated posture with his back against a truck wheel. Someone pressed a plastic mask over his mouth and nose.

Three deep breaths of oxygen cleared his head and energized him. He forced his eyes open, letting the sharp summer breeze clear them as he stared at his whole world literally floating away on a cloud of smoke.

And then he realized he was sitting in a pool of cold water.

-4-

When Ray walked into the house, he found Cindy perched on the edge of the sofa, eyes riveted on a News Channel Eight report on the fire. She wore a powder blue peignoir over a nightgown that stopped high on her bare legs. He wished she wouldn't dress like that when he was there. As he closed the door she turned toward him, one eyebrow cocked.

"So where is he?"

"Hannibal? He got a motel room."

"Oh." She sipped from a wide mug of coffee. "I just thought you'd bring him back here after."

"Good thing I didn't," Ray called from the kitchen, getting his own coffee. "You dressed like that. Or should I say undressed."

Cindy was on her feet to greet her father when he returned from the kitchen.

"I'm not a little girl anymore, Papa." Her hands on her hips forced her shoulders into a defiant shrug. "I love you, but this is my house and I'm not going to be uncomfortable in it. Now, is it true what they're saying on the TV? Did he really run into the burning building to save a little girl?"

"It happened like that," Ray said. "I think he's loco."

Cindy settled back into the sofa. She cradled her mug in both hands, filling her lungs with the aroma of the strong

Cuban brew. A warm smile lit her face. "So, just where did you meet this Hannibal Jones? He's no street hustler."

"Oh, you mean like the low lifes I usually hang out with, is that it?" Ray dropped heavily into the easy chair and kicked off his shoes. "Well, one of the boys down at the dispatch office gave me his card."

"You still going down there?" Cindy asked, her brows lowering menacingly. "Papa they fired you because they had too many drivers to keep busy. They're not going to take you back on unless things get a whole lot better than they are now."

"Jocinta you do not understand," Ray said.

"Cindy please, Papa. Why must you call me by that name?"

"I call you Jocinta because it is your name," Ray snapped. "It is a good, solid traditional Spanish name, with no H in it. And it is the name your mother gave you, God rest her soul. It is a tie to your past that you don't want, which is why you don't understand." He sat forward to make his point. "I go down there, as you say, because my friends are there. I like to be surrounded by other Cubanos and speak my own language. I'm not running from it like you. And also because it's good to smell the grease and the fumes. And because I like to be around men who are earning a living. It makes me feel..." He stopped because she was no longer listening. Her eyes had strayed back to the file footage of the blazing buildings lighting the television screen.

"I wonder what made him do it."

"Some people just like to help," he offered. "Not everybody wants to run away from all the bad things in life."

Cindy turned, stung by his remark. "Oh, like I don't want to help my people? Is that what you're saying, Papa? I know. You think I should have stayed in the neighborhood and been a nothing all my life. Papa, the whole reason I wanted to get away was so I could get into a position to help. I beg for pro bono work, helping our people start their own businesses, and then helping them hang on to them. They let me do way more than an associate at my level should dare to expect. And I contribute to..."

"It's not all about money, child. Like what Hannibal did tonight. Money and position didn't save that girl. You know, he told me he used to be some kind of government agent or something."

She sat back, her eyes turning inwardly dreamy again. "Really? A government agent. Well, maybe too many years in public service infected him with a compulsion to help others."

"Sounds like an infection all right." He swallowed a big gulp of coffee and watched firemen pointing their tiny hoses at the giant blaze. "That's the kind of virus that might turn out to be fatal some day."

-5-
TUESDAY

Hannibal's white Volvo eased into the left lane as it left Alexandria, heading north. In front of him, he saw Ray smiling in the rear view mirror, and watched him weave effortlessly through the stream of cars. He guessed Ray had driven a cab across this stretch of the George Washington Memorial Parkway countless times, taking fares to the Ronald Reagan Washington National Airport that they would pass in five minutes. Traffic wouldn't really get bad until they reached the ramp onto the Fourteenth Street Bridge, which crossed the Potomac into the District.

There had been an awkward moment when Ray arrived to pick Hannibal up. Hannibal hadn't really thought about how it would feel to have someone else drive his car. But a deal was a deal, so he nodded good morning to Ray and dropped into the passenger seat beside him. The Volvo sat still, idling, and it took Hannibal a second to realize that something was wrong. He turned an inquiring eye toward his new driver.

"Hannibal," Ray said, staring straight ahead, "I been driving cabs and limos for a long time now. I'm really a lot more comfortable if I have the front seat to myself. I mean, passengers usually ride in the back, you know."

Hannibal didn't want Ray to feel like an employee or a servant. Still, he did want him to feel as if he was earning the money that he'd get at the end of the week, so he climbed out and moved to the back. Later, when they pulled to the curb in front of Cindy's townhouse, she had slid in beside him without a second thought.

Now she sat next to him, bubbling like a talk show host in her navy blue power suit, perfectly made up with her hair tied back. In the opposite corner he absorbed the verbal and psychic energy she sent flying at him. He sat in his black suit and gloves, staring straight ahead at the Washington Monument, a white target marker in the distance.

"You know what your problem is?" Cindy asked, but left no space for an answer. "You're too darned used to things going your way. Think you're the only person ever put out of their home because of a fire? You had insurance right? Besides, after last night, you're a hero. That'll bring you business galore. Cheer up, for God's sake."

Hannibal thought of earlier hours of the morning, before Cindy had joined him in his car. He remembered walking through sodden, charred ruins in the dawn light. Furniture and decorations, the artifacts of people's lives, were made brittle by the fire and crackled beneath his shoes. The relics of his own existence had fared no better. His computer and disks were now slag and trash. Paper files and records, protected from the heat by a steel file cabinet, had been converted to lumps of pulp by well-intentioned firemen hosing down the building.

The only item he salvaged from his entire apartment was the woman's photograph, found face down, its brass cameo-shaped frame intact. Even that moment was soured by the look Ray gave him when he noticed the woman's blond hair. With all this on his mind, his eyes, mostly brown now, slowly rotated left, bringing the girl into focus. "Cynthia..."

"Cindy, please," she corrected him.

"Cindy. I'm homeless. Everything I own is on me or in the trunk. And I don't have a case right now. They were hard enough to get, new to the business, without even an office.

They'll be damned hard to get without an office or a phone. Or an address. This is not a time for celebration."

"You know, you get quite eloquent when you're pissed off," Cindy said with a smile. "Lucky for you, you happened to fall in with a real problem solver. We'll fix all that up this morning. Mister Balor's a big real estate developer now. I'm sure he'll give you a place."

Hannibal stared out his window, trying to keep his pessimism to himself. His mood seemed to match that of the commuters around him. Despite the traffic's density, Washington drivers did not use their horns like New Yorkers. They were as resigned to this part of their lives as they were to the gridlock inside the government buildings they passed. He watched old landmarks flow past as they inched down Fourteenth Street. The Bureau of Engineering on the left. Agriculture on the right. The pretentious Commerce Department building.

"The old neighborhood," he mumbled to himself.

"You're from here?" Cindy asked, apparently trying to draw him into conversation.

"Not really." He leaned forward to look past her. "Before I went out on my own, my work was my life. For eight years my whole world was right over there, between the White House and the Treasury Department building." Cindy turned to look. The two white marble structures stood practically next door to one another.

"It must have been a small world," Cindy said quietly.

"You some kind of treasury agent?" Ray asked. "A tax guy or something?"

Cindy sighed heavily with her eyes closed. "I rather doubt it, Papa, but I believe the Secret Service works out of the Treasury Department. That sounds more like Hannibal's style." Then she realized where they were. "Down that ramp," she ordered her father. "We'll park under the building."

They drove under an older sandstone structure, newly renovated, tall by Washington standards since skyscrapers are forbidden by law in the city. Cindy pressed an identification badge against a magnetic plate and nodded to the smiling teenager in a glass booth as the wooden arm rose. They rolled into a manmade cave beneath the capital city's streets.

Ray parked in an unmarked space and they all got out. Cindy pointed toward a door and walked off, her heels clicking on concrete. Hannibal followed, making no sound. Ray looked at them, and then looked down at his windbreaker, canvas pants, and rubber soled shoes.

"You two go take care of business," he called. "I'll catch a nap in the car."

A short elevator ride took Hannibal and Cindy to a richly appointed suite of offices. Audubon prints adorned the walls. They combined with fresh cut flowers to give the outer office an atmosphere much like the den in someone's home. Hannibal wondered why a law office would want people to feel as if they were visiting old friends. As they brushed past the receptionist, he slid his wraparound shades into place and tightened his gloves. Cindy pointed him to a vinyl chair while she went into the biggest of the offices.

Hannibal noted the antiseptic smell law offices always had, try as they might to seem homey. He could think of lots better places than a lawyer's office to sit for even a few minutes. Feeling like an invader, he smiled at the receptionist. She was a mature woman with her hair up in a bun, more likely referred to as an administrative assistant or office manager than a secretary. She looked like a pretty effective gatekeeper, and Hannibal anticipated a lengthy wait while Cindy somehow smuggled him past this barrier.

To his surprise, Cindy returned in less than a minute. She had stashed her genuine smile in her purse, replacing it with an imitation she used for business. "Mister Balor will see you now, Mister Jones." She waved him inside. He walked toward the big desk, but stopped just inside the door.

They entered a room paneled in dark maple, which matched the wide desk. Deep carpet, heavy drapes at the windows and waffled ceiling tiles absorbed sounds that would normally bounce off the walls.

It was a huge office, but the man behind the desk filled it. He was wide but not fat, medium height with too much thick, pepper-colored hair and way too much eyebrow. Bright brown eyes beneath all that dared you to say so.

"Dan Balor," he snapped, as if that explained everything. His handshake was fierce and strong. "You're Jones. Santiago tells me you lost your apartment in that terrible fire in Alexandria last night."

"That's right," Hannibal replied. He remained standing because Balor did. "I understand you might have one available."

"Let me call my building manager." Balor pushed a preset button on his executive telephone. While it dialed itself, he said "You saved a little girl's life last night."

"Miss Santiago exaggerates." Hannibal smiled, folding one gloved hand around the other.

"Maybe. I don't think the Post does, though. Except about Democrats."

After four rings, a gruff voice came over the speakerphone. "Balor properties, this is Mick."

"Mick? Balor. I need an apartment for somebody. What we got vacant?"

"Not a thing, boss," Mick answered. "All twelve buildings, all full up." After four seconds of dead air, he added "Course there's the place over the river where the ni..."

"We're on the speaker, Mick."

"Oh." The gruff voice softened a degree. "Sorry, boss."

"Across the river?" Hannibal asked.

"It's over in Anacostia," Balor said, waving the place away. "You can't live there. Nobody can."

"Why?" Hannibal stepped a few inches closer to Balor's desk. "Neighborhood too rough? Or too good?"

"Oh, no, it's not that." Balor suddenly realized Hannibal's meaning. Even through his Oakley's Hannibal held Balor's eyes, his skepticism clear. Finally, Balor dropped into his chair, bringing one hand to his face. He seemed to think a moment, and then looked up at Hannibal with the kind of openness one seldom sees on an attorney's face.

"Look, I bought this place cheap from HUD," Balor said. "Planned to renovate it. Now it's full but I can't collect any rent."

"I don't get it," Hannibal said, but he backed off and eased himself into the surprisingly comfortable visitor's chair.

"It's six apartments," Balor explained, "what we used to call railroad flats, in kind of a run down neighborhood. I figured if I fixed it up I could make it some low income housing, you know?"

"Sure, and it's full, so why can't you collect?" Hannibal asked.

Balor almost chuckled. "It's full of squatters. I think the place is a crack house, and I can't get them out."

Hannibal sat quite still, except for his left hand's middle finger, which tapped rhythmically on the arm of the chair. "Why haven't you called the police to move them out?"

"Do I look stupid?" Balor snapped, louder than he intended. "The police were my first stop. They won't do a damned thing. I got a court order for those schmucks to vacate the premises, but they won't go in and drag them out. That place is costing me money every month, and I get back zip."

"Well, then, maybe I can help." Hannibal pulled his card case from an inside jacket pocket, and dropped a card on Balor's desk.

"Thanks, pal," Balor picked up the card, "but you haven't seen the place. I already tried two detectives. They drove by and said the job's too dangerous."

"Sounds like real trouble," Hannibal said, standing up. "That's my specialty."

Balor looked at his visitor quizzically. He was thin, wiry, sharply dressed, but something in his manner said he could handle whatever came his way.

"You're not just a private eye, are you?"

"I'm not really a detective, although I do have a private investigator's license. And I'm not a bodyguard, although I have been known to protect people from danger. And I'm not a strong-arm man, but I do sometimes have to fight on the job."

"So what the hell are you?" Balor asked.

"Like the card says, man. I'm a troubleshooter. I help people out of tight spots."

Balor stared hard at the card for a moment, then raised his gaze to the light skinned black man sitting in front of his desk. Hannibal held a thin smile, radiating confidence. Balor spent a full minute making a decision. Hannibal stayed silent, his dark lenses staring out at the lawyer. Finally, Balor stood, extending a hand.

"If you think you can clear the squatters out, I'll hire you on the spot, pal. I like the look of you."

Hannibal met Balor's strong handshake. "I can take care of it, probably inside of a week. But I ain't cheap."

"Name it."

"I get five hundred a day, plus expenses," Hannibal said. "I sometimes need to subcontract specialists. They get paid separately. No questions, no restrictions, and I don't leave the job until it's done. Deal?"

"Done." Balor slapped a palm on his desk. "Santiago, draw up a contract like he says. Jones, by the time you reach my office manager's desk there'll be a two day retainer waiting for you, with the building's address."

-6-

A bright lance of sunshine stabbed into Hannibal's eyes, making him push his Oakley's back into place. His courtesy call at the police station had been as frustrating as expected, but he had to verify their awareness of the issues concerning Balor's property. With that errand out of the way he tried to get comfortable in his own back seat on his way to see the house in person. He really preferred to drive himself because he loved the way the Volvo handled, but now he had a chauffeur, at least for a few weeks. Anyway, it would hardly have mattered in the traffic, thick as shag carpet, flowing over the Douglas Memorial Bridge. They were crossing the Anacostia River, into the part of the District of Columbia carved out of Maryland.

They were nearing the far end of the bridge when Ray cleared his throat. "Hannibal, I realize most of what you give me will go to that loan shark, but what about you and me? I mean, Cindy, she told me you told Balor you get five hundred a day for solving people's problems. How can I..."

"She told you right," Hannibal said. "Five hundred dollars a day. That breaks down to sixty-five dollars an hour, which is just about how long your job took me. I'll take it out of your seventh week's check. Okay?"

After a long pause, Ray said "Gracias, mi amigo." Then he took a deep breath and sat a bit straighter. A moment later, in a lighter voice, he asked "So what did the cops say, anyway?"

"What I expected," Hannibal answered, leaning forward in the back seat. "Nothing they can do. No real crime being committed. Not enough manpower for stuff like this. And didn't I know how many murders and robberies they had to deal with, and, eh, like that."

"In other words, they just jerked you around."

"Basically," Hannibal said. "You know where you're going, right?"

Ray pulled off the highway, stopped at a red light under an overpass and craned his neck. "I been driving a cab in this town for five years, Chico. Say, Hannibal, you really think this gig is dangerous?"

"Well, let's see." Hannibal looked around to orient himself as the light changed and the 850 GLT pulled smoothly forward. "Down there. W Street, not a mile from here. A pair of brothers was shot to death Sunday in the sixteen hundred block. Both in their twenties. Family dispute, they called it."

"How you know that shit?" Ray slowed to let an old man cross the street at his own pace.

"There's a homicide within a block of here two or three times a week, I bet. I read the papers pretty close." He did not add that too often, when he read about murders he was reading about this part of the city. He knew Washington D.C. was a totally unique city, and some linked its oddities in different ways. It led the nation in violent crime most years, but did that stem from having a seventy- percent black population? Or could the crime rate have some connection to its gun control laws, the nation's strictest, preventing law abiding citizens from defending themselves. Or did being the central gathering place for America's politicians just make the town predisposed to violence?

As they approached their destination, he leaned back to absorb the neighborhood. In southeast D.C., the community was more like ninety percent black. There was not much activity on the streets during daylight. Here, old men still wore hats that matched their suits, worn shiny with age. Fashions for younger men included knit hats, he noticed, usually in red, black and green. The ladies still looked sharp, and most walked like they knew it.

Streets here were narrow, lined with sandstone row houses with red or gray exteriors. A few trees stood on each block, looking malnourished.

Ray pulled to the curb near the corner, put the car in park and lit a cigarette. "We're here, boss." He powered down the window. "Up there, second from the end."

"Uh-huh." Hannibal slid his sunglasses off and sat for a moment, apparently staring into space. In fact, he was scanning the street, exploring the environment before he threw himself into it. The target building was red brick and three stories tall with a basement showing a couple of feet above ground, just like every other building on that side of the block. On either side of the door, the front of the building bowed forward, like towers at the corners of a castle. Stone steps led up to the door.

Slanted stone walls stood in for railings on both sides of the steps, then continued to the building's front wall, closing in the stoop. A young man in a wife-beater undershirt sat on the left side of that stone wall, staring vacantly across the street. Hannibal knew that empty look. Cocaine did that to a man, about halfway between the immediate rush and the gnawing hunger at the other end.

In front of the tower-like curved walls small patches of long uncut grass waved. A low chain link fence contained the one on the left. Untrimmed knee high hedges enclosed the lawn square on the right. From looking at the grass, he guessed the building on the end was also abandoned. A cement path, maybe a yard wide, separated the building from its neighbors.

When he popped his door open, he heard the front door open as well. He had almost forgotten anyone else was around.

"Want some backup?" Ray asked.

"No, man, I'm more worried about the car in this neighborhood. Won't be a minute, anyway. Just a little recon."

Hannibal started toward the corner, staying across the street from the target house. Halfway down the block he was about to cross the street when a young voice caught his attention.

"Ain't seen you before."

He turned to face a boy sitting on the porch of an older single family house. He had a chocolate bar complexion and very short hair. His Redskins jacket was a size or two too big. Deep brown eyes shone with intelligence, but his mouth reflected a wary distrust of the world, probably born of experience.

"No, you haven't," Hannibal said. "My name's Hannibal."

"You Booolshittin'. Hannibal, like that dude in the movies that eats people?"

Hannibal chuckled. "No, like the general from Carthage who whipped the Roman legions with elephants in his army around two hundred B.C." After watching the blank look on the boy's face for a few seconds, Hannibal smiled as he would at an old friend. "I'm moving into that house up there. What's your name?"

"They call me Monty," the boy said, his face impassive. "You don't want to go in there."

"Really? Why not?"

"The Man runs that house." Monty started playing with a deck of cards. "Grandma says stay away from there. You could get hurt."

"Thank you, Monty. I still have to check it out, but I appreciate your warning."

Hands in pockets, Hannibal crossed the street and walked, neither slow nor fast, to the second house from the end. On the sidewalk, he slid his shades back into place. When he got halfway up the stairs the man on the stoop noticed him. The door guard, at least Hannibal figured that was his job, had very dark skin, with chipmunk cheeks and hair cut in a flat top. The whites of his eyes were lined and yellowed. His ashy right hand snaked down to close around the neck of a ball bat at his side.

"What you looking for, Jim?" he slurred.

Hannibal smiled pleasantly, leaving his hands in his pockets. "I'm from urban renewal, just checking out the real estate."

"I'm about to urban renewal your fucking head. Drag your narrow ass out of here."

"I'm not looking for any trouble, Bro." Hannibal backed off a step. "Just need to look around."

"Well then you just look the fuck around some fucking where else, dick head." Chipmunk Cheeks stood up. He was an inch shorter than Hannibal, but wider by enough to count.

"This is not starting well." Hannibal's voice grew more serious. "Can we talk about this? You need a break." His right foot crossed over his left, then swung in a high, wide arc across his body. Halfway through its journey it raked across the jaw of the man facing him. Chipmunk Cheeks dropped like a felled oak, slowly at first, then gaining speed until he toppled over the wall onto the small lawn. Hannibal took one hand out of his pocket and opened the door.

The hall seemed unnecessarily wide. A stairway with a heavy banister wound its way up the middle. One long row of rooms ran down each side of the building, each with its own door to the hall. He saw five doors on each side, but it looked as though the three in the middle were painted shut. Railroad flats. At one time the rooms were probably rented out separately. He tried to imagine what the building had looked like in its original form, when it was a single family residence. Time, and too many poor residents, had reduced the once-proud house to it lowest possible use and now he would have to probe its dirty little secrets and peer into its most embarrassing corners. He figured he might as well start at the bottom.

He found the door on his right unlocked, so he walked in. It was dark inside and the stench of urine burned his nose. Someone had boarded up the front windows on this side of the building. A small man in a tattered coat lay huddled against the front wall, under the two big windows. Inches away, two others lay curled in balls, with two empty wine bottles lying between them. Still, a sense of emptiness almost overwhelmed Hannibal. This appeared to be a haven for homeless winos.

Pink flowered wallpaper was crumbling from the walls, and the tile floor was chipped in several places. The two big sliding doors to the next room stood open. From the middle of that front room he could see through the other four to the back door. Each room had a door to the hall.

Across the hall the door was locked. He knocked politely and waited. A flurry of motion started behind the door, ending in a harsh voice calling "Who's there?"

"Meter man," Hannibal replied. More profanity came through the door, and more shuffling. Then a lock was thrown and the door slid open on a short chain. A beak like black nose poked through the space. Above it two wild eyes glowed. Beneath it hung a short revolver barrel, pointing at Hannibal's face.

-7-

Ray would rather have been walking into that building with Hannibal than leaning against his car at the curb. He was thinking of ignoring his instructions and following anyway, when a weathered Dodge pulled down the street and stopped in front of him. Only the light on the roof marked it as a taxicab. Its window cranked down and a thin Puerto Rican face poked out. Ray smiled in recognition.

"Yo, Nestor. Como estas?"

"Not good as you, Ray, from what I can see." The driver cut his eyes at the Volvo. "That yours? Nice ride, amigo. You using it for a chauffeur job?"

"Hey, it's a living," Ray answered. "But what about you? I thought you were through with that cab company."

"Soon, man, that's why I stopped. Me and Mal are looking at starting our own cab company. Sure like to have you with us."

Ray's eyes lit up and, for a moment, he forgot the string of bad luck that had dogged him since he lost his job. "I'm your man, Nestor. What'll it take."

"We can do this if the three of us do all the work ourselves, at least at first, and if we each bring three, maybe four grand." Ray's face fell a bit, then brighten again. "Well, give me a call next week and we'll see what we can put together."

Ray's ready smile faded as he watched Nestor's beat up car roll away. He knew he could get the money from his daughter, but he would never ask her such a thing. He was the parent, after all. And he would never gather even so small a sum of money driving Hannibal around town. In fact, he considered, he might not even collect his first week's pay if his employer got himself killed in that crumbling wreck of a house.

-8-

"Let me see your hands." The high-pitched voice came from under the wild eyes behind the door. "You don't look like you ought to be here."

"I was just thinking the same thing about you." Hannibal raised his hands to chest level. "Can I come in and look around? Obviously I'm not a cop."

"You sure as hell ain't no junkie," the gunman replied. "You the new mule? You got the stuff?"

"Maybe. You got the money?"

"I got the fucking gun." Wild Eyes flashed crooked teeth.

"Too true." Hannibal's left hand flicked out and closed around Wild Eyes' wrist. Hannibal tugged hard, fully extending the man's arm and pulling it through the space between the door and doorsill. Wild Eyes' face smashed into the door, slamming it on his arm. The pistol clattered to the floor. Raising his right foot, Hannibal kicked out with all he had, snapping the chain with a pathetic "tink" sound and sending Wild Eyes sprawling across the room.

This apartment looked just like the one across the hall, except no old men lay huddled in a drunken sleep. The third room revealed three bodies curled up on a double mattress lying on the floor. The fourth room was empty and the room farthest back was a kitchen.

Hannibal's stomach flipped and he burst into a sticky sweat under his clothes. This was the shooting gallery, the center of this tiny community. A woman thin as a television Somali sat on a folding chair in front of the stove, holding a spoon over a red electric coil. Her partner, his arm tied off with a catheter, was drawing a long needle out of the crook of his elbow. Oblivious to Hannibal, he filled the syringe from the spoon and handed it to the girl.

Hannibal had somehow fended off the smell of filth, the roaches, the trash thrown indiscriminately about. He had purposely not reacted to these things but now, with this sight, they all crashed in on him at once and his lunch pushed up into his throat. Refusing to throw up, he turned to go.

Fighter's intuition pulled his face back out of the arc of Wild Eyes' swinging right fist. Then instinct took over and he counterattacked. Right jab, a left hook and a side kick, in a seamless combination, without thought. He was bouncing on his toes when Wild Eyes collapsed, unconscious, on the dirty tile floor.

Bouncing in a circle also brought him around to face the stove. The girl had snatched a pair of scissors and was advancing slowly with them poised overhead like a dagger. Well, Hannibal didn't want to slap the crap out of her too, and he did have an alternative. He stopped his legs and reached under his right shoulder for his forty caliber Sig Sauer P229 automatic.

The woman froze, gradually lowering her scissors. Her eyes were those of a frightened child whose father had just pulled off his belt.

"What the hell is this?" she muttered, close to tears.

"This?" he asked, shaking his gun for emphasis while holding it in a two handed FBI grip. "Consider this your eviction notice. Now get your friends and your shit together and blow. I'm going upstairs, and when I get back, I expect you and your pals to be in the wind. Dig?"

She nodded. Her shooting partner started gathering their heroin and the tools of its use together, shoving things into his pockets. Hannibal backed through the kitchen's door to the hall, not holstering his gun until he was out of the room.

The staircase, like the hall, seemed wider than necessary. Despite his light tread, an echo followed him up. At the top he could hear rhythmic grunting from the left. A simple slam lock secured the front door. From his wallet, he drew a credit card. At least, it was the shape and size of a credit card, bearing all the expected color and lettering. The only real difference was that it was made of steel. He slipped the metal sliver between the door and its jamb, popping the door open.

On a bare mattress in the middle of the floor, a leggy girl, maybe seventeen, was trying to earn a living. She looked up, but her customer continued his desperate thrusts. Her face showed no fear or anger, or even embarrassment. It was more a pleading expression, begging him not to cause trouble.

Her face, unspoiled yet ruined, made Hannibal swallow hard. He backed away silently, pulling the door closed. After a couple of deep breaths, he tried a door across the hall. It opened, but the first room was empty. He picked up a sharp smell he did not recognize. Stepping silently forward, he peered through the two big doors to the next room. Twenty square panes of glass in two big doors separated him from a circle of young people, male and female, black and white. A small pipe moved from hand to hand, each person drawing on it as it moved, often relighting it. Disgusted, he returned to the hall.

"A shooting gallery, a hooker's crash pad and a crack house," He told himself on his way upstairs. "God, what else?"

The top floor's first flat was empty, end to end. He soon understood why. The toilet did not work, but someone, or perhaps several people, had insisted on using it anyway, until no one could stand to enter the bathroom.

Hip-hop music slipped under the last apartment's front door. Maybe, he thought, someone's in this house who isn't among the living dead. Shrugging, he again turned the knob and pushed open the door.

He took it all in very quickly. This room was well lighted, on electricity pirated from somewhere. It looked like a warehouse for televisions, VCRs and stereo equipment of all brands and descriptions. On the right, a black man with a crinkly beard and shaved head sat at a cheap metal dining table. The table held an assortment of equipment including soldering gear, files and a power sander. The man at the table was busy removing the identification plate from a boom box. He looked up briefly, snapped his fingers, and went back to work.

With a sound more roar than growl, a pit bull bigger than Hannibal imagined they grew flashed across the floor from the next room. Terror gripped his brain as he slammed the door shut and backed against the banister, his heart pounding and his hands shaking from the sudden adrenaline dump. He jumped at what had to be the sound of the dog hitting the door.

That was enough for one day.

-9-

Cindy Santiago opened the car door, tossing a briefcase in ahead of herself. As her hips sank into the upholstery, Hannibal thought he saw weariness on her face but as she turned toward him, it vanished.

"Well, how did the new detective team spend its day?" Cindy asked, situating her briefcase behind her calves.

"I spent the afternoon filling up my credit cards replacing my wardrobe," Hannibal said dryly. "You're almost twenty minutes late."

"Secretaries get nine to five jobs." Cindy eased out of her shoes. "I'm a professional, just like you. Oh, and you're welcome for steering you to the job."

"You really want to help me out, find me an apartment while I'm working it."

"He looked at Mister Balor's Southeast property today," Ray said while steering the 850 GLT out of the parking garage and into rush hour traffic. Darkness hung at the edge of the city, held at bay by street lamps and headlights. "Hey, it's got everything, you know? Crack. Heroin. Bums. Killer dogs. And, er..."

"Yes?" Cindy pressed. "What else could there be?"

Hannibal had no intention of bailing out his driver, but in the darkness Cindy's sweet woman scent reached him, and he wanted to talk to her.

"He means there was a woman. A woman of negotiable virtue."

"Negotiable? Oh. I see. A whore."

That brought a choking sound from Ray, and Hannibal's first real smile in several hours. As the car crawled toward the Potomac, the headlights of oncoming vehicles illuminated the Volvo's white interior. Cindy's bright eyes and intriguing smile reminded Hannibal that the entire world had not in fact turned to garbage.

"Actually, it was pretty bad," he said, more politely. "It's the local center for drugs, and houses a rather negative element. But I think I can convince them to go elsewhere if I talk to whoever's bringing in the drugs. I always try to end a case the easiest way first. So much for me. How was your day?"

Cindy pouted just enough. "Too long. Had to argue with the boss to take a case today. Guy got evicted from his little storefront. He and his family were also put out of the apartment they rented upstairs from the store, but he swears he paid the rent. Just didn't get receipts every month. He might be a while raising the fee, but he wanted somebody who could habla Espanol, you know? Anyway, fighting to get the case took more out of me than preparing it. I'm tired, and hungry, and my feet hurt."

"Well, all problems easy to solve." Hannibal stretched an arm along the back of the seat. "You have a place to sleep and you can get food. And I'll bet just putting your feet up would solve your physical problem."

"Thanks." She swung her stocking-wrapped calves onto his lap. Startled, he reflexively raised his hands. When they dropped, his left landed on her knees, just below her skirt's hem. He snapped his hand up, but she did not seem to care, so he gently lowered it back into place.

"So, do you want to take me somewhere for dinner?" Cindy asked. Hannibal thought her eyes were asking deeper questions, questions he had no answers for.

"Sorry, really, but I've got a previous commitment."

"Really?" Cindy said after a moment's silence. "Anybody I know?"

"Doubtful. I'll bet everybody you know has an address."

* * *

The Foggy Bottom Shelter, Northeast had spent most of its useful life as an A.M.E. Zion church. As the neighborhood became more and more rundown, its African Methodist Episcopal congregation had left for more God-fearing environs. After a few years as an empty vessel, the building became an easily invaded windbreak for transients. A coalition of charitable organizations and volunteers, short on funds but long on caring, turned it into a warm, dry place for those without homes. Now individual volunteers made it a house of love again.

Hannibal suspended his train of thought to watch Cindy thumb a long piece of her hair out of her eyes while she ladled stew onto plates he held in front of her. Her eyes had momentarily lost focus. He had figured out that it happened when she was lost in thought.

"So what's on your mind?"

"Actually, I was mentally writing a promotion of this place," she said through an embarrassed smile. "I'm thinking about making a presentation to the partners, to convince them to add this shelter to their list of donation recipients. Do you do this every week?"

"Just about," Hannibal said, "unless a case keeps me away." He stood beside her, jacket off and white shirt's sleeves rolled up. With a nod and a smile for each person shuffling past, he served them the food they needed with the respect they deserved. "Tuesday nights I serve the late dinner, and inventory donations." He handed a plate over the stainless steel counter to an older woman.

"You're just a compulsive helper-outer, aren't you?" Cindy asked, wiping perspiration away from her throat with a paper towel. The stainless steel serving area was scrubbed spotless, and light flashed from every surface. Their customers, however, were not so pristine. Hands and faces had been washed in every case, but some of their clothing bore the stains and smells of street living. Hannibal doubted that Cindy was this close to the homeless very often.

"You didn't have to do this you know."

"Are you kidding?" Cindy said. "I had to see you being humble. I wasn't sure it was possible. Besides, during the day you don't let anyone see those gorgeous eyes."

"Well, some of my customers in here find the shades a little intimidating," he said. Besides, he was enjoying his clear view of her in form fitting black jeans, fashion boots, and a denim shirt that, with its two top buttons open, buoyed the spirits of every man in the chow line.

Three men in a row said hello to him by name as they accepted their food, and asked how he was doing. Cindy waited until they had passed, then asked, "Lot of familiar faces?"

"Yeah, sorry to say. Sometimes it comes as a big shock, suddenly being homeless. Some guys have a hard time recovering. You'd be surprised, Cindy. Upstairs where the cots are, people mostly sleep. Down here, after chow, you can get a hell of a good chess game, or advice on the stock market, or a history lesson. Nowhere to go don't necessarily make a guy a bum."

"I know." Cindy carried her empty pot to the back. "That what you usually do after your work here? Play chess?"

"Sometimes, but I won't be today." He was gathering dirty cookware to put in the sink when their eyes met. Hers wrote an entirely different ending to the day than the one he had pictured. He was not sure if she stopped breathing or if it was just him. Clearing his throat got things working again.

"After I drop you off, I'll be back at my motel room early tonight. Your dad and I will be on an early stakeout in the morning. There's a man I need to meet."

-10-

A few blocks west of Cindy's office, a black Lincoln Continental rolled slowly down a ramp into a parking garage. Only a handful of cars remained in the huge cavern hidden beneath its midtown office building. The engine's roar echoed off the cement walls and floor to fill the hollow area with sound.

The car stopped near the center of the parking garage, a dozen feet from four men standing in line on a large painted arrow pointing the way out. Two of them looked like twins in expensive blue suits. Between them stood a short black man in khakis and sneakers. A taller man whose left arm hung in a sling stood on their right, eyeing the black man suspiciously. Widely spaced bare bulbs threw their long black shadows across the floor.

The engine died, suddenly filling the garage with silence. Both the limousine's back doors opened, and two men got out. One had the size and carriage of a heavyweight contender. The other was his boss.

The two newcomers walked toward the four waiting men, their clacking footsteps bouncing back at them from the walls. The older man's breathing was rapid. The air in the garage smelled musty to him, as if the cement walls had absorbed the exhaust fumes puffed out into the space every day. He got within inches of one of the well-dressed men before he spoke.

"Keep it brief. I got things to do," Anthony Ronzini said. He was used to getting answers quickly.

"This one works for you running numbers," one well-dressed man answered. "He got into a conflict with another of your workers in a game of dice. There was violence."

"He pulled a gun on me," said the man in the sling. "He shoots me over a dice game. And it ain't the first time he's caused trouble. This boy's out of control. He's a dangerous lunatic."

"And you a cheat," spat the black man, in a strong Jamaican accent.

Ronzini spun on the black man, stepping close enough to smell the grease on him. Despite his pasty face and gray rimmed hair, Ronzini seemed as full of energy as a man half his age.

"Your name?"

"Timothy." The black man, Jamaican from his accent, pronounced his name as if there were no "H" in it. Ronzini stared into his face for a moment, then turned to cock an eye at the well-dressed spokesman. He in turn tipped his head toward the man wearing the sling.

"Sir, we've used Randall here in a number of positions for several years. He's no cheat."

Ronzini turned back to the black man. Although Ronzini's face was in shadows, his eyes shone through. He still possessed the eyes of a calculating fox.

"I see why I was called." His voice was softly menacing. "You see Timothy, I can't allow infighting between my employees. On the other hand, I retain the right to decide on retribution. Now, did you shoot Mister Randall here?"

Despite his surface bluster, Timothy almost cringed. Just like thirty years ago, Ronzini's enemies were still more intimidated by his arrogant confidence than anything else. Timothy stayed silent.

"I see," Ronzini said after a moment. "You needn't answer, the truth is right there in your eyes. I think Vic here got it right. You're too dangerous to remain in my organization. I'm a businessman and I can't tolerate this kind of thing. Not here, with no real structure outside my own small organization." He nodded to the well-dressed men. Each gripped one of Timothy's arms. "You're fired," Ronzini said quietly. Then he turned back toward his car.

As he reached his driving companion he called back over his shoulder. "Freddy here was a golden gloves champion in his younger days. Freddy, hurt him. Don't break anything, and try not to let it show too much, but hurt him."

Ronzini was in the car by the time Freddy reached Timothy. Timothy looked at the men holding him, their faces bland masks. His arms were pinned solidly. There was no escape. Ronzini hoped in a way that Timothy was smarter than he looked. Then he would know that if he relaxed and let it happen it might not go too badly.

With Freddy standing in front of him, Timothy lashed out with his right foot, missing Freddy's groin but smashing into the inside of his thigh. Oh well, Ronzini thought. Some people just have to learn the hard way.

Freddy didn't even acknowledge being attacked. He just drove his right fist deep into Timothy's stomach. The well-dressed men pulled him upright and Freddy's left launched into the same target.

Doubled over and pulled back up. Ronzini watched the pattern repeated, knowing that for Timothy, this would be his whole life for the next ten minutes.

-11-

WEDNESDAY

"She really likes you, you know."

With his head against the driver's door armrest, Ray could lie with his feet against the opposite door. Being a bit taller, Hannibal found the back seat somewhat less comfortable. He turned his knees to the side and replied toward the ceiling.

"She's a beautiful girl, Ray, and sweet too," Hannibal said, "but she probably doesn't want to get involved with me. I'm just not good with relationships. My work, you know?"

"Same with her," Ray said. "Her job is her life, and that makes me sad. She needs someone to pull her out of herself."

"Besides," Hannibal quickly added, "when I'm on a case, it ain't easy to wine and dine a girl right. I tend to put in a lot of hours."

"You're telling me." Ray sipped from his coffee cup and returned it to its resting place on his rounded stomach. "God don't get up as early as you."

Hannibal smiled at that. At six o'clock, when he had pulled up in front of Cindy's apartment, he had already run five miles, showered, and changed into business clothes. Ray had staggered down the stairs, grunting a good morning as he got into the car. Hannibal reminded him then that his three hundred dollars a week was not a handout, and he would make sure Ray earned it. Ray had bristled, but controlled it.

They parked across the street from Balor's apartment building again, this time in the next block. Single family houses, most in need of repair, lined this side of the street. A small grocery store stood at the corner, with twin pay telephones outside which Hannibal thought ideal for making drug deals. He would simply watch and wait.

All the trees stood on the other side of the street. It was cool for August, and they were almost bare, lending a ghost town atmosphere to the block. Men in knit caps moved up and down as if they had nowhere to go. The women seemed mostly overweight, except for obvious working girls looking for their next John. He knew he was an intruder here, a threat to even the good people because he was about to upset the delicate ecological balance.

Soon after they were parked, the smell of fried eggs and bacon crept into the car. They waited only two hours, during which Ray fidgeted and they both ate fruit and chips. Once, Ray went up to the store, to ask to use the bathroom. He returned with a couple of sodas. Hannibal found the street surprisingly quiet.

He did not react when a Continental pulled up outside the store. It was the man getting out, though, who caught his attention. Man? He was a stove with legs, as big around as he was tall, but squared off and solid. A taller version came out next, black this time, and moved to the edge of the corner. Very alert, this one. Finally, an Italian about Hannibal's height and weight who looked to be in his early twenties.

The Italian wore a thousand-dollar suit and his hair was obviously styled rather than cut by a barber. The Man, for sure. The black man, evidently a bodyguard, preceded the smaller man into the store. Less than two minutes later, Wild Eyes came out of Balor's building. He walked swiftly to the store, glancing around occasionally. Hannibal sat up, sweaty from too much time on the leather seats.

When Wild Eyes came outside again, he looked paler than ever. He looked at the muscle man at the corner, and very quickly carried his two small packages back to his present home. Hannibal considered a moment, then slid his pistol out of its holster and held it over the front seat. Ray nearly jumped, but before he could speak, Hannibal dropped the gun onto Ray's belly.

"Now, no matter what happens, you stay right here. Capice?"

"Yo comprendo," Ray almost whispered.

As if he had an appointment, Hannibal wandered over to stand beside the outside guard. They looked each other over once, and went back to patiently waiting. Hannibal had brought his empty soda can out. He shoved it into the trashcan beside the steps leading into the store. A piece of wide yellow tape hung out of the can, the kind marked "Police Line Do Not Cross." The message was not lost on him.

The black guard came out followed by his principle. Hannibal waited until they both reached the sidewalk before he spoke.

"Can I have a moment?" Hannibal asked with excessive politeness in his voice. When the smaller man turned, Hannibal briefly wondered how a fellow so young could be the power in even a small area of this city. Hannibal also thought he saw a flash of fear on the man's face, but that expression was quickly replaced by a smirk.

"Are you trouble?" the man asked in a voice cultivated for toughness.

"Not today." Hannibal smiled as widely as he could and slowly lifted his jacket open. The other three men on the corner understood the significance of an empty holster. Everyone else nearby quietly moved indoors.

"Cop?" the other man asked. Both guards moved smoothly to bracket Hannibal.

"No kind of cop or G-man," Hannibal assured him. "I'm an independent and I just want to talk for a minute. Hannibal Jones is my name. And I call you..?"

"Sal. What's the pitch?"

"Real simple," Hannibal said. "It's that building down there, number twenty-three thirteen. Believe it not, that place belongs to somebody. The guy who paid for it wants it back. Luckily, we both know there's lots of other locations for you to do your business from, right?"

"So?"

"So, you name a price, I give you money, then you tell me your new location and I help your pals move. No police, no hassle. Cool?"

Sal turned his head long enough to light a cigarette. When he turned back, he was chuckling silently.

"You tell your boss, Hannibal," Sal filled his lungs with smoke, "tell him I like things right where they're at. He can't do dick, the cops won't do dick, and you sure as hell ain't going to do dick, so why should I change anything? Now, you a do-gooder, huh? Or a hero?" As Sal stepped closer, his two guards closed in. Hannibal did not react.

"I'm a businessman. Making you a business proposition. Wars are expensive and messy and they draw attention. I figured we could avoid all that."

Sal stopped within an inch of touching noses with Hannibal. "War? You talking war? Screw you. Ox, Petey, chew him up a little."

Sal turned away toward his car, but as he reached for his door the sounds of battle apparently stopped him. Maybe it was the familiar voice behind the grunts. He turned in time to see Hannibal bobbing and weaving around the black guard's massive fists. Then a left hook shook the guard's entire frame. The other man's arms wrapped around Hannibal but that didn't stop a front kick that flipped his partner's head up and landed him on his back.

Hannibal expanded his chest as if trying to break free of the guard's massive arms, which looked impossible. Then, suddenly, he exhaled, leaving the grip loose. His right foot slammed back into the guard's knee, and then stamped down hard on his instep. Hannibal seemed to slide out of the grip he could not break, turning to deliver three snapping jabs, a right cross, and a side kick that staggered his opponent.

A karate shout accompanied Sal's heel unexpectedly stamping into Hannibal's back. Off balance, Hannibal hit and toppled over the trashcan. He wrestled with empty potato chip bags and drink cans to regain his feet while Sal and his followers got into their car. He was still brushing cigarette butts and other debris from his clothes when the Lincoln pulled away from the curb. Hannibal's lips formed a tight line and his stomach clenched in rage. He had lost his Oakley's in the fall and bent to retrieve them. When he looked up, he found Monty standing on the store steps.

"So you came back."

"Yeah," Hannibal said. "Great reception too."

"Tried to tell you," Monty said with a shrug of his shoulders. "That dude is bad news. You ought to leave him the fuck alone."

Hannibal leaned his hands on his knees so he could stand eye to eye with Monty. "The problem around here," he said, loud enough for a wider audience, "is that everybody leaves him alone. They leave him alone to import poison to this neighborhood. Now me, I'm too stupid to leave him alone. I keep coming back, like a bad cold, you know? Not enough to kill you, but if it keeps coming back, it'll sure wear you down."

Heading back to his car, he made a point of not showing the pain in his hip where it had hit the edge of the trashcan. He could feel Monty's eyes on him.

-12-

Hitting the heavy bag hurt Hannibal's hands and feet, but not as much as hitting his two most recent opponents had. More importantly, the bag never hit him back. Wearing only the loose white pants of his karate gi he honed his punches and kicks, concentrating on speed and accuracy. He believed they were more important than power, even against men the size of those he had so recently faced. Glistening with sweat, he whirled, spinning into a devastating back kick.

"Hey, I didn't hire on to be a punching bag, man," Ray snapped, startled by a heel coming too near his face while he held the bag.

"I haven't hit you yet, have I?" Hannibal asked, launching into a series of jabs and crosses.

"No, but God, it's almost an hour and a half now," Ray whined. "Jump rope, shadow boxing, now this. You got to be getting tired, and that's when people make mistakes. Besides, I hate gyms. I ain't set foot in one in a long time, and I don't miss it."

"It's not a gym," Hannibal said, slamming a side kick into the bag that knocked the breath out of Ray. "This is a martial arts academy."

"Yeah, well changing the name don't fool me. It looks like a gym, it sounds like a gym, and worst of all, it smells like a gym.

Besides, didn't you get enough of a workout in front of that grocery store this morning?"

"That story's not over yet," Hannibal rasped, slamming hooks and jabs in combinations into the canvas bag.

"Uh huh. Well what can you do?"

"Well, I could find this Sal guy again and whip his ass. Or, I can make it too expensive for him to continue in that location, or just too inconvenient." Hannibal landed a roundhouse kick on each of his last three words. "Kick boxing isn't the only approach to getting a job done. All I need right now is a little more intel."

"You're dreaming, Chico." Ray watched Hannibal's eyes as his boss put boxing combinations into the bag. "Nobody in Southeast is going to talk to you about a pusher, man. Ain't you noticed how people just disappear around there?"

Hannibal stepped back from the heavy bag, his chest rising and falling like the drive arm on a locomotive's wheels. His heavy breathing made a steam engine noise.

"I think I might know how to cultivate a source." Then, as if to purposely change the subject, he asked, "Do you think your daughter might be free for dinner?"

"If I say yes, will you stop kicking me through this damned heavy bag?"

When Hannibal stepped back two paces from the bag, Ray shoved him toward the locker room. Hannibal expected Ray to return to the observation area but instead found his new friend at his elbow when he opened his locker. Ray reached in quickly, yanked Hannibal's phone out of his jacket pocket and thrust it into his face.

"Call her."

"Maybe after a shower I'll..."

"Now, Paco." Ray stared at him the way Hannibal remembered his father doing when he was little more than a baby. It was one of his few real memories of the man. Licking his lips, he punched in Cindy's number and waited through six long rings. His eyebrows shrugged at Ray, working to convey helplessness rather than reluctance.

"It's barely six," Ray said. "Try her office."

Hannibal dialed as instructed, reconciled now to taking action. Still, he was startled when he heard Cindy's voice on the other end.

"Er, hi. It's Hannibal. I guess I expected a secretary or somebody to answer the office phone." He sat on the bench and looked up to find Ray on his way out the locker room door. Then, despite the activity in the room and the odor of sweaty bodies around him, he mentally pulled himself into a private space to talk.

"Listen, Cindy, I was thinking."

"That's often a good sign," she said, sounding distracted. "What about exactly?"

"Well, I thought we should get a little better acquainted. I'm done working for the day so, maybe we could meet someplace. To talk. Over dinner or something." God, that sounded lame, even to him.

"Sorry, Hannibal, I've got a lot to get done tonight. I'm working on a new DPO. A direct public offering from one of our clients."

"DPO? Is that like an IPO?" Hannibal asked.

"Yeah, except the shares are sold direct to the public, without a lot of the registration and reporting requirements that IPOs go through. DPOs are a good way for small businesses to raise capital. But you don't want to hear about that stuff."

"No, it's interesting," Hannibal said.

"Anyhow, I'll be here for hours putting this thing together. Sorry, but I have to decline."

"Okay. I understand." Hannibal squeezed his eyes shut and when he opened them the walls of his private space had crumbled. A fellow three lockers down was looking at him, his face beaming the sympathy that comes from shared experience. Hannibal nodded and was about to say goodbye when Cindy said something he almost missed.

"Rain check?"

"Sure, sure," Hannibal said. "Maybe you can explain all that DPO stuff to me tomorrow night."

"If we both have time." Hannibal heard papers shuffling. He could feel her attention pulling away from him, back to the job at hand. Almost absently she said, “So how’s the case going? Any progress?”

“I need to find out more about what’s going on down there,” Hannibal said. The reminder of work made him suddenly aware of his fatigue. “Shouldn’t be a problem though. I met somebody today who sees it all. Maybe he’ll give me what I need.”

-13-

THURSDAY

"Hey, yo, Monty," Hannibal called through his rolled down window. The boy spun on his skateboard, identified the source of the call and rolled to the car.

"Back for another beating? You must like getting hit."

"It's an acquired taste," Hannibal said from inside the car. "What you up to?"

"What's it to you?" Monty looked into the front seat, as if making sure Ray was the only other occupant.

"Well, if you're not too busy I thought I'd buy you lunch."

"Where?" Monty asked. Hannibal found it interesting that the first question was not "why."

"Your lunch. You call it."

Monty stared around, as if surrounded by options. Finally, while facing the front of the Volvo, he said "There's a Micky D's four, five blocks up that way."

"Fine. Climb in."

"Nuh-uh." Monty stepped back, eyeing the white car's sleek lines, clutching his board tighter. "I don't get in nobody's car I don't know. Besides..." The boy glanced up and down his home street as if it were suddenly foreign.

"Besides," Hannibal said, almost to himself, "it kind of looks like a pimp's car. Okay. Ray, meet you there."

Hannibal slid out onto the street. Today he wore black jeans and a short sleeved knit shirt, his shades in place. He looked up at Monty's house, badly needing paint, but its yard clean. He glanced back at a group of older boys hanging by the phones in front of the store, then across at number twenty-three thirteen, fully occupied yet abandoned. He remembered reading in one of his psychology classes how people, like animals, are shaped as much by their surroundings as by genetics. If that was true, how could this bright young man survive in such an environment? How had he?

"Yeah, so what you looking at?"

"Your Skinner box, Monty," Hannibal replied. "So let's walk."

Hannibal's car pulled away, giving him time to examine his companion. Monty wore a new looking ball cap, its bill pointed over his left shoulder, but his Redskins tee shirt and blue jeans had been washed too many times, their colors dull and faded. On these streets, against these buildings, dull and faded might be the best camouflage. As they walked, he felt Monty checking him out as well. Had he guessed Hannibal's reason for being here? No, Hannibal saw only curiosity in the boy's eyes.

When they opened the door, Hannibal's stomach lurched at the smell of grease, but he noticed Monty's first genuine smile. Young people in here laughed and ate quickly to the sound from boom boxes parked on their tables. Old men, curled into a few booths, stared at the wall, ignoring and ignored by everyone else. Loud talkers, loud rappers, and cooking noise almost blotted out any real conversations, except in the far corners. Although not overcrowded, the place still made Hannibal slightly claustrophobic, as if too many were trying to do too much living in too small a space.

Hannibal ate more slowly, but Monty had much more food, so they finished at about the same time. The boy did a good job on a double quarter pounder with cheese, large fries, a large drink, some chicken nuggets and an apple pie. During lunch

Hannibal found out he lived with his widowed grandmother. He did not know what he wanted to be, and found the phrase "when you grow up" offensive. As he swallowed his last few fries, Monty pulled a deck of cards from his hip pocket.

"Okay, so what's the scam?" Monty asked, idly shuffling the cards.

"Scam?"

"Well, shit, nobody buys for nothing." Monty absently cut the deck and started dealing blackjack. "Or is this National Buy-A-Poor-Kid-A-Burger day?"

"If I wanted something, it wouldn't be too bright to give you the lunch first, now would it?" Hannibal was more than a little amused. This kid could ride a long way on ego.

"Yeah, well you don't look too bright. You need a bag man? A mule? Maybe a lookout? I'm a damned good lookout."

Now Hannibal knew how he would play this. Monty saw himself as a streetwise player. To an extent it was probably true. In any case, he would have to treat Monty like the adults he had dealt with in this same situation. He pulled a roll of bills from his pocket, which immediately got Monty's attention.

"Okay, you've got me pegged," Hannibal said. "What I want, pal, is a little chat with you about what goes on in your block."

Monty suddenly began looking around their unpadded orange and yellow booth as if it had abruptly moved to the truck lane on I-95 and he expected seventy-mile an hour company.

"I figured you'd know what was going on," Hannibal rushed on. "You're an alert fellow."

"Word," Monty replied, slouching just a bit. "I know all the shit goes down."

On an impulse, Hannibal peeled a bill off his roll of fives. He laid the bill down in front of Monty, but did not take his hand away. "This one says, no more profanity when you're talking to me."

Monty said, "Shit," and Hannibal pulled his hand back, with its prize. "Okay, okay, the golden rule, man." Monty snatched the bill, shoving it into his pocket.

"Golden rule?"

"The man with the gold makes the rules, man," Monty said. "You got the gold. Now, what you want?"

When it came out, Monty's smile was infectious. Hannibal caught it. "You a trip, Monty. Your grandmother call you Lamont?"

"What? No man, she calls me Gabriel. That's what my folks did to me before they split."

"Gabriel?" Hannibal asked. "How do you get Monty from that?"

"They call me Monty because of this." He showed Hannibal the top card on his deck, the ace of clubs, then laid the top three down, left to right. "Three card monte is how I get my chump change." Monty quickly slid the three cards around, changing their order.

Stifling a laugh, Hannibal laid down another bill. Again, his fingers held it in place. "Okay, you little hustler, how long has our friend Sal been around? He just don't fit in, in the hood." As if for emphasis, he tapped the card on the left.

Monty picked up Hannibal's card, a red queen, then showed him the ace in the center and picked up the bill. "Sal only moved in about three months ago. He's The Man, and nobody f...messes with him." Monty dropped three more cards and Hannibal dropped another bill.

"His people loyal to him, or his money? Or his drugs?" Hannibal tapped the center card.

Monty showed the center card, a loser, then the flashed card, on the right. "Ain't no loyalty for junkies and crack heads, brother." Monty said it as if quoting an obvious axiom. "It's just everybody's scared of him."

"He didn't look all that bad to me." Hannibal wondered if he would get anything for free.

Monty flashed his top card again, a red deuce, and dropped the top three cards, more slowly this time. "Oh, he's a bad dude, but he ain't scary bad. So you can figure it ain't him. It's whoever's behind him."

"Thanks," Hannibal said, impressed by he boy's insight. "So, does he do the deal same time, same place, every day?

What I saw yesterday seemed kind of obvious." Another bill, and another wrong card chosen. Monty pocketed five more dollars.

"It ain't that easy. Never the same time and place twice." Then Monty dealt again, flipping the cards very slowly this time, as if to prove that no one could get confused about the whereabouts of the black king he had shown Hannibal before he started. Then he looked up, waiting.

Hannibal looked around quickly. People here seemed very good at minding their own business. And this kid was playing him like a pro. There must be more. He peeled off another bill and laid it on the table. This time he moved his hand, and tapped the right side card.

Monty slowly lifted the right card, a red trey. "Different every day, but if a guy pays attention he'll see there's a pattern. Sal, he ain't too bright." Now, slowly, Monty eased a finger under the center card and flipped it up, revealing the wandering black king. "Tonight, for example, he ought to be parked a block west around ten-thirty. If you want to know." Monty waited for a slight nod from Hannibal before he picked up the bill on the table.

"I think that's all I need," Hannibal said, pocketing his money roll. "You ready to go?"

Monty looked over his shoulder dramatically. "Maybe we better not leave together."

Hannibal wondered if playing spy was a universal obsession among boys. He remembered getting so wrapped up in the game in his own youth that he lost track of reality. In his case, it happened at the center of the James Bond world of spies, the Berlin Wall.

As a child, he got lost in passing imaginary top secret notes to deep cover agents crossing the border between East and West. With no father and few friends, he had gratefully slipped into a world where nothing was as it seemed. A world where his father might not be dead, but a prisoner, part of some monstrous conspiracy. Or better still, maybe his dad was the heroic spy, undercover so deep he could not even contact his own son.

Hannibal had lived within walking distance of the Brandenberg Gate. Almost every weekend he would go to the plaza and watch the armed guards on the other side. Books, movies and the oppressive atmosphere in his hometown had made Hannibal suspicious of every Slavic looking face he passed. Reality had merged with his view of the world.

But that was all half a lifetime away. In the present day case, Hannibal was not sure how closely Monty's reactions matched up with his reality.

"Well, Ray's right outside now," Hannibal said. "Why don't we just follow you back in the car? Just in case somebody saw all that green you just stashed in your slide."

* * *

Ray had never seen an indoor firing range before and he was none too comfortable. The drive to Virginia and out I-66 had brought them to a huge blue and white building. Ray followed Hannibal inside, very aware that every face he had seen since they arrived was white. The place was clean and comfortably air conditioned, but Ray still felt himself on the edge of sweating. Walking deeper into the building, down carpeted halls full of NRA members, was enough to make him nervous. But as they approached a shooting station he could see that Hannibal had other things on his mind: his gun, and his recent encounter with the boy he called Monty.

"I'm telling you, he's a grown man in a kid's body." Hannibal said, carefully pushed twelve bullets into a magazine.

"Maybe he's a midget," Ray said. "I think you just got hustled, Chico." He twisted his neck to read the box Hannibal was pulling shells from. Winchester, it said. Forty caliber, one hundred eighty grain Black Talon SXT hollowpoint ammunition. To a man who had never even held a firearm, they sounded big, nasty and powerful.

"He's a hustler, but I don't think he's hustling me." Hannibal said. He traded his sunglasses for amber safety lenses and pulled on headphone type hearing protection. "This kid's ego is tied in to knowing what's going on in his hood. He knows he can't be a player, but he sure as hell can watch the game. I'll bet he knows every deal that goes down in Southeast D.C." Hannibal slapped the magazine into his automatic and stepped to his firing station.

Ray stepped backwards as far as he could to distance himself from the action. Standing against the back wall, he looked past Hannibal at a man-shaped paper target twenty-five yards farther on. Even with earplugs in, he was buffeted by the pistol's blasting report. Hannibal seemed even more relaxed than the other shooters, firing neither hurriedly nor very slowly. Ray was surprised at the amount of smoke filling the target area. It was ducted away, but he didn't know pistols created so much smoke to begin with. After twelve shots, Hannibal pushed a button, summoning his target to him.

"So, you going to send the cops?" Ray asked, looking over Hannibal's shoulder. Grid lines on the paper showed him all the holes were within two and a half inches of each other.

"For what? This is my job."

"Theirs too," Ray reminded him. "They might like a little gift like this."

Hannibal stared down into the perforated target, and Ray wondered if he saw anyone's face in particular there. "See the one in the paper this morning?" Hannibal asked. Ray shook his head. "It went down last night, around nine o'clock in Union Station. It's pretty crowded that time of night. Two guys are arguing, right there in the food court, downstairs. They're shouting at each other, right? So another guy walks up, grabs one of them by his jacket, puts a gun to the back of his head and bang."

"Why you take it so personal?" Ray asked. At first he was not sure Hannibal heard him, but he soon realized his friend simply had no answer. After a few seconds of silence, Ray asked, "Cops get them?"

"Oh, they got them, all right. Couldn't identify either of them. Or the victim. Nobody knows why it happened. What do you think?" His eyes drove into Ray's.

"Got to be a gang thing," Ray said. "Probably over drugs."

Shaking his head slowly, Hannibal jammed his pistol into its holster under his right arm. "They can't protect anybody, Ray. They might want to. They might want you to think so. But they just can't. I don't need any noncombatants getting blown away tonight, okay?"

"Yeah, but Hannibal, how much can you hurt these guys?"

"Hell, I don't know," he admitted. "But that's not the point. What I need to do is just be a big enough pain in the ass that they finally decide this one place ain't worth it. All I need to be is stubborn. It's that simple."

"Yeah, simple." Ray stared down the line of Anglos firing at man shaped targets and understood why Hannibal was comfortable here. These people were like him in one important way. They were prepared to take care of their own troubles themselves. "Except, what if you're not the only one stubborn?"

-14-

There was one hell of a party going down. Hannibal could hear the music, loud and driving, pulling everyone within a one-block circle into the celebration, whether they wanted to be or not. Three or four couples had walked past him in the dark, already drunk or stoned, moving toward the source of the beat like George Romero's hungry zombies toward living flesh.

If anyone saw him, they would probably think he was in the same condition. He sat with his back against a building's cold sandstone stoop. A row of three overly full trashcans separated him from the street.

The chance of anyone seeing him was slight. He wore black jeans, pullover, running shoes, gloves and a shell windbreaker to conceal his weapon. Unmoving, he disappeared in the shadow of the garbage. Years of Secret Service work had taught him how to remain still for extended periods of time, and with that patience he had gained the ability to withdraw.

When you worked crowds with politicians and dignitaries, your best defense was invisibility. A wise instructor had told him camouflage was only the beginning. The art was to learn to withdraw your personal aura, so people looking right at you did not see you, unless you wanted to be noticed.

From the shadows he watched a long black Lincoln Continental take possession of the street, pulling up within ten yards of his surveillance point. First the black bodyguard got out and looked around. The occasional passerby ignored him. Then Sal, wearing arrogance like a cloak, stood up and walked out several feet in front of the car. His face told a story of impatience and distrust. The other guard remained in the driver's seat.

The black guard said something Hannibal couldn't hear. Judging by Sal's body language, he answered with some snide remark. Hannibal remembered his time in the Secret Service, thinking how quickly these boys would be looking for work if pushers held to the same standards. How often had he traveled with the Vice President's family without ever seeing them? When you protected someone, you looked at everything except your principle. Also, you checked the area before your man left his vehicle. That's why no one could ever have been lying in wait for anybody Hannibal had been assigned to protect. Not the way he waited now.

Even worse, as they approached their meeting place, they almost surely drove right past Hannibal's car just three blocks away. The white Volvo was certainly not inconspicuous. Ray would wait there for half an hour, then return home if Hannibal did not show up at the car. That eventuality seemed remote. Since they had failed to recognize his car, they had no clue that Hannibal was present, and in his mind they deserved what they would get.

Hannibal felt the party music filling the street the way the music does in old voodoo movies just before the climax. His heart was thumping like the base line as he eased himself up into a deep crouch. He pulled a black ski mask from his belt and stretched it over his head. Now the night air was filtered through woven cotton. With his attention focused on the big man inside the car, he felt adrenaline flow into his bloodstream. He had spent years on the other side of this situation, waiting for someone to attack, but this sure felt different. Being the attacker gave him a rush like nothing he had ever felt in bodyguard work. And he had to admit that most of his work in the Service had been exactly that – personal protection duty, which was just glorified bodyguard work.

It had not seemed so humid before he sprinted for the Lincoln. Now his lungs could not grab enough air. The two men outside the car did not know he was there until they heard the passenger door yanked open. Sal turned to see a shadow on the front seat holding a gun against his driver's head.

"Get the fuck out," Hannibal rasped in a guttural voice. "Out, or I swear I blow your head away." The driver's door opened and Hannibal stiff-armed the other man out onto the asphalt. Sal shouted something garbled, and the other guard rushed around to the passenger side of the car, drawing his gun as he moved.

"You boys react too slow," Hannibal said to himself, pushing the car into gear and stomping on the gas. Both doors slammed shut as he pulled away from the curb. Three bullets smacked the rear window. He heard their impacts over the screaming tires, but the glass held.

In his rear view mirror he watched Sal ranting at his two giant flunkies. The Lincoln's big V8 engine gave out a deep-throated roar. Hannibal was certain he was driving a car full of illegal drugs. He planned to dump them down a convenient sewer and ditch the car a few blocks away. That easily, he could get Sal's attention and open serious negotiations. It shouldn't be hard to convince him that this was a bad place to do business.

Then, as he crossed the first intersection, headlights came on behind him. They drew his attention because the engine behind him snarled loudly, but the sound was even deeper than roar of the one he was driving. Just as it was leaving, the adrenaline rush kicked back in.

As the Lincoln passed the loud house party, he watched his rearview mirror. In the light cone of a street lamp he saw a black Camaro pulling up on him. At that moment, he appreciated the Lincoln's apparently bulletproof skin.

The Camaro pulled up close to his rear bumper, and then pulled a bit closer, giving him a small jolt. Hannibal's head snapped back. That was a warning, he thought. A taste of things to come if he did not pull the Lincoln over. That little contact threw him off balance. This car, for all its size, was hard to control.

So Sal the drug dealer had posted a back up vehicle in case of trouble. Maybe he was smarter than Hannibal thought. How had the Camaro's driver known Sal was not inside? Could he have seen Hannibal take the car from him? Maybe, or maybe he expected a signal Hannibal did not give.

A red light glared at the next corner, and Hannibal simply rolled under it. A loud horn blared on his left, sounding like a train whistle as it passed behind him. Then a woman, walking with the weight of too much drink, stepped into the street. He stood on the brake, and again received a crunching impact from behind. The woman looked through the windshield as if trying to see if anyone was driving, then went on across the street.

The driver behind Hannibal was bald, with tightly stretched skin, as if someone had pulled it all taut under his neck. He held a small telephone in his right hand. He said a few words into it, then dropped it to pick up a small revolver. Hannibal pressed the accelerator, his bumper making a strange, crying noise as it twisted loose from the Camaro's bumper.

Hannibal needed both hands for driving, so he could not even consider gunplay. The Camaro stayed with him. A third corner came up. He maintained a lead on his pursuer, but he was leaving Ray behind. He wanted to turn around. With no pedestrians nearby, he didn't think it would too hard.

Hannibal hauled on the wheel turning right at the corner, only to find the Camaro coming up on his right side. The Camaro smacked into Hannibal's car with a squealing crunch, and then surged ahead. His diaphragm paralyzed, Hannibal cranked the wheel to the right, trying to stay in his lane. At the next intersection he turned left, leaving the other car behind.

God, that idiot had actually run into him. He was sweating freely now, wishing he was not driving steadily away from his only backup. He had to get turned around. At the next corner he would...

A liquor store sat at the next corner. A uniformed policeman had just stepped out of that store carrying a package and was getting back into his blue Metro Police car. Hannibal briefly considered stopping and asking for help. But then he remembered that the man pursuing him was only guilty of reckless driving. Hannibal was the one driving around in a car undoubtedly full of illegal drugs. He slowed down, not wanting to get stopped for reckless driving himself. He hit his turn signal and, feeling the cop's eyes on him, made a left and headed back toward his own car.

Streets were narrow and short in Southeast D.C., with some laid out at odd angles to the rest. It took a few more turns for Hannibal to really be pointed in the right direction, not far from where Ray sat behind the wheel of his Volvo. He had not seen the Camaro behind him for a while, and the street in front of him looked clear. Up ahead three or four men stood clustered around a big boom box. They were jamming the O'Jays. He remembered the last time he heard that tune. He was wet under his arms that night, just like now, except then it had been from dancing.

Hannibal's focus returned to the road when a slow moving Cadillac turned onto his street up ahead of him. It was driving away from him but sitting right in the middle of the street. The Cadillac slowed to a crawl right in front of him. Hannibal locked his brakes, even as he saw lights behind him. It had to be the Camaro.

With a squeal of rubber, the Lincoln hit the car ahead, but without much impact. Hannibal turned to stare out his back window. The sports car behind him swerved left. Hannibal dived for the passenger side door. Tires made their screeching sound as the Camaro's driver wrenched his two thousand pound steel bludgeon to the right toward the driver's door of the Lincoln. Hannibal heard the engine pumping closer as he grasped the door handle.

Then there was a deep base thump of steel punching steel and the high hat cymbal sound of shattering glass, and a concussion tossed him through space. The cement sidewalk slapped his back like a giant, over-friendly hand. His eyes did not want to open and the air forced out of him by the impact seemed reluctant to return. He yanked off his mask thinking that might help. It did not, and he noticed his face felt wet on the left side. He tasted blood, wondering as he had so many times before why its taste reminded him of copper. He rolled over, he thought onto his knees, though he could not be sure. Thoughts were slippery, hard to get a grip on, but he had a feeling that sitting still would put him in some danger.

Then the music changed. No, one kind of music stopped and another took its place. No more O'Jays. This new song sounded too high and shrill, and somehow familiar.

For the last fourteen years a police siren had meant assistance to him. For half that time he had often been the source of that siren. But now, in his confusion, his muddled brain reached back to his childhood, when that sound had only meant danger. He was caught.

Hannibal lurched to his feet and forced his eyes open. Through a fog that had risen awfully suddenly, he saw the Lincoln, smashed, leaning slightly toward him in the street with its trunk popped open. Its nose was still pressed against the tail of the Cadillac, like one big dog sniffing another. The Cadillac's driver looked at him for a second before jumping into the Camaro as it roared off. They were running. Maybe that wasn't a bad idea.

It took his muddled mind a second to determine the direction of the source of the siren sound. A small smile curled his lips when he had it pinned down, then he turned and started walking away from it. The smile kind of hurt, but at least he could feel his face. Glancing over his shoulder, he saw the music lovers on the corner looking over the wreck. One of them looked up and waved him on, hooking a thumb in the police car's direction. Hannibal nodded at the fuzzy man and started jogging. Hannibal wasn't worried. His figure, covered in black from head to toe, would be invisible to anyone more than half a block away.

The area looked familiar but he was not sure where he was. All of Southeast Washington D.C. would seem familiar, he reasoned, an unchanging rundown landscape of dingy houses and cracked sidewalks on poorly lighted streets. Still, he thought he recognized this street.

A thin man, very tall, was weaving like a Redskins lineman in front of him. Hannibal tried to dodge, but he could not see too clearly and they collided. The man felt as if he was rooted to the ground. Hannibal bounced onto his back and lacked enough balance to get up.

"Come on. One more block."

He knew that voice. "Monty?"

"Come on, man, get up," Monty said. "You ran full out into that light pole." Hands that felt much too small grabbed Hannibal under his shoulders. With Monty's help for balance he managed to stand shakily and let the boy guide him forward.

"Man, you look like they really fucked you up." Monty dug his fingers under Hannibal's belt behind him for support.

"Watch your mouth." Hannibal noticed his words had come out slurred and tried harder. "We had a deal," he said more slowly.

"Okay, dude. Don't talk. I'm taking you home."

Walking helped him to breathe more deeply. The dizziness faded, and Hannibal's vision began to clear. Concussion? Yes, he must have gotten a concussion. But he knew he was recovering control, so it could not have been bad. A passing thing. No nausea, no headache. Must be okay.

But when they reached the porch steps both nausea and a throbbing headache caught up to him. Still, with the railing for support he reached the door.

Monty knocked on the wooden panel. Hannibal checked his jacket, making sure it stayed zipped up far enough to completely cover his holster. He stared into a window in the door, which was covered on the inside by a heavy curtain. Not good security, he thought. Anyone could punch in the glass, reach in and unlock the door.

Then the curtain moved away. A round, dark face stared out at him. The woman's gray hair was pulled to the back of her head. Some sadistic sculptor had spent sixty years engraving worry lines into her kindly face. Fear shone in her eyes. Not fear of him, but rather for him. She looked down at Monty, then past them both, as if the devil might be following. When she saw no sign of him, she began unlocking the door, a four-step process to Hannibal's hearing.

Woman and child helped him into the room and onto the couch. While her strong arms helped him into a seated position she filled the room with "Lord today," and "have mercy Jesus." Then she shuffled off on flapping mules.

His mind now clearer, Hannibal glanced around the modest room. The passage of time had dulled the paint and faded the wallpaper, but otherwise the house seemed immaculate. The sofa was not as supportive as the woman and boy had been, as if the inner springs had simply given up trying to do their job. All the furniture was overstuffed and reupholstered more than once, in the kind of eclectic decor that comes from collecting pieces one at a time at bargain prices.

"Don't worry," Monty told him. "Grandma fix you up." He stood very close, as if protecting his charge from whatever might attack next.

"What were you doing out there?" Hannibal asked, squinting his left eye. His cheek was beginning to throb.

"Just wanted to see if you'd really go." Monty never quite smiled, but his cynical expression lightened just a bit then. Hannibal leaned forward to smack him, but just then the woman returned with a large porcelain bowl full of steaming water and a handful of soft cloths. She wet one, wrung it almost dry, and swabbed at Hannibal's cheek, against his weak protests.

"You don't have to do that Mrs..."

"Call me Mother Washington." She sat down on the sofa beside him. "Everyone else does. Except Gabriel of course."

"Aw, Grandma!" he protested, but love shone through his rough tone.

"This isn't too bad," Mrs. Washington said. "Looks like you just got a little bit of a scrape."

"My face was covered," he said, then cut himself off. She could misunderstand his wearing a mask. "Ma'am I appreciate your hospitality, I really do, and your grandson was a big help, but I can't stay here. I have to be honest. There might be people looking for me."

"Young man, hush." Against his will, he found himself pushed back into childhood by her voice. "I've tended knife wounds, gunshots and a whole passel of split lips right on this here couch. The Lord won't let no evil come in this house after me."

He moved her hand, holding the cloth against his own face. "There's always a first time. Mother Washington, can I use your phone? There's some people be worrying about me."

Mrs. Washington raised an eyebrow and pointed toward the kitchen. "Go on, son, call your woman."

Not wanting to argue, he simply got up and went to the kitchen. The linoleum was chipped beneath his feet, and the lighting was dim, but like the rest of the house, the kitchen was sparkling clean. The sweet aroma of freshly baked fruit made his stomach ache for a taste of home. Only a homemade apple pie could smell so good. He dialed the wall phone, and one and a half rings later, heard Ray say "Hello!"

"Ray? Hannibal. Things didn't go too good. No, I'm all right. Yeah, but I didn't get far. In fact, I'm less than a block away from the house. Yeah. No, no. Well, because I don't know how alert the bunch in the house is and I don't want anybody to see me coming out of here. No, the car's too conspicuous. Just wait right there. I'll give it about fifteen minutes and I'll jog on up, okay? Right. Out." As he hung up the phone he found a small round face staring up at him.

"You got a backup man, don't you?" Monty asked. Hannibal smiled and nodded on his way back to the sofa. Monty followed like a kid behind the ice cream truck.

"I didn't think you were on this job alone," Monty said. He waited until his grandmother passed them to go into the kitchen herself before he continued. "See, I spotted your ride parked around the way. I bet your partner's in there. You a fed?"

"Gabriel!" his grandmother snapped from the kitchen, embarrassed by his question.

"No, son, I'm not a fed," Hannibal said. "I'm just a guy who wants those drug dealers out of that house."

"Praise the Lord." Mother Washington walked past him to set a slice of pie and a steaming cup on the coffee table. "Now you sit down here and eat something."

"Mother Washington, I've got to..."

"Sit!" she ordered. Hannibal dropped onto the sofa behind his plate. Mother Washington slowly lowered herself into an armchair. She moved as if her feet bothered her, or perhaps her knees.

"Young man, there's some decent, God fearing people live around here," she said. "They's poor and they's loud and sometimes they gets out of control, but mostly, they's good people. Now them people with they drugs, just come in here and took over. What we got to do, we got to take our street back. Somehow." Her conversation had built into preaching, but dropped off with the last word.

"Well, maybe I can help a little," he said around a bite of pie. "Really, though, I don't think this kind of thing will ever really go away unless everybody around here just stops buying drugs." He stood up, still just a little dizzy. To his dazed vision, the house wore poverty like a drape, but beneath it, a certain nobility lay hidden. "Again, I thank you for everything, but I really must go. I'll be back tomorrow and if you like, I'll stop by. Now, can I use your back door?"

Mother Washington raised her hand as if giving Hannibal a benediction. He nodded and moved back through the house. As he reached for the knob, Monty tugged on his jacket. "You coming back to mess with The Man?"

"Well...yeah. He's got to leave that house."

"What you going to do?" Monty asked, backing away with hands spread wide. "You ain't no fed. They ran you off the road."

"Gabriel, leave the man alone, now," Mother Washington called from her chair.

After a brief hesitation, Hannibal dropped onto his haunches, closer to Monty's eye level. "Look, pal, I know it looks like the biggest guy always wins, but I'm telling you it ain't like that. Look." He had the boy's attention now, but what could he tell those wide, cynical brown eyes?

"Look," he began again, "When I was your age I was in a lot of fights. Not gang action, like the kids do these days, but one on one. What I found out back then is, the winner isn't necessarily the biggest guy, or the strongest. It's the guy who won't give up. If you don't quit, you can't lose. I don't quit. And I'll take that house back. You'll see." He stood up and was about to call goodnight to Mother Washington, but she was very still with her eyes closed. Asleep in her chair, he thought. Or praying.

Hannibal slipped outside and the night swallowed him. He hurried through the tiny backyard down the narrow alley. When he reached the street he scanned it with all his senses. He saw no one on the street, if you didn't count the single wino moving unsteadily on the sidewalk. After a deep breath Hannibal began a slow jog toward the corner, staying close to the buildings. The cool air cut into his lungs, each inhalation shocking him awake.

He homed in on the only white car shining in the dim moonlight. He heard the car's door lock click open just as he reached for the handle. Ray must have been watching for him. He dropped heavily onto the seat, breathing hard. The short run had done him good, filling his lungs and getting his heart going, but the dizziness had come back. Mild concussion for sure, he concluded. He had something to tell Ray, something that seemed important but he could not recall it right then. Maybe if he just lay back in the seat for a minute.

-15-

FRIDAY

"Coffee." Before he had really thought it, Hannibal had said it. He awoke needing some, like every day. His next thought was that he wasn't at home. Where he was did not feel like his apartment. Then he remembered he no longer had an apartment. But it did not smell like a hotel room either. He cracked his eyelids, suppressing the headache and glanced around. He lay in double bed, in a strange room. A pleasant, clean, neutral room. He saw prints on the walls, the kind of pictures that end up in calendars, but no photos on the furniture, no cigarettes or magazines. A guest room.

Swinging his feet to the floor made him feel a little better. He wore only briefs, but a terry robe lay across the foot of the bed. Despite some soreness, he managed to squirm into it. Then he reached for the doorknob, figuring there must be a kitchen and in it he could find some...

"Coffee?" Cindy met him at the door holding a large mug toward him. Its aroma was heaven, making all his senses predisposed to happiness. Perhaps that's why she looked so good to him. She wore her hair down, with the slightest curl at the bottom. It was a completely natural look that must have taken her hours to achieve. She wore her skirt and blouse just tight enough to leave room for his imagination. He smiled like an idiot, accepted the cup and gulped down a third of it.

"Good morning," he said when he came up for air. "Thank you. Why am I here?" He tried to be gracious, but as he spoke it sounded rude to him.

"You were hurt," Cindy replied, her smile flipping over into a pout. "I couldn't let him take you to some hotel."

"Him is your father, I assume." He stepped past her to sit on the couch. "Where is he? Come to think of it, that must be his room. Where'd he sleep?"

"Oh, he took the couch." She sat beside him. She was being far too sweet and he wanted to be mad.

"That wasn't necessary." He took another big gulp of coffee.

"You were hurt." She was playing with him, and he did not know how to react. "Come in the kitchen and join us for some breakfast. Then you can drop me at work, then go get checked out by a good doctor."

His Seiko told him it was nine-thirty. "Aren't you late?"

"I'm an attorney," Cindy replied in her haughtiest voice. "I told them I'd be in when I got in. I wanted to wait until you were up. Now there's juice and toast and bacon and juevos rancheros in there, you know what that is? Good. Anything else you want?"

"Yeah. I want my pants." But she had managed to make him smile.

* * *

The Hannibal Jones who walked into Balor's office was all business. Hannibal had waited fifteen minutes for a client to leave, but he showed no signs of impatience. This Hannibal wore the same dark glasses and gloves he had worn during his earlier visit, but now he was dressed in black jeans and a pullover, running shoes, and a black shell windbreaker. He presented a very different image from the dapper young man who had walked into Balor's office three days before. Balor looked closely at the abrasion on Hannibal's face. Hannibal hoped it wasn't a show of weakness, but rather that it would emphasize his tougher image.

"Morning," Balor said, taking a seat. "That's not a rash on your cheek, is it? Things get rough over there in Anacostia?"

"Yeah," Hannibal replied, continuing to stand.

"Uh-huh." Balor nodded with resignation. "And now you come to tell me you want out."

"Not a chance." Hannibal saw in Balor's eyes that he had overreacted, and toned his voice down a notch. "I come to tell you things are going to get rougher. You got to stay behind me, no matter what, you understand? I'll clear that place out tonight. In a week, you'll be able to start renting it. First, I got to prove to the squatters that they can't come back. When they settle somewhere else, then I'm off the case."

Balor leaned back, taking a long hard look at the man in front of him. He focused on Hannibal's dark glasses, as if he wanted a better look at his eyes.

"You know, I pride myself on being able to read people," Balor said. "I don't really know you, but I can read your body language all right. Your whole attitude tells me you're serious. You really are just getting started, aren't you? Okay, what can I do to help?"

"That's easy," Hannibal said. "You can turn the place on."

"What? I don't..."

"Turn it on." He rested his hands on Balor's desk. "The lights, the gas, the phone. All of it. And be prepared for the cost of those renovations you said you planned to do. Oh, and I need you to whip up a dummy lease for me."

"You moving in?" Balor asked with a smile.

"You couldn't pay me to live in that place for real. But for right now, the only way to keep those junkies and winos out is to be there to chase them away."

"Kind of an elitist attitude, isn't it Mister Jones?" Balor picked up a cigar, but never flicked his lighter because he saw Hannibal stiffen at his remark.

"You know, I've heard that stuff all my life. Man wants to stay in his slum, that means he don't want to get ahead. Man wants to leave the slums behind, he's got an attitude, betraying somebody. Just you remember you're fighting this battle long distance, Bro. I'm the hose flushing that place out."

-16-

Raul's body language told Hannibal that he recognized the white Volvo 850 GLT when it pulled up to the curb, and after a moment he clearly recognized the driver. While Hannibal stepped out of the back seat, Ray slouched up front, as if trying to disappear. Hannibal stepped up to Raul, staring up into his tiny pig eyes. The bright sunshine glinting off the car behind Hannibal might have been the cause of Raul's squint, but Hannibal doubted it.

"Adolfo's expecting me," he said, holding a neutral expression. Then he kept his movements slow and easy on his way down the stairs and into the office. The two front bruisers sat at one desk playing cards. He walked past, ignoring them.

Adolfo Espino was pushing a forkful of taco salad into his face when Hannibal leaned one hip up on the desk and pulled a roll of bills from his pocket. While staring off in another direction, he peeled off a pair of hundred dollar bills and dropped them on the desk.

"What do you know," Espino said around a mouthful of food. "And it ain't even noon yet." He returned his attention to his food but looked up a few seconds later when he realized that Hannibal was still there.

"So, Adolfo," Hannibal looked down as if he had not heard what the other man said, "you know this guy Sal who runs a little business over in Southeast?"

Espino slowed his eating and pushed back slightly from the desk. "I might know him."

"Well, between you and me, he's a punk, you know?" Hannibal smiled, but behind his Oakley's his eyes were cold. "He must have some heavy backing to keep from getting squished."

"So?"

"So, who?"

Espino shook his head and shoved fingers into his greasy hair. "Boy, I don't know how you walk, you got so much balls. What you want to mess with little Sal for?"

Hannibal spread his hands. "Hey, what do you care? It's business. I just want to know what I'm getting into." Espino stood up, turned and paced to the back of the room. He came back with his hands in his pockets, shaking his head again. The only sound in the room was the slap of pasteboards on a desk at the front of the office. Eventually the silence shook something loose.

"I'm going to do you a favor, Paco. You're right about this boy Sal. He's just playing. Nobody messes with him, because of his old man."

"Yeah?" Hannibal dropped to his feet to pace with Espino. "Who's he?"

Espino stared up into Hannibal's glasses. "Mr. Ronzini could crush you like an ant under his thumb."

"Think he cares about what Sal does down in Southeast?"

"Care?" Espino laughed. "He probably don't even know. But he won't let anybody mess with his only boy. Bet your ass on that."

"Okay, Adolfo, thanks." Hannibal slapped the little man's shoulder. "See you next week."

"I can't wait. Oh, by the way, about your friend."

Hannibal stopped, turning with one eyebrow cocked above his glasses. "My friend?"

"Yeah. Santiago, Raymond. The guy you paying the bill for. Word got to me that he told his bookie he's working again. He's already looking for credit. Them guys play rougher than me, you know. Hate to see this become a full time job for you, know what I mean?"

* * *

A pensive Hannibal returned to his car and directed Ray to head south. He had some gear to pick up from a very specialized supplier. It didn't take long for the urbanized Washington landscape to give way to the tree-lined Virginia countryside. A forty-five minute drive took them to the Woodbridge exit off I-95. On the way they found a Popeye's fast food restaurant with a drive through. Ray negotiated the vicious Northern Virginia traffic with a soda between his legs and curly fries in his door's map pocket. He talked around bites of chicken.

"You know, Hannibal, Cindy asked me if you were coming back tonight. She makes a good breakfast, eh?"

Hannibal, also biting into chicken pieces, had covered himself with napkins. "Don't worry, bro, I'm not planning to take your bed."

"Hey, I wouldn't mind."

"I don't think it's a good idea for me to just move in." He was trying to be gentle. "Besides, I'm sleeping at twenty-three thirteen tonight."

There was a pause while Ray chewed and swallowed. "You sleeping with them druggies?"

"No," Hannibal said, "they're sleeping elsewhere. I'm going to evict them."

"And just how you going to do that, tough guy?" Ray slowed down to look in his rearview mirror at Hannibal.

"That's what this trip's for, bro. To get the gear I need to exterminate the place. Now hit the CD player, will you?"

"Where is it?" Ray asked, staring at the dashboard radio.

"Never mind." Hannibal reached between the front bucket seats and poked buttons. David Sanborn oozed smoothly from eight speakers. Hannibal did not feel he needed to explain that the compact disc player was in the trunk, loaded with a six pack.

The snappy jazz of Sanborn's horn followed them away from the highway and into the lush green of Virginia's countryside. Soon Hannibal directed Ray to a solid looking two-story house with no visible neighbors, built back against a hill. It was an older home, unusual enough in this bedroom community that was merely a distant suburb of Washington. A well cared for lawn lay behind a short stone wall. Ray turned onto the gravel driveway and stopped in front of the garage. Hannibal climbed out of the car and stretched his legs while he inhaled the fresh-mown atmosphere. He thought the house had character. Maybe it was the stone chimney rising on one end. The same stones made up the front wall and the path leading to the front door.

"Come on in," he called to Ray, waving him on. "You'll like Frasier. He's wild." He pushed the bell and stood staring ahead. He could feel the eyes on the other side of the tiny peephole examining him. If someone had taken him there under duress he had a signal he would give involving scratching his nose and looking to the right, then left. Eddy Frasier was a very careful man.

When the door flew open, a stocky man in aviator glasses grabbed Hannibal's arms and lifted him inside. Words poured forth, rapid fire and high energy.

"Hannibal Jones, how the hell are you? I ain't seen you in a dog's age. Whatdoyousay, pal? This business or pleasure? Who's your friend?"

"Take a breath, bro," Hannibal said. "Eddy Frasier, this is Ray Santiago." The men shook hands. Ray fidgeted, clearly uncomfortable under Frasier's wild-eyed gaze.

"Ray works with me," Hannibal said while Frasier went to the bar in the living room and set out three fluted glasses. "He's a great wheel man. Ray, Frasier here used to be DIA. Now he helps independents like me with outfitting."

"I just like to play with the toys." Frasier stood three bottles of Samuel Adams beside the glasses and opened one. "Take a look at this, Hannibal." Frasier held out his left wrist while his right hand poured beer.

"Okay, a quartz digital watch." Hannibal sipped at his own beer glass. "So does it blow up or something?"

"Camera." Frasier wiped his lips with a napkin. "Uses seven exposure cartridges. Takes thirty-five millimeter black and whites. And the watch works, timer, alarm, the whole bit."

"He serious?" Ray asked quietly.

"Oh yeah," Hannibal said. "When it comes to the toys, Frasier is always serious." Turning to Frasier, he asked, "How much?"

"For you? A thousand bucks, and I'll throw in the developing kit."

"How about for somebody else?" Hannibal asked.

"A thousand bucks."

Hannibal shook his head. "Maybe next time. Today I'm looking for something special."

"Should have called." Frasier emptied his glass. "I'm not a warehouse, you know."

"I know you got what I want," Hannibal said.

"Which is?"

"A bloop tube." Hannibal let his eyes wander. Frasier's house always looked to him like a hunting lodge. He kept expecting to find something's head hanging on the wall.

"Downstairs." Frasier stood as if his chair had spikes in it, and pulled open the door leading to his basement. Hannibal and Ray quickly followed.

Below Frasier's living room they entered a comfortable finished basement. Frasier leaned against the paneling on the back wall and cut his eyes toward Ray. Hannibal nodded. Frasier shrugged, put both hands against the wall behind him, and slid the panel aside. With his back against the steel door now revealed, he turned a combination dial, which his body hid. Hannibal listened to the ratcheting, then the click. When the door swung inward, Frasier backed inside and his guests followed him.

The hidden room, built into the hill behind the house, looked twice as big as Frasier's living room. The walls were covered by brackets holding rifles, shotguns and a variety of edged and bludgeon weapons Hannibal recognized but figured Ray would not. No museum could match Ray's collection of exotic weaponry. Steel filing cabinets lined one wall. Wooden bins and chests formed aisles in the room, giving it the appearance of a bizarre supermarket of mayhem. The air was unusually dry, and Hannibal could hear the soft hiss of ventilation. Across the room, Frasier lifted what looked like a single barreled shotgun down from brackets. With its wooden butt the weapon was not quite thirty inches long.

"Here you go, Hannibal. M79 grenade launcher. Forty millimeter."

Hannibal broke open the shotgun-style weapon and looked down its aluminum barrel. "Very nice. Now, I don't want to own this beauty, just rent her for about twenty-four hours. I'll also need a half dozen smoke grenades."

"Parachute type?" Frasier pulled open a drawer in a file cabinet.

"No, ground markers," Hannibal said, "I need the ones that go off on impact.

"Roger." Frasier handed Ray a cardboard box of grenades, which looked like aluminum shotgun shells. "That it?"

"Afraid so." Hannibal clicked his weapon back together. "Got to run. I'm on the clock."

"No problem, man. Pay me when you bring the stuff back. Hey, Gretch is going to be mad she missed you."

"Give her my best," Hannibal said as they left the hidden room. From outside Ray stared back into the weapons vault until the steel door swung completely shut.

"Can I ask you a question?"

Frasier smiled. "Hey, he can talk. I was beginning to think you were like Zorro's sidekick in the old TV show. Well, what's on your mind?"

"Where do you get all that stuff?"

Frasier's conversational tone never varied. "Well I could tell you, but then I'd have to kill you."

Frasier chuckled to himself maniacally while showing his guests back up the stairs and to the door. There he hugged Hannibal tightly, slapping his back like a long lost brother. Ray shook Frasier's hand with clear reluctance just before he and Hannibal finally left. Hannibal did not say anything when they got in the car. He could see Ray took Frasier far too seriously, and he had no intention of disillusioning him. They were back on the highway before Ray spoke again.

"So you got your plan and you got your toys, so what now?"

Hannibal leaned forward. "Now, Ray, I've got a favor to ask. We need to hit a few stores for me to pick up some necessities for tonight. But after I get that stuff jammed into the trunk..." he hesitated, rethought it, and went on. "After that, I'd like to take Cindy to a nice seafood place. Kind of..."

"Alone?" Ray asked. "No sweat, chico. I'll just take a nap and you can pick me up after, to head out to the house."

Hannibal leaned back smiling, and said "thanks" so low Ray barely heard it.

-17-

It wasn't at all what Hannibal expected. When he told Cindy that he wanted to take her to her favorite place, he expected her to name an expensive seafood restaurant in the suburbs, or maybe on the Maryland coast where eateries competed for who could claim to have the best crab cakes. His first surprise arrived soon after he picked her up at her office. Their destination was only a few minutes away, just west of Dupont Circle. They got lucky and found parking on the street just a block away.

They were not in the suburbs or on the shore, and as they stepped through the door Hannibal realized this was not to be an expensive meal. The restaurant was little more than a café, really, snuggled down in the basement of a townhouse. The decor was modern and stylish in an unpretentious way. As fancy as they were, the chairs were still folding chairs. The lighting was dim, but the colors surrounding them were so bright that the walls and decorations seemed to shed their own light.

As they settled in at their laminated table, he also realized that she had not steered them here to order a lobster or fresh caught crabs or even that local favorite, a salt baked rockfish. Salsa Thai was not a seafood restaurant, but he had guessed that by the name.

"First time here?" Cindy asked, picking up a menu.

"I'm pretty much a steak and potatoes kind of guy myself."

"We'll fix that," she said through a smile. In the soft light, Hannibal saw Cindy's face as if for the first time. He had never noticed that she wore makeup and now he realized that what she did wear was very subtle. Her lipstick was nearly worn off by this time of the day and for some reason he found it amusing that she had not bothered to freshen it before her meal. Her hair was down and its ends looked tired, drooping from a long workday. Yet her eyes belied the other signs. They were full of life, wide awake and ready for more. And as he picked up his menu he noticed that she was watching him as closely as he had observed her.

"Something?"

Cindy nodded. "That's a nasty scrape on your cheek. It didn't look that bad this morning."

"Occupational hazard," Hannibal said. "I don't think it will be a scar, though."

"Oh." He wasn't sure if she was relieved or disappointed by that news. But she seemed to be smiling as she looked over her menu. "Did you have a doctor take a look at it?"

"It wasn't bad enough for that," Hannibal said. "I'm kind of used to taking care of the small injuries myself. I put some NuSkin on it. You'll hardly notice it tomorrow." He looked down at his own menu in some confusion. He recognized a lot of the words, but not many of the actual foods listed. It wasn't just his first visit to this Thai restaurant, but rather his first time in any Thai restaurant.

"Since, this is your favorite place, why don't you order for us?"

"It's my favorite mostly because it's close," Cindy said, signaling a waiter. "And the food is really good, if you like hot stuff. Do you like hot stuff, Mister Jones?"

He smiled broadly. "Are you always so full of innuendo, Ms. Santiago?"

"Is that what I'm full of?" she said in response. Then, to the waiter she said "Bring us some of those Pinkies in a Blanket for starters, and a couple of Chang beers. Then the wild pork for me, and for the newbie here, hmm, I think beef with basil leaves and chili. And make everything Bangkok hot."

Their beers arrived first, and Hannibal smiled at the two elephants apparently butting heads on the label before tipping the bottle's contents into his glass. It produced a bubbly head, but the head shrank rapidly, which Hannibal did not take as a good sign. Cindy surprised him by taking a substantial swallow from hers.

"Authentic Thai beer," Cindy said. "Brewed in Thailand but imported by a D.C. company."

"And you obviously like it a lot," Hannibal grinned.

"Hey, in my business you have to be able to drink."

"The practice of law requires a good alcohol tolerance?" Hannibal asked, taking a tentative sip from his glass. The beer was thin, and bitter enough to make his head shake. Maybe he didn't have what it took to be a lawyer.

"Well, business law, specifically, requires a lot of dinners and cocktail parties with clients. You've got to be able to both drink and hold your liquor. A shame really. I know a lot of alcoholic attorneys."

Hannibal took another sip. Despite an aftertaste he would find hard to describe, it really wasn't too bad. It seemed light of body to him, but that could just be in comparison to the German beers he had drunk so much of.

"Yes, you did say something about working with businesses," he said, watching her drain her glass to one-third its original contents. "Is that what you did at the last place too?"

"Oh there was no last place. I joined Nieswand and Balor as an associate right out of law school. But enough about me. I want to know why nobody has heard about a hero like you. Don't you have a publicist?"

The girl made him laugh, and he was doing so, quietly, as their appetizers arrived. At first glance they looked like nothing more than egg rolls. Hannibal picked one up as he spoke.

"Cindy, low profile is the very essence of the Secret Service. Especially in the protective service, which is where I was.

People see you a dozen times on television or at a speech, but they still shouldn't recognize you." He stopped to take a bite, and smiled as the flavor spread through his mouth.

"That's a Pinky in the Blanket," Cindy said, selecting one for herself. "Really, just shrimp fried in an egg roll wrapper, but boy are they good. Dip it in that stuff. And tell me why you left the service."

Hannibal swirled his bit of food in the dark red sauce Cindy indicated. "I had a disagreement with my boss," he said. "I don't want to get into specifics, but it had to do with whether I had a duty to protect the principle's reputation as well as his life. This all came up after a particular incident. I didn't think my duty included covering up stupid actions. My supervisor did. The friction between us just grew and grew." He paused to take a bite.

"So what happened?" Cindy asked. "Did you get into an argument?"

"I slugged him. Hey, that's really good. And hot. I mean really hot, not like the stuff they usually call spicy in a restaurant."

"Wait a minute," Cindy said. "You hit your boss?"

"Well, yeah. Knocked him down, actually." Hannibal dipped another appetizer, bit it in half, and followed it with a swallow of beer. Now it tasted pretty good.

Cindy was smiling fully now, her head tipped to the side just so in a way that seemed awfully charming to Hannibal. "I take it they frown on that kind of thing in government service."

"Actually, the guy was known to be a bit of an asshole so they were pretty easy on me," Hannibal said. "They allowed me to resign, and helped me get my private investigator's license. All of a sudden, I was self-employed. That was only a few months ago. Say, don't we need a couple more beers?"

Before Cindy could respond, their entrees arrived. Aside from delivering their main plates, the waiter spread small containers all over the table including plenty of steamed rice. Hannibal knew the rice would come in handy to absorb the spice if all the food was as hot as his first sample.

"Man, everything looks good," Hannibal said. "I guess it was dumb for me to expect you to want the standard stuff. I even considered trying to find a Cuban restaurant but I see you've moved well past that stuff."

"Don't jump to any conclusions," Cindy said, choosing a fork to attack her wild pork. "Despite what my father might think, I haven't turned my back on my heritage. In fact, nobody can do the Cuban cooking thing as well as I can in my own kitchen. Maybe some time soon I'll let you sample my own paella."

"Now that's an invitation I couldn't say no to," Hannibal said. "If I ever eat again, that is. If we finish all this stuff they'll have to roll us home when we're done."

"Or at least back to the office, for me," Cindy said,

Hannibal's eyes lowered to his own plate. "Your office? You're going back to work after dinner?"

"I have things that just need to be finished," Cindy said. In the dim indoor twilight the restaurant maintained her eyes sparkled alluringly. There was enough room noise to make Hannibal lean forward when her voice lowered. "You know, I could possibly change my plans. That is, if you're free for the rest of the evening."

"No," Hannibal said, almost in a sigh. "I'm afraid I'm working tonight too. You're not the only one with unfinished business to pursue."

-18-

Nine o'clock seemed late to be knocking on Mother Washington's door. Hannibal fidgeted on the porch and unthinkingly straightened up when he heard her coming.

"Who is it?" the woman called in a strong voice.

"It's Hannibal Jones, Mother Washington," he called through the door. "I was here last night."

A chain rattled and three locks clicked before the door opened. Monty stood behind his grandmother, a dubious backstop in case all was not as it should be. She wore a pleasant face, but mumbled something about bothering old people at this time of night. Hannibal smiled and stepped in, to be greeted by the warm aroma of chocolate chip cookies. When he stopped in front of the sofa the room became suddenly quiet, as if Monty and his grandmother were waiting for him to make the first move.

"It's actually Monty I came to see. I need a favor."

"What you need, child?" Mrs. Washington instantly became interested when it sounded like someone might need help.

"I'm fine, Mother Washington, really," he assured her, not sitting. "I really need Monty to just do something for me. I'm going in number twenty-three thirteen."

"Oh, wow!" Monty said, but Hannibal's statement put a look of horror on Mother Washington's face.

"I'm going in there in a few minutes," Hannibal continued, "And when I do I'd like to have lots of company, and I think I know how to arrange it. Can Monty make a phone call for me?"

Hannibal had left Ray parked around the corner. Now he stood in the backyard of Balor's contested building, looking up at long unused clotheslines that still hung slack from three of the open kitchen windows out to the row of tall trees behind him. A rusted fire escape, little more than an iron ladder, snaked down the wall beside those windows.

Glowing ghostly under a full moon, the yard was a field of knee high weeds, as wide as the house but not very deep. The little yard was alive with a chorus of crickets. It smelled of decay and rust, and long ago visits from untrained dogs. Neighboring yards looked little different. What was it like there, he wondered, before the despair that comes with unemployment stripped away all pride of ownership?

Almost tripping over a rusted tricycle, he set down his shopping bag. Then his black form sank into the weeds, all but disappearing. He knew what he planned to do would draw attention, but he wanted people in the house behind him to be able to say they could not see him.

Next he pulled the M79 from the bag, breaking open its black anodized barrel and shoving a cartridge inside. He clicked his weapon together, flipped up the leaf sight and got comfortable with the stock against his left shoulder. He used the skeletal tricycle to support his grenade launcher. A quick look at his watch told him that if Monty was sticking to the schedule he had just dialed his grandmother's telephone. Hannibal had no doubt that Monty would sound suitably hysterical to the people at the other end.

* * *

Sylvia was so nervous she spilled a drop of the precious fluid from her spoon. Sitting in that first floor kitchen, her eyes flashed from left to right.

"What's the matter, baby?" her partner asked, staring not at her but at the trembling spoon full of melted junk.

"It's that man," Sylvia moaned. "That man that crashed in here, waving a gun in my face. He did this to me."

"Relax babe. You're all right now."

All right? Was she? Resting the needle against her arm Sylvia noticed, as if for the first time, how thin she was. Just bones wrapped in dark brown skin. It was only one sign of her spiraling dive toward hell. Her hair was falling out. Her teeth were bad. And the pain came around on schedule every night about this time.

Despite all that, she had never considered going to the hospital for help until that man had pointed a pistol at her head. Now, thanks to him, she was terrified.

Sitting there, just about to shoot up, she suddenly felt as if somebody was watching her. Impulsively, she dropped her needle and spun toward the windows. Deep blackness hung against them, yet the feeling remained.

"What the hell's the matter with you, girl?" her partner asked.

Was it just the paranoia again, she wondered. She wrapped her bony fingers around the edge of the sink and stared wide-eyed into the darkness behind the house. Her own reflection stared back from inches beyond the window. Fear twisted her face into a ghoulish mask, but she was not sure what she was afraid of. If one more thing happened, she silently swore, she would run to that hospital and beg for help.

* * *

Surrounded by tall grass and weeds, Hannibal raised his barrel, lining up the left top window in his sights. When he squeezed the M79's trigger, it rewarded him with its signature thumping sound which, although impossible to describe, had earned the weapon its nickname.

By the time the first grenade landed in one apartment's kitchen, he had reloaded. On his second try he aimed a little high, breaking a raised window. Just before his third shot, a light came on behind him. Some neighbor he assumed, trying to figure out what was making that weird noise.

Thick smoke billowed out from the top left window before he sent a grenade into window number four. He heard a high female voice behind him say "What the hell is that?" but he was sure no one could see him. He had the final window lined up, but froze because he saw a face behind it. It looked like the skinny female junkie he met there.

When she turned away from the window, he pumped his last shell into it. Voices were rising in the building now, a general panic evident from inarticulate screams. A small smile curled the edge of his mouth. Moving in a crouch, he turned and quietly left the backyard.

*   *   *

At his car, Hannibal tossed the shopping bag into the back seat.

"You ought to see your grin," Ray said.

"I just like it when the easy stuff works. I'm going around. I want to see some faces, dig? Bring her around when the fireworks are over." This time, the sound of approaching sirens made him smile.

Hands in his pockets, Hannibal strolled around the corner, whistling an O'Jays tune he had heard the night before. The air on the street smelled far sweeter than the atmosphere in the backyard. An occasional blank-faced person rushed past him and disappeared into the darkness. He reached the front of the building in time to watch the last few rats desert their sinking ship, just before competing sirens heralded the approach of the first fire truck. A small circle of neighbors had gathered in the street to watch the smoke pouring from every orifice of the supposedly abandoned building. As emergency vehicles rolled into place they fell back to the sidewalk across the street.

Two long red trucks blocked the street, their sirens still wailing, their occupants pouring out like ants from a poisoned hill. Hoses were hurriedly attached to hydrants and pulled into position, but not opened up.

A white boxy ambulance stood nearby, two of its emergency personnel leaning against it. A police car stood at each end of the street for crowd control. Once everything was in place Hannibal wandered down to the nearest police car. A blue uniformed man spoke into a bullhorn, telling the yawning crowd to remain calm.

"They don't seem to be fighting the fire," Hannibal remarked. The policeman turned to him. He had the look of a ranger, with a lean frame, close cut hair and piercing eyes.

"Don't think they will. That smoke's too white to be from a house fire. Looks like signal smoke to me. They sent some guys inside to check it out."

"What do you know," Hannibal said blandly. "False alarms must be a bitch, officer..."

"Kendall," he supplied. "And if the guy who did it called it in, he's in deep shit. Probably, though, somebody saw the smoke start to come out and just called. Can't jump on that citizen."

"You got a good attitude, Sarge." Hannibal leaned against the car. "And since I live there, I'm in a position to keep this from being a wasted trip, at least for you."

The cop lowered his bullhorn, looking again at the man in front of him, staring hard at the black windbreaker and gloves Hannibal was wearing on this August night.

"You live there?"

"Well, just starting today," Hannibal said. "In fact, I'm the only legal resident. However, I checked it out earlier and I happen to know there's a major cache of stolen goods inside."

"Well, what do you know," Kendall shot back. "Now, if I just had a search warrant I could go in there and bring it all out."

"You don't get out of it that easy." Hannibal wagged a finger at him. "You were called here for an emergency. Just like those firemen can go in to look for the cause of the fire, so can you, to investigate the false alarm." Kendall looked at him, hesitating for a minute. "Come on. It's free."

What little crowd the commotion attracted was dispersing, just like the smoke from the house. Kendall followed Hannibal up to the stoop of twenty-three thirteen. Firemen had just about secured their gear, and one truck had already left. One disgruntled firefighter walked past Hannibal carrying five spent shell casings in a plastic bag. It had not taken them long to find the source of the smoke.

Hannibal had just about convinced Kendall to open the outer door and walk in when a bald black man with a crinkly beard mounted the steps behind them. He started past them, on his way into the building, but Hannibal grabbed his arm to stop him. When he turned, anger flashed in his eyes, but not recognition.

"Lose your dog?" Hannibal asked. "Listen, man, you can't go in there."

"Yeah?" The man's eyes bounced off the policeman's uniform and returned to Hannibal. "And why is that?"

"You're trespassing," Hannibal said confidently.

"No, brother, I live here."

"Really?" Hannibal stepped slightly to the side, almost sandwiching the man between himself and Kendall. "The owner told me I had the only valid lease here." He pulled the folded form from his hip pocket. "I'll show you mine if you'll show me yours."

"I don't carry my lease around," the bald man said, turning to go. Hannibal held his arm tightly.

"No problem," he said, holding a thin-lipped smile. "We can go up to your flat and get it."

Now the bearded man stared hard at Hannibal, memorizing his features. "I think I lost it," he said slowly.

"Shame." Hannibal met that hard gaze. "We can just contact the landlord and straighten all this out. What's his name again? And where do you send the rent check?"

The bearded man snapped, "Fuck you," gave the cop a hard glance and walked off into the night. Kendall's eyes followed him for a moment, then returned to Hannibal.

"You want to tell me the rest of it?"

"Why not? My name's Hannibal Jones, I'm a PI, and I'm currently in the employ of the owner of this building." While he talked, he produced his license and let Kendall have a good long look. "He really did sign this lease, I really do legally live here, and I really am the only legal resident."

"And the stolen goods?"

"Third floor, left." Hannibal started up. "Come on, this is on the level. In fact, that guy that just left is the fence, maybe the thief. You could go arrest him."

"Sure, if I had some real evidence." Kendall started inside. Hannibal followed. Kendall's flashlight led them up the stairs. On the last flight he stopped and faced Hannibal in the darkness.

"Know what I think?" he said. "I think this is all your gag. I'll bet I could pinch you for that little practical joke with the smoke."

"Sure, if you had some real evidence." The two men exchanged smiles in the dark.

Hannibal was pleased to find the door unlocked, evidence the owner had left in a considerable hurry. After a few seconds flailing around in darkness, he found a lamp and turned its switch. Powered by pirated electricity, the bulb burst into life. Officer Kendall whistled one long, descending note as he looked around at the disorderly shelves and stacks of electronic components.

"Didn't even know Crazy Eddy's had a branch in D.C." Kendall said. "It'd take me a week to get this stuff out of here. It'll take the department a month to try to find the rightful owners."

"Yeah. Wanted to talk to you about that." Hannibal opened both windows in the room to clear the remaining smoke, crossed the room again and shoved his hands deep into his pockets. He decided to lean against the door sill, presenting the least threatening picture he could manage. Kendall dropped into the tattered sofa, smiling, waiting for the sales pitch.

"I been wondering just what you're up to."

"Then let's play it straight," Hannibal said. "This place is a crack house. There's a shooting gallery downstairs, vagrants crash here, streetwalkers bring their Johns in here to take care of business. As you can see, it's also a warehouse for thieves and fences. I'm here to undo all that, to turn this place into a money making proposition for the owner. Now don't misunderstand me. I don't think my employer has me down here because he's full of community spirit. He paid good money for this place and he wants to make money off it. But you got to admit, if I do my job right, it'll have some pleasant side effects for the hood."

"Let's cut to the chase. You want help, is that it?"

"Nothing weird," Hannibal assured him in his softest voice. "I can take care of myself, but I could use some time. How about you get some of your fellow officers in here tonight to seize and impound all these stolen goods? They'd have to list and catalog it all and check for ID tags and such, right?"

Kendall stopped for a moment to think, which Hannibal found very encouraging. In his experience, uniformed cops rarely did such things. When he looked up, it seemed he had gotten the idea. He pulled a pack of Camels from his shirt pocket and lit one.

"In other words, you're looking for a high profile police presence," Kendall said. "And while we run interference, what? You move in, set up, and start turning this place into a fortress, is that it?"

"Something like that. Actually, I figure if I can just get settled, the problem will go away in a couple of days. Junkies and bums ain't known for their determination, or their attention span. They'll find an easier place to crash."

"Sure hope you're right." Kendall stood, shaking his head.

"Meantime, maybe you can use this cache as an excuse to increase patrols in the hood?"

Kendall stood up, took a long drag on his cigarette, and rested his other hand on Hannibal's shoulder. Hannibal made a special effort not to react.

"You know, if we maintain too much of a presence around here, it can make things worse with the local citizens. I'll goose it up as much as I can without anybody thinking we're trying to, you know, be a bunch of Nazis or something."

Hannibal nodded and eased his shoulder out from under Kendall's hand to head down the stairs. The cop followed. When they reached the front stoop, Hannibal's car stood out front. While Kendall headed for his patrol car to file a report, Hannibal stepped up to his Volvo. Ray, very nervous, powered down his window.

"You sure about all this?" Ray asked.

"All of it," Hannibal assured him. "Just pop the trunk, okay? The sooner we get this stuff unloaded, the sooner you can go home."

Ray pushed the necessary button and Hannibal raised the trunk lid. By the time he pulled out his sleeping bag and air mattress, Ray was standing beside him.

"It ain't too late for me to stay here with you, Paco."

Hannibal's gear was packed into a large duffel. He shouldered his burden and turned to his friend. "Ray, if you stay, my car will be here. My beautiful Volvo. I am not prepared to try to defend the house and watch the white tornado all night."

While Ray stayed near the car, Hannibal went inside, settling his bedding in the first floor apartment on the left, the one the heroin crowd previously used. It wasn't even close to clean, but it did contain a couple of rusted metal chairs from an old kitchen set. He quickly ran through the flat, looking for drugs. It was no surprise to him that the users had not left a single grain of powder behind. However, he did gather quite a collection of needles, both new and used, and catheters, the rubber tubing the addicts used to tie off their arms. Odd, he thought, how something as deadly as heroin could make a comeback. As if crack cocaine wasn't bad enough. It sometimes seemed that the bad things in life never really went away. They just changed their shape or found a new audience.

Not knowing how long it might take the police to arrive, he sprinted upstairs. In the apartment full of stolen goods he found a dresser that the previous resident had used to store tools and spare parts. He dumped the drug paraphernalia on top of a variety of screwdrivers, closed the drawer, and hurried back downstairs.

He had chosen a first floor flat because he thought people might try to reenter through windows. On the first floor he could patrol likely entrances. Besides, he knew it would take a day or two for the utilities to be turned on. He knew that apartment's electric stove worked, which meant that at least in the kitchen he had pirated electricity. He would let one of his new neighbors pay his meager power bill for a couple of days.

He returned to his car, retrieving a couple of large shopping bags from its trunk. He had packed a variety of necessities for his stay at the house. On his third and final trip from the car, Ray slammed the trunk and stood facing him.

"Hannibal, mi amigo, this is loco. These people kill each other like it's nothing."

"These people?" Hannibal asked.

"These drug people," Ray explained. "They'll cut their best friend's throat for a dime bag, man. You know they'll dust you like nothing."

"Ray, I'm perfectly safe inside. Now let me get set up. I'll be looking for you at noon tomorrow. You got the list? The cleaning stuff is especially important." Ray stood in his path as if he had more to say. Hannibal, standing with hands on hips, blew one heavy breath at the ground. In a gentle voice he said, "Look, I'll be careful, okay?" He slapped Ray on the shoulder, and got a half smile in return before Ray returned to the car.

Hannibal watched his own car pull away through the big front window of his new home. He was just thinking how alone he was when another vehicle pulled up out front. A glance out a window told him a police van had arrived. He smiled at the long blue line snaking out, heading for his building.

Then he turned to making his home livable. Wandering the flat, he placed an Airwick in each room. A shopping bag yielded a small foot pump, with which he began inflating his air mattress. That done, he pulled out a telephone and plugged it into a wall jack. With it pressed against his ear he heard silence as expected. He left it off the hook, knowing that a most annoying noise would let him know the second service was established.

He had some fresh oranges, pears, apples and bananas to cover his first couple of meals. His fruit was sealed in plastic bags, which he hoped would suffice to keep out the roaches and any rodents he might be sharing the house with. He sat three books beside his bed. Next he carried one of the big shopping bags into the kitchen. Guided by moonlight he pulled out a coffeepot and a small, shadeless lamp. Using a cube tap, he plugged the lamp and coffee maker into the fixture supplying the stove. Once he had light he filled the coffee basket with grounds. The next thing out of the bag was a water filter that he screwed onto the faucet. After letting the sink run for three minutes, he filled the coffee pot's reservoir. When the aroma of fresh brew hit his nose, he wandered into the hall. There he watched the river of televisions, VCRs and radios flowing down the stairs until he spotted Kendall.

"Hey, pal, come in and take a load off for a minute."

Kendall stopped, stereo components under each arm. "Little busy right now, Jones."

"Okay. Can you just tell your friends I belong here? And, look, I'm leaving my kitchen door open. There's fresh coffee in here, and Styrofoam cups, spoons, sugar and creamer in packets. Everybody in blue can help themselves. Just ask them to hit the trash bag with their garbage."

Kendall was on the edge of laughter by the time Hannibal finished. "What, no donuts?" he asked. Hannibal chose not to answer, instead going back inside long enough to pick up one of the overloaded shopping bags. He had things to do, and he wanted to move around while the presence of so many policemen made unwanted interruption unlikely.

Secret Service work had taught him the importance of securing his area. Good security meant paying attention to details. Carrying a long, police type flashlight he went next door, to the other first floor apartment. Starting in the front room, he moved around the flat, nailing each window shut. The kitchen presented a different challenge because, aside from the window over the sink, there was a door to the backyard. Hannibal pulled two blocks of wood from his bag and nailed one across each of the outer corners.

Back in "his" apartment, he found three policemen in the kitchen, sipping coffee. Less than half a cup remained in the pot. Hannibal resisted the urge to make a caustic remark while pouring the dregs into a cup for himself. Then he pulled out the box of Gevalia Stockholm roast and started a fresh pot.

"Thanks for the java," one cop said, making conversation. "You know, I thought druggies were still using this place to shoot up."

"Yeah, I know," Hannibal answered, starting to nail the kitchen windows down. "I'm hoping they'll find a new place for that after tonight. And I hope you boys appreciate the help."

The cop crushed his cup and tossed it at the trash bag. "Don't get me wrong, but it don't do shit for us. I mean, yeah they're gone, but they'll just pop up somewhere else."

"Maybe," Hannibal said, rinsing out the pot. "If you'd have come in here and busted them, maybe not."

The silent policeman pulled his talkative partner back out into the flow of stolen goods while Hannibal kicked three rubber wedges under the kitchen's back door. He wanted one escape route that was not permanently closed.

Policemen were still carrying hot items out when he finished. A few detoured for a cursory search of the premises, adding drugs to their haul. Hannibal took this opportunity to explore the house more thoroughly. After checking its fixtures he was sure he had dropped his gear in the best flat. His base of operations contained the building's only functioning stove and sink. Not that the apartment was fully habitable. The pipe leading to the bathtub sprayed water around the room when he turned it on. The only tub in the building with running water that did not leak was on the second floor, so he would be spending some time up there. For other needs he would have to plan ahead. The third floor flat so recently used as an electronic storage area contained the only operable toilet. Considering how hospitable its previous occupant had been, Hannibal wondered what everyone else in the building did when nature called. Then again, maybe he didn't want to know.

An hour later, Hannibal stood in the door to his new apartment, watching the last blue uniforms waving their way out the door. Kendall stayed until all the others were gone.

"Not sure if I admire or pity you, Jones," Kendall said, shaking Hannibal's hand, "but I sure do wish you the best."

"Thanks," Hannibal said. "Don't take this the wrong way, but I sure hope I don't have to see you here again."

Hannibal closed the hall door behind Kendall, noticing the forlorn and impotent click of the latch. Back in his apartment he watched through one of his front windows as the police van pulled away. He could almost feel the street heave a sigh of relief. It was not a feeling he shared. Suddenly aware of the extent of his aloneness, he returned to the hall and jammed three rubber wedges under the front door before returning to his inflated bed.

Hannibal had always been a loner during his Secret Service days, so even after eight years in this city he was quite used to spending his time alone. He pushed his mattress to the front of the room, just below the big windows. Attaching a spring clamp to the front windowsill and hooking his flashlight into it, he created a second lamp. He pulled off his jacket, folding it into a pillow shape. He pulled off his shoes and placed them together at the foot of his bed. Otherwise fully dressed, he got comfortable in his sleeping bag and turned to the first page of one of Walter Mosley's novels about Easy Rawlins. Black detectives, he reflected, were almost as rare in fiction as they were in real life.

Not just the music, but the very beat of the city seeped into his tiny corner of the house. The neighborhood throbbed and pulsed with life, but Hannibal was not in sync with it. His ears were tuned to any sign of an attempted break-in. He gathered scant cold comfort from the gun pressed against his ribs. Watching occasional movements on the walls outside his cone of light, he wondered if Monty and Mother Washington were asleep. It was a warm night, the air still, the moon bright.

As he faded into a watchful state between sleep and full awareness, he imagined a crawling mass of drug users, homeless winos and petty thieves, flowing over the house, flowing over him like roaches gathering at the edge of the light. His exhausted mind became confused about whether he was in, or in fact was the narrow light they tentatively approached.

-19-

SATURDAY

By the time Hannibal knew he was awake, he was sitting up with his pistol in his fist. His eyes opened wide, gathering every scrap of light in the room. In the darkness he tried to feel any vibration coming through the floor that might signal a footstep. A quick glance at the luminous hands of his watch told him it was three-thirty.

Certainly the sound of breaking glass had triggered his internal alarm, but now he received nothing but silence. The sound had been distant, memory now revealed. Could the noise that awoke him have been a window breaking next door, or across the street? No. He had more faith in his instincts than that.

Just standing made Hannibal feel more confident. After slipping his feet into his shoes he went to the front door, all his senses turned up to maximum. A slight vibration in the floor tied ideas together into a picture. He mentally cursed himself, remembering a hole in his defenses that he had not thought to jam a stopper into.

With his weapon thrust in front of him, Hannibal moved down the hall. At the back of the building and beneath the stairway stood a door he had never opened. He turned its knob now and very slowly pulled it toward himself. The blackness of the cellar seemed to stretch right down to the center of the earth. He heard the scurrying of tiny clawed feet, and maybe the rustling of a bigger animal.

Hannibal opened his mouth to quiet his accelerating breath. He stood still for a moment, forcing himself into calmness. He withdrew his aura and narrowed his eyes to narrow slits. When he had reached the state of relaxed alertness he was looking for he lowered one foot with painful slowness onto the first wooden step inside the door. Gradually he shifted his weight onto that step until he was certain it would hold him without creaking.

Settling his other foot two steps further down took even longer, but now that he was more fully below the level of the first floor, he was certain he had company. He figured that someone had slithered through one of the narrow basement windows. His mind spun into random calculations, wondering if any of the previous residents would be so ambitious, or if Sal had already heard about earlier events and sent a team to recover his crack house.

While his mind handled administrative details like who and why, Hannibal's senses focused on where. He had a pen light in his pocket, but that would pin down his location faster than theirs. The basement was as dark and close and damp as a cave. Water dripped from pipes clinging to the ceiling like horizontal stalactites. Hannibal stepped farther into this dank, mildew clogged environment, ignoring a wide cobweb his arm thrust through. Breathing became more difficult. Fear, so comfortable living in the dark, tried to crawl into his ears, carried by the sound of rats patrolling their territory.

Something scraped against a cement wall, causing a tiny dribble of crumbling dust. Hannibal thrust his gun in that direction and thumbed back its spur hammer. Then he deepened his voice and, with all the confidence he could gather, did his best Clint Eastwood imitation with a hint of James Earl Jones for resonance.

"Step over here to the base of the stairs before I get mad and blow your fucking face off."

He heard more rustling, and a sound like sneakers padding across a wet sidewalk. Hannibal pivoted, tracking the sound like a radar screen until the movement stopped almost in front of him. He pulled the pen light out and turned its light on the man in front of him.

The man was a boy, barely sixteen, Hannibal guessed. He held his hands up beside his face. His eyes were round despite the light, twin white circles with black dots in their centers glaring from a round black face.

"This is my building," Hannibal said through clenched teeth. "What are you doing here?"

"The pipes," the boy muttered, voice shaking, eyes riveted on the gun pointed at his chest.

"Pipes?" Hannibal asked. "What, like crack pipes? You a druggie?"

"No, man, these pipes," the boy stammered, pointing at the ceiling. "The copper, man. We can sell the copper."

Tension drained out of Hannibal, leaving a relief almost like going to the bathroom. This was no deadly enemy, just a frightened thief. "Well, you picked the wrong place," he said. "You alone?"

"Yeah," the boy said, but his eyes cut to the right, into the darkness. Hannibal heard a subtle movement and realized he had dropped his guard too soon. He turned the light off and dove forward. His chest slammed into the boy at the bottom of the stairs as he heard a bullet crack the wall behind him. Sliding across the floor with the boy pinned beneath him, Hannibal swung his left arm up toward the flash he had seen and squeezed the trigger twice.

The gun's concussions slammed Hannibal's ears, as if someone had boxed them. Through the echo he heard a cry of pain, then the words "Oh shit!" in a stunned voice. Two seconds later, a metallic clank told Hannibal the gun had flown quite a distance.

The boy beneath him was frozen with terror, panting so hard Hannibal thought he might hyperventilate. He pulled the boy up, dragging him a few feet away from the stairs.

"Let's see how tough your partner is," Hannibal whispered. Pressing his gun against the boy's chest, he turned toward the darkness.

"Can you walk?" Hannibal called. No response, but he could hear ragged breathing from the darkness. "Can you stand?" Still nothing. One more chance. "Want me to shoot the boy?" Hannibal could not have asked for a better gasp of fear than he got when he pressed the gun into the boy's throat.

"No," a voice called from the darkness.

"All right then. Come over here and slide past me up the stairs."

After a five second silent pause, more scuffing and grating sounds came from the dark. Hannibal pulled out his pen light, turned it on and aimed it at the stairs. A tall, gaunt figure shuffled toward them. As the man reached the base of the steps he looked back into the light and simply said "my boy?"

Hannibal could smell the poverty on the man. He wore no armor, even lacked the basic defense of a thin layer of fat under his skin. He was no predator, but rather a scavenger. Breaking in here may have been an act of desperation, and Hannibal felt small watching blood dribbling down his leg.

"Go help him," he told the boy. "You two get up the stairs. Head for the front door."

The man put an arm over the boy's shoulders and mounted the stairs without a word. Hannibal walked in the trail of blood, following the pair to the door. He kept the gun on the younger intruder while he kicked the wedges away and turned the lock.

"Let the boy go." The man pressed his hand futilely against his mid thigh. His eyes bored into Hannibal's. Did he expect Hannibal to take them to the police? Maybe he expected to be gunned down in the street for trespassing. Whatever his thoughts, he seemed ready to take his punishment, but not ready to share it.

"Oh, hell." Hannibal reached into his hip pocket. Fumbling with his wallet one handed, he dropped it in the process of pulling out a bill. Enough moonlight dripped through the glass on either side of the front door to make the twenty dollar bill in Hannibal's right hand visible.

"Here's the deal," Hannibal rasped, still working at sounding tough. "No cops. Take this. Get to a hospital. Don't come back. And put this in the street. This building don't get no uninvited visitors."

The man's hand did not move, but the boy reached for the money. Then Hannibal opened the door, letting the city's rhythm flood the hall, and waved them out with his pistol.

This time he left only two wedges jamming the front door closed. The third he used to brace the basement door, just in case. Back in his own room, he opened his sleeping bag and shook it out before sitting on it again. He turned to stare out the window and slowly slid his pistol back into its holster, wishing for company, wishing for a shower, wishing not so much for an end of this case, but for an end to the forces that had caused it.

-20-

A sharp, angry sun shoved Hannibal into full wakefulness. In the first light hours, he noticed the view from his front window could pass for any city street scene anywhere on earth. Who would guess he was sleeping in a war zone? But then, that was just as true when he was much younger, waking up every morning in Berlin.

His first order of business was coffee. The multi-legged animals were not nearly as active in daylight hours, but he still heated water and washed everything before using it. While his brew was brewing, he pulled off his holster and clothes. The kitchen tiles were cold against his feet. Standing naked and feeling just a little vulnerable, he quickly took what his father used to call a "whore's bath," using a cloth and a bar of Ivory soap to wash only the essential body parts: face, underarms, crotch and pelvic area. Later he would scrub the bathtub upstairs and enjoy the real thing, but this would do for now.

Clean and essentially dry, he pulled out an apple and crunched into it. After a couple of pieces of fruit for breakfast he planned to explore his building more thoroughly, listing necessary renovations. He might start work on this one apartment today, but as soon as he was sure the danger was past he intended to hire a team to clean and renovate the entire building.

All night, Hannibal had been prepared for angry intruders trying the doors and windows. Now, a knock on the door took him completely by surprise. Pulling on trousers, his shoulder rig, and his windbreaker to cover it, he went to the front, opening his window to see who had knocked at the door. Monty stood there, looking quite impatient. Grinning, Hannibal hurried to the door and pulled it open.

"Morning, Monty. Sorry to keep you waiting."

"Grandma wants you to come to breakfast," Monty said without preamble.

Monty's face revealed no emotion whatever, but Hannibal suspected this might be important. Important relationships so often hung on such small things, and cultural mores were never Hannibal's strong suit. He licked his lips and assembled his answer carefully.

"Monty, I would love to have a real breakfast this morning, and of course I'd be honored to join you and your grandmother. But I'm afraid if I left this building for more than a minute, I'd find it infested again when I got back, if you know what I mean."

"A lot of them won't come back," Monty said, still deadpan. "Everybody knows you put Mister Lincoln in D.C. General this morning. Now me, if I get shot, I'll make them take me to Suburban, over in Bethesda. Too many brothers don't come back from D.C. General." After sharing this important advice, Monty turned and bounced down the steps to the street.

With Monty gone, Hannibal picked up a note pad and began his inspection. His own apartment, as he began to think of it, could do with a coat of paint and new flooring. In the second room someone had broken through the plaster, exposing the wooden slats beneath, like bare ribs under a grazing gunshot wound.

All the light fixtures were gone, and the refrigerator was just an empty metal box. The oven was beyond cleaning, so he would need a new stove. The bathroom sink, like the one in the kitchen, would need hours of scrubbing, after the plumbing got extensive repair. He could only wonder if the wiring was intact, or if the furnace and water heater downstairs worked.

Worst of all, in Hannibal's mind, was the general filth these people had lived in. He wished he could hose out the entire place.

Another knock on the door pulled his thoughts back into focus. After again checking at the window, he opened the door for Monty. He stood at the threshold wearing the same bored expression, but holding a foil-covered plate like an offering. Hannibal raised his eyebrows in silent questioning.

"Grandma say you need breakfast anyway." Monty walked in without waiting for an invitation.

Hannibal and Monty sat in a shaft of sunlight, sharing the sleeping bag seating. The plate balanced on Hannibal's lap was overflowing with bacon, fried eggs, grits, and corn bread already buttered. Hannibal ate as if he had not tasted food in weeks. While he did, he noticed two starlings arguing noisily in a big tree out front. He thought the tree was mostly dead. Friendly conversation floated in the window on a breeze that led Hannibal to believe that the whole block smelled like the breakfast that Mother Washington had made him. He reflected how, with this one building's previous occupants gone, it was not a bad neighborhood at all.

When Hannibal finished his food Monty took the plate and asked, "What you doing today?"

"Today, when my gear gets here, I'm cleaning this place up some."

"Need some help?" Monty asked.

"Yeah, if you want. Come back around noon, and I'll have plenty of brooms and mops."

"Alright," Monty said without pronouncing the letters "l" or "r." "I'll be back but what's the point of all this cleaning?"

"It shows intent," Hannibal said, walking Monty to the door. "By Monday, I figure even the thickest junkie will understand I'm here to stay. Then the owner can start fixing the place up for real and get some of these apartments rented out."

"Here to stay?" Monty asked, one hand on the doorknob.

"Well, not me personally, but some honest people, you know?"

Monty nodded and left. He seemed vaguely disappointed, but Hannibal could not be sure why. He watched from his window as Monty headed up the street. His view of he boy was interrupted by a blue patrol car rolling past. Hannibal checked his watch. Kendall had been as good as his word. Their patrols had shrunk to just over an hour apart. They never stopped or talked with anyone, but Hannibal figured the increased presence gave the bad guys a case of the crawlies and maybe, gave the good folks a little more security.

Hannibal returned his focus to cataloging the ills of his new home. It seemed that the more he looked the more he found, and he lost all track of time during his inspection. He also began to gather any useful items he found and tote them into his own apartment, including a functional card table that, until the day before, had been covered with electronic equipment on the third floor. It was hot and smelly work, and he was glad he could leave some windows open on the upper floors for ventilation.

When he finally checked his watch he was startled to see that noon was seconds away. He hastened to clean up his area and roll his sleeping bag. He was just deflating his air mattress when the familiar sound of his own car's horn put a smile on his face.

His smile dropped as soon as he opened the front door. As expected, Ray was on his way up the stairs with a suitcase in one hand and a pail full of sponges and cleaning supplies in the other. Behind him, and not part of Hannibal's plan, Cindy carried brooms, mops and more cleaning gear. Even with a cloth tied over her head, she just did not look like a cleaning lady. Hannibal turned a stern expression on his driver.

"Ray, what's she doing here?"

"Hey, it's good to see you too," Cindy said.

"I didn't mean it like that," Hannibal said as they came in. "But considering the hours you work, you've got to have better things to do with your Saturday afternoons. Besides, I just don't think this is a good place for a girl to be today."

"Really?" Cindy unloaded her arms on the card table Hannibal had brought down from the third floor. "Well that's one hell of a sexist attitude. It's no more dangerous for me than it is for you. Besides, I don't think there's a man alive who knows squat about cleaning."

"Speaking of sexist attitudes," Hannibal said, pulling off his shoulder holster and hanging it on the back of a chair.

"Come on, Hannibal, this place stinks. You know you could use an extra pair of hands here."

When she turned toward him, his resolve weakened. Her shorts really were, revealing her nearly perfect legs. Her Star Trek tee shirt barely fit her, and her body was badly distorting the Enterprise's shape. Then she flashed that smile at him and he forgot whatever else he wanted to say.

"Your little friend is downstairs," Ray said, as if nothing whatever was going on. "He says for five bucks he'll watch the car all day. Where you want to start?"

Hannibal sat back on the windowsill, wishing those damned starlings would shut up.

After Hannibal changed into shorts and a tee shirt they started cleaning in the kitchen. His plan was to work forward and get this one flat livable. If nobody started any real trouble the next day, he would then be comfortable bringing in a cleaning team. They could start across the hall and work their way to the top. Once he had a decent place to stay, there would be no rush for cleaners, plumbers and the like to get their jobs done. But even with every window open, that one place was rough going. When Hannibal moved the refrigerator away from the wall they all gagged, but somehow enough hot water and disinfectant soon had an effect.

The three did not work hard, but rather continuously. Ray got a bag of ice and a case of soda from the corner store. By four-thirty, when they reached the front room, their drinks were almost gone and sweat coated all three cleaners. Hannibal had to admit that Cindy even glistened with style, and she had a smudge on the tip of her nose which he found just too cute to tell her about.

"Okay, okay, okay." She fell back against the wall between the front windows. "That's enough. We need to stop, get cleaned up, and go somewhere nice for dinner."

"Sorry, doll, but the tub that works is upstairs." Hannibal began sweeping his front room. "How about you and Ray go eat and bring me something back?"

"How about I go get something for all of us to eat here?" Ray countered. "You got a table here. There's two chairs in the kitchen and I know there's more upstairs."

"All right, look. Just hop down to Popeye's and get us some..." Hannibal had his hand on his wallet, but Cindy's wave stopped him.

"Hey, I got it," she said. "Least I can do. Popeye's, right? Chicken, biscuits and some of them funny fries? Got you covered."

Ray started through the door with his daughter following. At the last instant she ducked back into the room, reached for Hannibal, and dropped a small kiss on his lips.

"You're doing something really special here, chasing those drug people away," she whispered. Then she was gone.

Hannibal watched the Volvo motor off from his window perch. She was a special lady all right, lovely to look at, bright as a new penny, a hard worker and damned sexy on top of all that. And she seemed to like him. Too bad he was not in the market for a woman of his own.

As he turned away from the window, his inner voice asked, *since when are you ever not in the market for a woman?* He was laughing silently at himself when he heard feet on his front steps. For a moment he wondered what they had forgotten. Just as he heard a thumping knock on the door, he realized he had not heard a car pull up. Returning to the window, he found a familiar, well dressed figure on the stoop. He smiled at the expensive suit, so out of place in that setting.

"Well, Sally. I been wondering when you'd drop by."

"Open this Goddamned door, spook," Sal shouted. "My boy missed his appointment this morning. If you got to him, I'll kick both your asses."

"Language, language, Sally." Hannibal stared at Sal's two bodyguards standing behind him, filling the stoop. "Ain't you heard? Your friends moved out. I hope they didn't take anything you personally need with them. Like white powder, for instance."

"Hey, I don't touch that crap," Sal said. "That shit's for the weak, for losers. And I ain't weak. They all get their stuff from me."

"Well then, I wouldn't sweat it. They'll find you. You know they want what you got. Certainly nothing to fight about, since they're elsewhere. Now, why don't you and your muscle just move it on off my porch before I call the cops and have you picked up for trespassing?"

Hannibal was enjoying Sal's face, wondering how red it could get before his head exploded, when he heard a whump sound, like one of his Papa's artillery rounds. He was already running toward the kitchen before he identified the sound. Something had hit the back door, something big. Magnified through the long tunnel of the apartment, the sound had gained impact.

One room before the kitchen, Hannibal saw a gloved fist crash through the window nearest the kitchen door. The other window imploded seconds later, as the man in gloves climbed in the first window.

Without slowing down Hannibal drove his right foot up and forward, crashing into the first man's face, crushing his nose, driving him back out the window. The bruiser halfway in the other window grabbed Hannibal's ankle. Without hesitation, Hannibal spun, raking his free heel across his attacker's face. The man grunted in pain and Hannibal was free, but his spinning kick left him face down on the floor. At the other end of the apartment he saw Sal's black guard clambering in through a front window, into the room Hannibal slept in.

The room his gun was in.

Ignoring the men behind him, Hannibal dashed forward. The flat suddenly seemed many times longer than it was minutes ago. The black guard was just picking up Hannibal's shoulder rig when Hannibal reached the front room. Without losing momentum, Hannibal long jumped into space, bringing his right heel around in a side kick to the man's jaw. The guard staggered, and the holster flew.

Hannibal's now green eyes trailed his automatic's arc. It landed on the open windowsill. As he dived for the holster straps, the gun slid over the edge and down. Hannibal's chest hit the sill, his arms reaching down, hoping he might just snag the straps.

Like the claw that picks up prizes in an arcade machine, a giant hand gripped Hannibal's throat. Sal's white bodyguard, Petey, stood below the window. Hannibal saw his gun under Petey's right foot. Blue dots crowded the detective's vision. Sal's laughter filled his ears.

A slow rage began to build behind Hannibal's eyes, and since he couldn't reach Sal, he directed it toward Petey. Hannibal grabbed the guard's pinkie with his right hand. His left wrapped around his right fist and he pulled down sharply. With a howl of pain, Petey released him. As Hannibal slumped forward, gasping for breath, he felt a hand wrap around his belt. There was just enough time for fear to begin to grow in his mind before his body whipped around like the teacup ride in a carnival, stopping abruptly against a wall, just missing the door out of the room.

His right side on fire, Hannibal looked up to see three of the biggest men he had ever angered converging on him. One swung a foot, but Hannibal managed to pull himself up and dive into the hall, avoiding a cracked skull. Lying at the base of the stairs he felt his mouth go parchment dry. Eye level with the bottom of the front door he fully realized his predicament. He could never move the wedges in time to get the door open and get through it. Even if he did, Sal waited outside with who knew how much help. On the other hand, the three linebacker types who were stalking toward him represented an impenetrable human barrier. He knew he had no chance of getting past them to escape through a back door or window. Only one avenue remained.

Legs pumping, Hannibal darted upstairs. His pursuers followed, but they were in no hurry. They must have realized he had no place to go. He would likely break a leg if he tried jumping from a second floor window. He could only hope he would find a weapon of some type.

As he moved, Hannibal cursed his own stupidity. He had gone to the window unprepared for defense, not wearing his gun since he changed for the cleaning. The fact was, he expected single assaults by drug crazed idiots. He never really believed Sal Ronzini would fight for this building once his clients had been convinced to leave.

A quick look back further reduced Hannibal's confidence. Ox, the black guard, waited at the head of the stairs on the second floor while his two partners searched one of the apartments. They moved with smooth professionalism, and Hannibal knew they would make sure one flat was clear before they investigated the next. After making sure the second floor held no surprises, they would corner him on the third floor. That did not sound at all like fun.

* * *

Scant minutes later, Ox stationed himself at the top of the stairs on the third floor while one of his partners led the way into the flat on the right side of the house. As he pushed the door open, a gray steel folding chair smacked into his face. He fell back, almost but not quite flipping over the rail.

As the second muscle man charged the door, Hannibal swung his chair low, edgewise. It hit the man's knees with a sickeningly loud crack, and he went down like a chain sawed pine. Unfortunately, in falling forward he wrenched the chair from Hannibal's hands. Ox stepped over the other man and into the room. With so little room to maneuver, both fighters knew the situation favored the bigger man.

"Can't afford to let you get past me, stud," Ox said. "You understand?"

"Yeah, I get it. It's just business, right?" Hannibal looked for a way around Ox, but the man filled the doorway.

"Naw, Jack," Ox said. "This is personal. You gave us trouble before, and I got a feeling you're the same nigger held a gun to my partner's head and took off with a car full of Sal's best superfine China white. Now old man Ronzini don't like his little boy getting humiliated."

"So what are you, the baby-sitter?" Hannibal feinted to the left, then right. Ox ignored his movements. He wasn't giving away a free inch around him that could lead to an escape.

"I've worked steady for the Ronzinis for nine good years. They count on me to solve their problems. And you a problem, Jack. You understand now?"

Hannibal nodded because he did understand. Maintaining solid eye contact with Ox, he dropped into a low crouch and raised his fists.

"Okay," he said through clenched teeth, "but it won't be free."

"I'm tired of playing," Ox said. He swung his huge fists in a one-two attack at Hannibal's head. Bobbing and weaving, Hannibal felt only the wind from the two blows. He countered with a sharp uppercut to his foe's jaw, followed immediately by another. A front kick pushed into Ox's solar plexus and for the first time, Hannibal thought he might slip by the bigger man. As he ducked past on Ox's right, a huge hand wrapped around his upper arm and he realized he had missed his chance. Again he was airborne, and again he crashed into a wall. Stunned, he could only watch as the monster's shoulder came crashing into his midsection.

But the big man was slow, maybe tired. Hannibal gathered what he had left to bring a knee up hard into Ox's face. The bigger man pressed a hand against Hannibal's chest, clamping him in place against the wall. When he looked up, blood dripped from his nose.

"That hurt." Ox looked at Hannibal with contempt. Taking his time, he cocked his other arm back and smashed his fist into Hannibal's face.

Dazed, Hannibal could barely make out his target as Ox pulled his fist back for another shot. Before he could strike, Hannibal lifted his own leaden right. With a loud shout, he delivered three rapid fire jabs into Ox's face. The pressure against his chest eased and he dropped below the arm and moved as quickly as he could for the door. He was panting and his legs were a little wobbly, but he pushed the weakness out of his mind. The stairs were his only chance at survival. He felt a sort of crazed relief as he stepped into the hall.

Then the man Hannibal had hit in the face with a chair brought a fist around and down against the side of Hannibal's head. When he hit the hallway floor, Hannibal knew the fight was out of him. He mustered his last reserves to survive what would surely come next.

His mind slipped back to when he was seven years old. It was not his mouth that got him in trouble then, just his skin tone. At the hands of bigger boys with blond hair and blue eyes, he had learned that after a while, if you just hold on, your body starts to reject the pain messages. The feeling reminded him of sitting in a dentist's chair. You know a high-speed drill is making a hole in your tooth, you feel it, you might even smell smoke, but the hurt is gone. Well, not gone really, but banked up for later.

With some surprise, Hannibal looked up to find himself staring out the open front door. He did not think he had hit enough stairs to reach the first floor, but there he was. Clenching his teeth, he pressed up to hands and knees. He just wanted to make sure all his limbs worked and no bones were broken. Sal Ronzini, just now walking in, took it as an act of defiance.

Maybe that too.

"Kind of hope you got the message this time, shithead," Sal said. Hannibal could not lift his head, but he did not need to. Shadows told him two men stood on either side of him.

Through a red haze he saw the pointed tips of Sal's handmade Italian loafers. Crawling forward five inches put him within reach. He swallowed, disturbed by the fact that his lips were not dry. He was dripping red splotches on the floor. He coughed and cleared his throat.

"Something to say, shithead?" Sal asked arrogantly.

Sal's voice was all the help Hannibal needed. Sal's Italian loafers made perfect goal posts. Hannibal swung his right fist up, directly between Sal's pointed toes. It was not much of an impact, but it got him a satisfying gurgling moan. Sal dropped onto his knees beside Hannibal. Behind Hannibal, Ox roared. Then that weightlessness feeling returned. Ox and one of the others had no trouble making Hannibal fly.

Some part of Hannibal managed to smile inside. As big as that doorway was, they missed it twice. On the third pass he did not hit the door or its frame, but sailed out onto the sandstone steps which delivered him to the sidewalk. Footsteps followed him. Someone lifted him again. Hannibal opened his eyes, and a face came into focus through a shifting red curtain. It was the black guy. Again that slow motion fist wound up, but this time Hannibal could not even raise a hand. Hannibal kept his eyes on the knuckles, anticipating their impact with his face.

"The police."

It was a very young voice, with the accent on the first syllable. Monty? Then he heard some angry mumbling, followed by faster steps away down the block. A final hard slap, and Hannibal tucked and rolled trying to keep his head from hitting the concrete too hard.

-21-

Black confusion clouded Hannibal's mind. Not a new feeling, but the first time since high school boxing. It was different this time, because there was travel involved. Moved. Moved again. Ow! Something rubbing his face, his chest. Moved one more time. Slowly the aches started seeping in. Not like beatings in school. Those boys just did it for fun. The guys who did all this damage were experts. A very professional working over, he thought. Everything hurt, nothing broken.

He heard voices. Frightened voices. One female voice seeped through. He tried to assure her. I'm okay, Ma. Don't worry, they can't hurt me. Scheiskopf. He called me scheiskopf, Ma.

The cloud was slowly lifting. The world waited patiently for him. He always hated this part. He forced his eyes open. He had a sideways view. Cindy stood with her back to him, but as she pulled her tee shirt over her head she moved a little to one side. Then her bra dropped and she stood revealed in profile. Magnificent, proud, thrusting. Almost worth getting knocked out for. Then she wiggled out of her shorts. When they dropped to the floor he saw that the front of them was splotchy with blood. They landed beside her cast-off tee shirt, which was even more broadly stained red. That brought tears and a strong, unreasoning sorrow for having made a mess.

Hannibal tried to speak while she pulled on another tee shirt. Breathing got difficult. He realized it might be phlegm, or it might be blood. Either way, he had to clear his throat. Try to cough. Come on, you can do it. Cough. Get that stuff out of your throat before you drown, or suffocate.

One cough cleared Hannibal's throat and sent a tremor of pain through his ribs and chest. Cindy turned, shouted "Madre de Dios" and a long string of Spanish he did not understand, ending with calling "Papa" three times. She cradled his head in her lap, stroking it gently. While her tone moved from soothing to accusatory and back she dabbed very gently at his mouth with a tissue. The tissue felt rough and scratchy, but her thighs were warm and baby soft against his ear and cheek.

The first thing Cindy said that he clearly understood was "Damn you, Hannibal Jones, you scared the bejesus out of me."

"Where?" He noticed he was slurring. His lips must be a mess this time.

"My place," Cindy said. "We headed for the hospital at first, but you kept saying get you to the base. Papa figured you meant here."

Hannibal smiled. It was too complicated, but he would need to explain why he feared ending up in a strange hospital, where they might not understand him. Tomorrow.

"Good to see you're in one piece," Ray said, entering the room. Hannibal felt guilty for taking his bed again.

"Monty okay?"

"Sure," Ray said. "He saw what happened. Says they were going to kill you, but a cop car came down the block just in time."

"Yeah." Hannibal's mouth hurt when he talked. "Heard him tell them about it. That got them off me." Turning his head, he looked up past Cindy's overhang to make eye contact with her. "I'm really sorry I got blood on your shirt. It'll never come out."

"Paco, you got blood all over everything," Ray said. "I looked like I worked in a meat packing plant after I drove you over here."

"Sorry." The word had barely left his mouth when the full meaning of Ray's comment sank in and Hannibal sat up too fast. "My car!" he shouted, then clutched his head as pain surged upward, slamming into the underside of his skull. Keeling over, he muttered "white leather upholstery." On his back, he brought the ceiling into focus and tried to do the same with his thoughts.

Cindy stood and Ray turned his back, hold out a pair of jeans. She squirmed into them, talking all the while. "There's a doctor on his way over here. When we found you lying there I guess I went a little crazy. I called Dan at home."

"Dan?"

"Mister Balor," Cindy said. "He says end it. He doesn't want you to get killed over a piece of real estate."

"Out of the question." Hannibal hated the drunken sounds his torn, swollen lips made. "You tell that bastard we had a deal. I told him, first day, I'm on the job until it's done."

"But Hannibal..." Cindy began.

"Just have to work harder," he muttered. "I still don't get it."

"What?" Ray asked.

Hannibal looked over at his friend. "I really figured once I was in, that would be it. A couple of junkies might come to the door, or vagrants trying to climb in a window."

"Poor Hannibal. Never took a physics class, did you?" Cindy asked, smiling for the first time. When he looked at her quizzically, she added "That place was full when you got there, right? You emptied it out, but you couldn't fill it up. With just you in there, it was still a big, empty space. They had to rush in. Nature abhors a vacuum, remember?"

At first, Hannibal rolled his eyes and blew air between his teeth, making a "sheesh" sound. Then his face sobered and his jaw slowly dropped in understanding. A slow, shallow smile spread across his face.

Cindy Santiago had given him a revelation, an epiphany, a vision of how it would have to be, and he wanted badly to be able to sit up and give her a big kiss.

-22-

SUNDAY

Mirrors never lie, but Hannibal sure hoped the one over the dresser was exaggerating just a little. His skin showed multiple bruises from his face to his waistline, but he reminded himself that he bruised easily. His left eyebrow was badly swollen, but at least the cut over his left eye was closed. A purple ring as big as a donut surrounded his right eye. He again thanked the Lord for a nose too small and flat to easily break. His lower lip was still three times its normal size. His jaw was not broken but it hurt like hell. He stared at himself and managed a crooked smile.

In part, he was smiling at Cindy's doctor. When he arrived the night before, it quickly became obvious that he had never worked a boxer's corner. He over reacted to Hannibal's superficial injuries. After an examination he still wasn't convinced there was no serious damage. He taped up Hannibal's sore ribs, and even offered anesthetic before the three or four stitched he used to close the small cut over Hannibal's eye.

While all that was going on, Cindy had made her father bring Hannibal's things from his motel. He found his socks and underwear in the top dresser drawer. Rummaging through it, he found the photograph he had salvaged from his burned out apartment. He lifted it now, feeling new warmth just holding it in his hand.

Very curly script at the bottom of the photo said "To my honey." The woman's face looked younger in the picture than he remembered it, but then it was taken before the loss of her man, single parenthood, and the unearned disrespect of others had taken their toll. He leaned the small framed photo against the dresser's mirror, kissed a fingertip and touched it to her face.

"Well I look like hell," he told the photo. "It ain't as bad as it looks, though, and I heal pretty quick. Still the tough guy."

His ego drove him to make one other small change, but he knew that what he needed would not be in the room he was using. While he was alone in the house, Hannibal tentatively invaded Cindy's bedroom. He could not avoid the impression of how feminine she had made it. Pink pillow shams and bedding on a four poster bed dominated the room. He did notice that the bed was made, and that the closet doors and even her bathroom door were closed. He avoided looking on her dresser at all, aware of just how much of a invasion that would be. Besides what he needed would surely be on her white, wrought iron vanity.

He opened and closed cases and kits, working hard to leave everything exactly as he found it. More than once he looked over his shoulder, unnecessarily. Finally he found the tube of beige gunk he was looking for. He squeezed a dab of it into his palm and mixed it with a little hand cream. Stifling his pained noises he spread the paste over his black eye, expertly laying it on, moving out a bit past the bruise and blending it smoothly into his own skin tone. This would not hide the injury completely of course, but it would make it a lot less obvious.

Backing up a bit from the mirror, he could see purple around his waist below the tape, as far as his view allowed him to check. There was no sense in trying to hide these bruises, and they would fade soon enough. Stretching exercises would be torture but he would do them, slowly and thoroughly, after he made one telephone call. He moved into the living room, stood beside the couch and picked up the phone.

When he heard the greeting Hannibal focused on not slurring his words. "Mister Balor this is Hannibal Jones. Sorry to bother you at home on the Sabbath, but..."

"Jones. Are you all right?" Balor asked. His concern sounded genuine. "Don't worry about the day, it's not my Sabbath anyway. But Miss Santiago told me you were, well, that you'd been hurt. Pretty badly."

"I figured I'd better report in." Hannibal very slowly lowered himself onto the sofa. "Just bumps and bruises. I've been examined by a doctor, and he gave me a clean bill of health. No broken bones, all senses are functioning normally and I'm not passing any more blood."

"Any more?" Balor muttered. "God. Isn't this when you call the police? At the very least, we've got these guys for breaking and entering and assault, right?"

"You tell me. You're the lawyer. Do you expect the police to react somehow differently this time? It's my word against theirs, there's no physical evidence, and the other side took some lumps too. Can't prove who started it all. Will the cops make it right?"

After a pause, Balor said "You have a point I'm afraid."

"And while I'm in court for weeks everything returns to the status quo in that house."

"Maybe it should end here," Balor said. "I told Santiago if you want out..."

"I'd like to finish this," Hannibal said, as diplomatically as he could. "However, I realize I'm operating on your bankroll, and this job is about to get expensive. I'm afraid I'll need to subcontract some help on this."

"I don't care about..." Hannibal could hear Balor reordering his thoughts, as a man does when expressing thoughts foreign to him, "This isn't about money, Mister Jones. This is about somebody taking something that belongs to me. I'll spend my last dime to get it back. But it isn't worth people getting hurt."

"People are always getting hurt. If I get my head handed to me, well, it's my head. I knew it'd be dangerous. This is what I do. Now, do I go ahead and do my job, or not?"

Hannibal suffered through a long silence. He heard Balor draw on a cigar, could almost see his lawyer's eyes examining the consequences of his next decision. When he finally spoke, he sounded very tired.

"Look Jones, I'm sorry. These people you're up against are just too dangerous. I'm not taking a chance of having anybody's death on my conscience. It's over, understand? Naturally I'll pay you for your work up to this point, and of course I'll cover any medical bills or other expenses. But it's over." There was no goodbye, just silence and, after a moment, a dial tone.

-23-

Hannibal had just hung up when Ray and Cindy returned from church. He reacted to seeing her in a light blue summer dress. She reacted rather differently to him wearing only jeans, with his ribs wrapped in white tape and bruises covering his body like Dennis Rodman's tattoos. He read her concern for him in brown eyes grown wide.

"You look worse than before," Cindy said, rushing forward but stopping short of touching him. "I don't think you should be walking around too much. I hate the people who did this to you. Are you all right?"

"Oh, sure," Hannibal said. "I got my ass kicked, I'm sore everywhere, and I just talked to Balor. I'm out of a job." His eyes were hooded, his brows tightly knit. He stood up slowly and went into the guest room without looking at anybody. While he gathered clothes with one hand, he pushed the door closed with the other.

Just before the latch caught, the door flew open. Hannibal turned to find Cindy glowering in the doorway.

"So that's it? You just quit?"

"I never quit!" Hannibal snapped. "I was fired!" He turned his back to her, breathing deeply. "Right now I wish I could buy the damned building, then I wouldn't have to stop, but I work for somebody else. That's the business I'm in. I do what the client wants, whether I like it or not. Now, please let me get dressed."

Hannibal slowly eased a tee shirt over his head and pulled it down. Then he gathered up his blood soaked shirt from the night before and stood staring at the bundle in his hands. He was trying to decide if it belonged in the trash.

"Where you going?" Cindy asked from the doorway.

"Don't know. Out."

Cindy brushed past him to reach into a dresser drawer. "Didn't mean to sound like I was accusing you. I don't really think of you as a quitter. Here, I got you a new shirt."

"Sorry I yelled." Hannibal accepted the white, long sleeved shirt from Cindy and started pulling pins from it. He unfolded it and removed the cardboard and plastic through an uncomfortable silence. After fumbling the buttons open he slid one arm into a sleeve.

"Not sure I get you," Hannibal said. "I mean, I thought you wanted me to stay away from that place."

"Yes." Cindy's head dropped and she examined the toes of her shoes. "No. That was before. I just don't want you getting hurt anymore, and they'll hurt you if you go back."

"It'll kill me if I don't."

Cindy tentatively reached for him, but pulled her hands back as if a touch might hurt him. "I can see that now. But more, I think maybe I see why. What you were trying to do, it's important. I mean, I knew that before, but maybe I didn't know how important until I saw the look on that little boy's face when he saw you lying there, all beat up. Somebody needs to show him it's not all hopeless."

"So?"

"So, don't give up." Cindy began buttoning his shirt once he had it on. "You're a fighter, right? Then fight for what you know is right. Go get your job back."

"You didn't hear him." He fumbled with his cuffs until he got them buttoned. "I don't think I can change his mind. He was pretty damned clear about this. The case is closed."

Without raising his eyes, Hannibal stepped quickly to the door, waving to Ray on his way out. Cindy looked past her confused father, staring at the closed door as if she could still see Hannibal.

"Maybe you just need a good lawyer."

*   *   *

Hannibal sat in his car watching the free enterprise system at work across the street. People streamed into and out of the little corner store, gathering the necessities of life in small daily quantities. They were friendly, honest, courteous people, deferring to older neighbors at the door, helping women with their packages.

A dozen feet away, a smiling young man with a shaved head and an earring chattered to passersby like the scalpers outside the MCI Center when Hannibal went to watch the Wizards play. Only this guy was not pushing overpriced tickets. He was hawking drugs.

Free enterprise.

Hannibal had bought a new black blazer. Afterward he wandered the city aimlessly for an hour before his wheels brought him back to Southeast. He was not sure why he was there, or why he had parked down the block from, but out of sight of, Balor's building. The store seemed to be the center of activity in the neighborhood, and maybe he just wanted to see his situation in terms of people, not property.

Even with his window down, the temperature in his Volvo was rising fast. He looked down to wipe a handkerchief across his dripping face, careful not to wipe away the makeup around his eye. Reluctantly he started the car, raised the window and punched the air conditioning button. When he looked up, he saw Monty rolling down the sidewalk on his board. That ignited a smile. Maybe he would go say hello, maybe offer to take him to one of the parks which lined the Potomac on the Virginia side. After all, there's more than one way to save our youth, he thought.

Monty flipped his skateboard into his hands at the door into the store. The boy with the earring called to him. Monty turned to face him, then turned away. The older boy called again, waving to him. This time Monty reacted more caustically. Hannibal could see contempt on his face.

Hannibal watched the conversation through his driver side window, almost as if it was on a television screen. Only this was real. The older boy was holding a joint out to Monty and smiling, right out in the open. It was as if they were in their own little world, invisible to passersby. Hannibal could not hear his words, but his face and hands were saying Monty should take it. It was free. What was he so afraid of? If he did not like it, at least then he would know he was not missing anything. After all, what kind of a chump turned down free stuff.

Hannibal slid his sunglasses into place and got out of his car.

"Give it up, Aaron," Monty said, waving a hand as if dismissing the taller boy. "I ain't about to even start taking any of that junk from you."

"I ain't trying to hear that, see," Aaron said, pushing his sample closer to Monty's face. Then a hand reached in from outside their world and wrapped around Aaron's wrist.

"Try harder."

Aaron's eyes scanned up and down Hannibal's form. Hannibal figured he was probably a complete mystery to the boy, obviously not a policeman, but just as obviously not a competitor. "Who the fuck are you?"

Hannibal snapped his hand around, locking Aaron's arm at full extension. The boy's mouth flew open in shock. "I'm the local Chamber of Commerce. You're out of business." Showing almost no effort, Hannibal snapped his foot up into Aaron's exposed ribs. Aaron howled in pain. That was gratifying, so Hannibal kicked him again.

"What you doing?" Monty said, yanking Hannibal's jacket. "Let him go, man. He's just a hustler. You don't beat a brother up for running his hustle."

Hannibal released Aaron, turning to Monty. Fear and surprise wrestled for dominance on his face. "Monty, are you so far gone you think what this kid's doing is okay?"

"At least he's trying to get something for himself," Monty said, fists on his hips, head tilted at a defiant angle.

"You can't look up to dope pushers like this scum. He's no better than Sal."

Monty shrugged. "Sal rides around in a Continental. Who should I look up to? Winos in the park? That bunch of homeless guys down the block? I got to get the milk Grandma sent me for." Monty ended the conversation by walking into the store.

"Some of those homeless people are miles better than these drug dealers," Hannibal told Monty's back. "At least they're honest and..." He stopped, realizing nobody was listening. At that moment, a great deal was going on behind his dark Oakley's. As he turned toward his car, he came face to face with Aaron, who now had three large friends with him. Hannibal balled his fists and stalked toward his car, which was beyond the four young men. They stared into his face as he approached, but as he reached them they parted to let him pass.

Behind the wheel, Hannibal dialed his phone even before turning the Volvo's key. He was talking as he pulled away from the curb.

"Ray? Hannibal. I'll be there in about half an hour and I need you to drive. Yeah, you still got a job, whether I do or not. Yeah, well, it ain't just about money, is it?"

* * *

Balor's home was in McLean, barely ten miles northwest of the District and a world away from the property he owned in Anacostia. It stood at the end of a long winding drive through an elm and maple covered dale. To a Realtor it was a traditional double wing colonial. To Hannibal, it was a million dollar brick monstrosity.

"I'll stay and watch the car," Ray said as Hannibal got out.

"I guess it's pointless to argue," Hannibal replied. "I need to do this alone anyway." He pushed his shades into place and straightened his posture.

"Cindy swears she'll have a place just like this one day," Ray said through his open window.

Hannibal stared up at the imposing structure for a moment. "Why?"

*   *   *

"Good day," Hannibal said, surprised by the age of the woman who answered the door. "My name is Hannibal Jones. I'm working under contract for Mister Balor and I need to speak to him on a matter of some urgency."

"Oh, my. How formal," the woman said. She was short, slight and silver gray, with an open face and perfect posture. "Please come in. I'm Beth Balor. Have a seat and I'll see if Dan's available."

Hannibal chose to remain standing, but he pulled his glasses off. The decor was traditional pastels, all the furniture overstuffed. The house was brightened, not by paintings on the walls, but by several small vessels of fresh flowers and small framed photographs. Staring around the stadium sized sitting room, he wondered where the servants were. Surely Balor's wife could not keep a house this size alone. Then he remembered it was Sunday and wondered if the Balors gave their Christian house workers the day off.

"He's waiting for you in the sun room," Mrs. Balor said when she returned. Hannibal started forward before he realized she was not alone. Cindy's face flashed an oddly brave kind of guilt, like a wronged wife caught with another man.

"What are you doing here?" he asked before he had time to think. "Sorry. None of my business." He rushed on, trying hard to focus on his mission.

Hannibal stalked into the sun room as confidently as he had entered Balor's office when they first met. He stood as straight and tall as he could, ignoring the pain around his ribs. Balor stood up from his chair and stared out the French doors leading to the deck. Beyond it, mature shade trees reached for heaven. Hannibal realized he was expected to speak first. No problem.

"Mr. Balor. You've got to let me finish what I started."

Balor stared at his carefully landscaped rolling hills and lit a cigar. "We've had this conversation. I don't think the job can be done. That pile of brick and boards isn't worth seeing people get hurt. And if you go back there, if you keep this up, I'm telling you, you will get hurt."

"So?" That response turned Balor around. Hannibal suddenly realized Balor was looking into his hazel eyes for the first time. "People are always getting hurt," Hannibal added.

Balor pushed the French doors open. The scent of hyacinths flooded the room, replacing his cigar smoke. He stared out at his private forest until Hannibal wondered if he was forgotten. Then Balor stepped out onto the deck, and Hannibal followed. Balor turned toward him, taking another pull on his cigar.

"Tell me something, will you? Why do you do this?"

Caught off guard, Hannibal spread his hands. "You mean my work? It's who I am. It's what I do."

"I see." Balor left another pause, then said "This thing's personal with you, isn't it?"

Hannibal had not thought of it until that moment. "Yes," he said. "Yes, I guess it is."

"Of course it's not your problem, it's mine," Balor said. He seemed to be considering a purely theoretical situation, his eyes a thousand miles away. "You could just walk away. No harm, no foul."

Hannibal could not see the theoretical playing field Balor was looking over. "The problem won't go away, whether I do or not."

"Perhaps the problem isn't that important to me," Balor said.

The air seemed unjustifiably sweet out there, inappropriate for the conversation. "Perhaps," Hannibal said more softly, "But it isn't only your problem."

"Right," Balor said. "You probably see it as a community problem, or a purely moral issue. And I guess you'll probably keep at it, even though I called the whole thing off." Balor started pacing and Hannibal thought he was talking primarily to himself. "In which case, lacking resources, you'll probably get yourself killed." Then Balor looked up at Hannibal, his face set in stone. "Okay. You win. I'm in. I'm in until you've had enough."

Just like that, Hannibal thought. He had not noticed he was holding his breath. Now he released it, then inhaled deeply and nodded in Balor's direction. "I told you it'd get expensive from here on out. I'll have to get some help."

"Do it."

"It's dangerous work," Hannibal went on. "Anybody working for me gets two-fifty a day."

Balor shrugged. "Thirty something an hour. Hell, I think my plumber gets that. Draw expense money at the office."

"And there'll be expenses for equipment. And you'll have to start the renovations early."

"That part goes through Mick Denton, my property manager. Look, just do what you got to do and send me the bill. Besides," with a chuckle, "It's all deductible."

* * *

Outside, Hannibal held the car door for Cindy, then walked around to get in the other side. He had not even touched the seat himself when Ray turned around toward him.

"So? You talked to Balor?"

"Yep. Good man. Gave me the go ahead and a blank check."

"So you're going back to Anacostia?" Ray put the Volvo into gear.

"Yeah, but not today. Right now, if it's okay, we'll go back to Cindy's. I need to take over your room again and stretch for about an hour. Can't let these bruises cramp me up. Then a hot shower, then I head for the homeless shelter."

"The shelter?" Cindy asked. "I thought you went on Tuesday."

"Oh, this isn't volunteer work," Hannibal smiled.

-24-

The three of them arrived at the shelter just after dinner was served. Because of the reason for this trip, Cindy looked at those inside differently this time. She noticed, for instance, just how high a percentage of them were women and children. She saw the effect on the body of a nourishing but not satisfying diet. She saw the anger lying just under the skin.

Hannibal moved about them at ease, as an outcast among outcasts. She felt like an outsider, and was looked on as such by people huddled around their food as if to protect it. He exchanged smiles and nods with several men, while she could only keep her eyes moving, trying to avoid making contact. Her father, she knew, was at home in almost any situation. He took a seat at a table with a checkerboard painted on it. Very soon a man his age sat on the other side. Cindy sat beside her father, watching Hannibal settle into a chair at a table with three men eating in silence.

Hannibal neither knew nor really cared what was going on in Cindy's mind right then. His focus was on figuring out the best way to broach the subject he had in mind. The men he chose to sit with wore clothes worn out as much from washing as wearing, and he had found the level of cleanliness to be a pretty fair gauge of men in the shelter. The man beside him looked like a no-nonsense character, so he decided to try the direct approach. "I need some help."

"Sorry, I'm tapped out," the stocky black man with the receding hairline said.

"Money I got," Hannibal said. "Manpower I need."

"You talking work?" the tall white man with the angular face asked, looking up from his soup. "Is it legal?"

"Legal." Hannibal leaned forward on his elbows. "Legal, but dangerous. Might last a day, or a week."

"Risky stuff, eh?" The muscular black man reached out a big hand. "You look like you already started. Well, you got my attention. They call me Sarge."

"Good to know you. Hannibal Jones." They shared a firm handshake.

"I've seen you. You come in here a lot," the taller man observed. "I'm Quaker. So, what's the job?"

"I'm turning some druggies out of a house over in Anacostia," Hannibal said, keeping his voice low. "It's worth two-fifty a day to me to have some good men at my back."

"You saying two hundred and fifty dollars?" Sarge asked. "A day? Cash money?"

Hannibal nodded. Suddenly, it seemed all eyes in the room focused on him. He gave a faint smile. This would be easier than he expected. "Look, I only need maybe a half dozen guys," Hannibal said. "And I'm dead serious about the risk. It might mean some fighting. Maybe even getting shot at. These drug types, they play rough. And the dealer over there? This guy don't dance. You can see that just looking at me. Whoever comes with me, you can bet they'll earn their money."

"Tell me something I don't know." Sarge pushed his chair back as Hannibal did. When he stood, both Sarge and Quaker got to their feet as well.

"Fellows, there's a nice, quiet little bar down about a block away. I think we should go talk. Drink beer?"

"You buying?" Quaker asked. Hannibal nodded.

"Then I'm drinking."

Hannibal took Cindy's arm on his way out, and tapped Ray's shoulder to follow. Sarge and Quaker walked out behind them. Several men in the room fidgeted, but only two others actually got up and headed for the door.

*   *   *

In the bar's semidarkness, everything seemed clearer. Hannibal slid into a booth. Cindy followed. Sarge squeezed into the opposite side, with Quaker on his outside. Ray pulled a round table over to them. Hannibal ordered a pitcher of draft and filled a glass for everyone. All the men took a swallow right away, but Hannibal noticed that Cindy never touched hers. He hoped she would not feel ignored, but after all, this business did not really concern her.

"So, how come they call you Sarge?" Hannibal asked.

"Two tours in Nam," Sarge replied. He rolled up his sleeve far enough to reveal the Marine fouled anchor tattoo on his muscular forearm. Hannibal gulped his beer and blessed his sudden turn of luck, in the right direction for a change.

"Well, Sarge, we're talking about an assault here," Hannibal said. "Something I suspect you know something about. I'm working for the owner of the building. Right now the place is a crack house, a shooting gallery. It's got hookers. It's got winos. It's got..."

"We get the idea," Quaker interrupted. "You tried it by yourself, didn't you? Heard about it last night. Got your ass kicked too, didn't you?"

"Shut up, Q.," Sarge snapped. "We talking guns, here, Jones?"

"Call me Hannibal, man. And I'd like to keep the shooting to a minimum. Besides, I got a license to carry. Do you?"

"Don't need one," Sarge muttered. "I'm between gigs right now, but when I can get work, it's usually as a bouncer. Got my own Louisville Slugger and my own two hands, and they usually do me."

"You talking about staying in this place a while, ain't you?" Quaker asked.

Hannibal noticed a new man, black but shorter than the others, had joined Ray's table. He was sitting up straight, trying to exaggerate his height.

"Cindy, we need another pitcher over here, and a couple more glasses," Hannibal said, then turned toward Quaker. "We'll stay for a few days, until the bad guys get the message they can't come back."

Cindy started to speak, but her father yanked her elbow, pulling her nearly out of the booth. She stood and locking eyes with him for a crucial moment. Finally, she curled her lips in and stamped off toward the bar, as best she could stamp in heels. Hannibal waited for her to reach her destination, knowing he could not get the men's attention while she was walking.

"This place is a dump, ain't it?" Quaker asked.

"Well, it ain't no palace, but it'll beat sleeping in a cardboard box," Hannibal answered. "It's dry, and it keeps the wind out. Actually, I was planning on fixing it up while we're there."

"Oh, you want labor too." Sarge emptied his glass.

"At these prices, the job's twenty-four seven. Like I said, we'll already be there, and after this last little bit of action, I'm not comfortable asking anybody else to be hanging out there unless they're prepared for violence. I'm just not sure I could protect a bunch of Merry Maids, or even regular contractors, that is, if they'd even come in to work in that place. So, yeah, I figure we'll do as much as we can ourselves before we call in experts for the serious renovations."

"Might not ever have to," the newcomer said, in a strong Jamaican accent. All eyes turned to him. "I'm a journeyman plumber. Times is hard. But I can do the work, and I can fight, mon." After a moment he added, "And it'd be good to earn me money. Me name's Timothy." He pronounced it without an "H". Hannibal made introductions all around. Cindy returned, dropped a glass in front of Timothy and put the pitcher down beside it.

"You lucked out, Slick." Sarge reached across to refill his glass. "Q's done some carpentry work."

"Neat, ain't it?" Quaker said, grinning.

"What more could I ask?" Hannibal said.

“How about an electrician?” a new voice asked. He was a big man, hovering over Cindy but bent forward, as if he might fall over. He could have been anywhere from thirty to fifty years old, with the yellowed eyes and puffy black hands Hannibal had seen too much of lately.

“Don’t know if you’re the man for me, Mister...”

“Adams,” the man replied in a deep, gravelly voice. “Virgil Adams. And I know what you’re thinking, but I ain’t no junkie. Not anymore, anyway. It cost me everything I had, but now I’m clean and I want to get on with my life. Only...”

“Only nobody will give you a chance, is that it?” Sarge asked. Virgil nodded, but his eyes stayed on Hannibal.

“I guess we can use one more man.” As Hannibal spoke, Cindy poured a beer and handed it up to Virgil.

“I don’t know, kid,” Sarge said. “You’re going to need real fighters if I understand the situation here. A perimeter to secure. Guards to post. In a hood that’s more like Saigon than suburbia. We’re talking about people who hold life kind of cheap. You know how many murders there are in D.C. every year?”

“Yeah,” Hannibal replied, meeting Sarge’s eyes. “Four hundred forty-six last year. In an area not quite seventy miles square. Look, I appreciate your experience, but before you take the operation over, understand you ain’t dealing with no amateur here. I was a beat cop in New York City, then a city detective, so I’ve spent my share of time in rough neighborhoods. And I spent eight years in the secret service, protecting people obsessed with making contact with strangers. I know how to set up a perimeter.”

“Okay.” Sarge raised his hands in mock defense. “Don’t get your...” his eyes cut over to Cindy and back. “Don’t get yourself in an uproar. I’m just saying we all ought to know the layout.”

“You’re right,” Hannibal said, calmer now. “It ain’t really that bad. It’s a row house, with a narrow path on each side, so there’s only the front and back to defend. It’s three stories, with a little bit of a backyard. The front stoop’s elevated. Good field of view there. And the neighbors might not help but they ain't against us."

"Cool," Sarge said. Everyone at both tables took a long drink while they looked around, as if considered the others. Sarge finally said, "Well, I'm in if you want me." Quaker, Timothy and Virgil all made similar noises.

"Good," Hannibal said, raising his glass to them. "I want to get back in there fast, before the squatters have had time to get too solidly settled back in."

Sarge nodded and leaned back in the booth. "Hope you won't mind discussing the best way to do this."

"Not at all," Hannibal said, his voice tight with excitement. "In fact I think we need to get together for a long planning session, after you guys put your things in order for a long stay. We'll go over the floor plan and so forth, and we won't make a move until we have a solid plan of attack we can all live with."

"Well, you don't want to do that at the shelter, man," Timothy said. "You got a place we can crash?" Hannibal's mouth hung open for a moment.

"Of course he does," Cindy said. "With only one car we'll have to make a couple of trips to get everybody there. While my dad drives back and forth I'll make us some snacks or something."

"Cindy, are you sure?" Hannibal asked.

"Relax," she said, bumping him with her shoulder. "We got enough sofa and carpet space for everybody. We could pick up a couple of sleeping bags."

"Sounds like a plan," Virgil said.

"Yeah." Sarge looked at his watch. "Let's make it twenty hundred hours at the shelter. That's eight o'clock for you civilians. Solid?"

"Yeah, solid, I guess," Hannibal stammered out. "Meantime, I'll get on the horn and get us some gear. Those of us who don't have our own bats, that is."

"Good deal," Sarge said, rising. "Just remember, in an assault like this, the readier you look, the less casualties you get. Looks is important."

Hannibal watched his newly hired thousand-dollar-a-day attack force move off to gather their things at the shelter, walking a little taller than they had an hour before. He turned to Cindy with all of his admittedly limited humility.

"Listen, baby, thanks a lot for what you did just now. You sure don't owe me any help, after the hell I've already put you through. But if we can stay together and get to know each other a bit, tomorrow will just go that much better. I guess I should have thought of that sooner."

"Hey, I don't mind." Cindy snuggled in closer, gently nuzzling his cheek. "Got to respect a man who don't give up after what they did to you. And these men too. You know, it's funny."

"Can't see much funny right now."

"I meant the weirdness of our society that turns skilled, able bodied men into, well, the homeless."

"It's an old story, babe," Hannibal said. "Every country has its refugees. Homeless don't mean useless."

"They each have their own story," Cindy said, staring pensively into her beer, "And they're all different."

Hannibal smiled. "Yeah, well right now I'm writing a new story of my own. Since you're so impressed by my new friends, do you want to cook for this crowd, or should we just order pizzas or something?"

"We can talk about it." Cindy slid out of the booth again. "Right now I need to find out if this place has a ladies room."

Hannibal watched with admiration as she walked away. Maybe he was in the market after all.

As Cindy moved out of sight, Ray slid into the booth opposite Hannibal. He smiled the way men do when they're embarrassed and don't know how to broach a subject. Hannibal wondered if it involved his growing closeness to Cindy, or maybe he had misgivings about having four homeless strangers stay in her apartment with her overnight. Unsure, Hannibal poured them both a fresh beer.

"Okay, Ray, did I do something I should apologize for?"

"No, no, it's just..." Ray's voice trailed away as he turned toward the bar. Hannibal let the silence hang until Ray turned back, eyes on the table.

"I got a chance to go into business, like you, only with two partners. I need to be earning a real living again, and get my own place. This business idea is the way, and it's what I want to do. Naturally, I need some seed money. So anyway, this job with you, I mean, how come you didn't ask me, Paco?"

"Oh, Ray." Hannibal suddenly felt very small. "I didn't think..."

"I know I'm not no bent nose, but I been taking care of myself for a lot of years, man." Once started, Ray rolled on. "Besides, those guys are strangers. You know me, man. I could use…"

"I didn't think I should risk you on this. And I don't think Cindy would…"

Ray plowed on. "I could use that kind of money, man. Besides, what if some of these druggies don't speak English, you know?"

"Okay, Ray, I'm sorry." Hannibal offered an embarrassed smile. "Of course you're in. I need you on this. And when it's over, I'll help all I can with you setting up your business. If you need more capital, I'll help you get a business loan."

The Budweiser sign over the bar flashed bright red, but when Ray Santiago looked up, a new light showed in his face.

"But there's a condition to all of this." Hannibal looked so serious, Ray's smile faded, as if he sensed new found independence could be threatened.

"What kind of condition?"

Hannibal checked over his shoulder to make sure Cindy was not on her way back. "You tell your bookie he just lost a customer. I mean permanently. And no more trips up to the track, either. I know what you told Cindy, but we both know the real reason you got fired. You spent too much time up at Pimlico and even Charles Town when you were supposed to be picking up fares. So for you, the horses are out, for good."

"You want to take all the excitement out of my life?" Ray stopped because Cindy was just dropping into her seat next to Hannibal.

"Trust me Ray. I think in the next couple of days you'll see just how exciting life can be."

-25-

MONDAY

Ninety three million miles away, the sun cannot distinguish between Georgetown and Anacostia. This particular day, the same hot rays blessed both places, glaring through clear skies that seemed endlessly high. No breeze disturbed the urban air and even at dawn, a haze began rising from the streets. Starlings woke each other in the big tree down the block from number twenty-three thirteen. The sweet aroma on the air did not reflect blooming flowers, but rather that it was trash day.

Along with the first rays of sunshine, a white Volvo 850 GLT came to Southeast Washington D.C. Its purring motor became the dominant sound on the block when it pulled up directly across the street from number twenty-three thirteen, but it soon died down. Inside sat six men, identically dressed in black jeans and tee shirts. Hannibal, in the front passenger seat, turned to his team with an excitement born of confidence that payback was at hand.

"All right gentlemen, let's do it just the way we planned it."

The dark man Hannibal called Chipmunk Cheeks had returned to his lookout position. Hannibal assumed that, confronted with police or superior numbers, his job was to run inside and alert everyone to hide their drugs. Surely only lack of understanding made him hesitate.

He stood slowly and watched as six men stepped leisurely from the Volvo. The car's trunk popped open, and each man reached into it before stepping up onto the sidewalk.

Hannibal had done them up right, following Colin Powell's theory that an overwhelming show of force often meant less conflict. A late night visit to Eddy Frasier's home had yielded everything he needed to impress anyone who saw them. Each team member wore a flak vest. Each man held a black riot baton, except Sarge and Hannibal. Sarge held his own baseball bat like an old, trusted friend.

Hannibal's left fist was wrapped around a twelve-gage riot gun. At Frasier's suggestion, it was the Magtech Model 586P combat shotgun. Hannibal swung the six shot pump gun's barely legal nineteen inch barrel across the back of his neck and stood just off the curb. Sarge moved directly in front of him. Virgil stood on Hannibal's left, while Quaker went to his right. Timothy took a position behind Virgil, while Ray watched Quaker's back. Once in this formation they stepped forward as one man, stopping just before the bottom of the stoop.

"All right, son," Sarge called up, "hit the bricks. You don't want none of this." When the guard picked up his bat, Sarge swung the head of his into his left fist. The smack sound jolted the watchman into action. He vaulted the side of the stoop, hit the grass, rolled, and darted down the street.

Hannibal glanced around as the team mounted the sandstone steps. In neighboring buildings windows opened and closed. Hands pulled drapes away from a few windows. He felt good. Their appearance posted notice to the whole neighborhood that they meant business. And his anger rose when he stepped on a bloodstain he himself left on those steps two days before.

Sarge wrapped a hand around the doorknob and looked over his shoulder. Hannibal guessed the old NCO was checking his team for nervousness, fear, lack of confidence. He would see a good tension level, Hannibal knew, but nothing to worry about.

"This is it, men," Sarge said. "We drive for the top and flush downward. Stay together. And if you're in the rear, watch the rear. Oh, and, er, follow the boss' instructions."

Hannibal and Sarge exchanged smiles. Taking a deep breath, Sarge shoved the door open, swinging around with it, holding his bat vertically with both hands, as if it were a rifle at port arms. Hannibal swept the hall with his shotgun at waist level. No response. Just like last time, it was likely that no one knew they were there.

The smell of drugs was everywhere. Early morning heat kept an air of unwashed humanity hanging in the building. Moans from people who never really sleep well pried into his ears, unasked, like some remote form of rape.

He felt fluttering wings in his stomach again, the same ones he felt but always denied when he used to walk through a crowded lecture hall with the Vice President. That feeling of being surrounded by unknown danger, knowing no one could defend against it all but knowing it was his job to try.

Inside, the building was as quiet as a morgue at midnight. The group climbed both flights of stairs without seeing an unfriendly face, followed by only the sound of their own footsteps. At the top, Sarge moved to the first room on the right. The sound of rap artists leaked under the door. They were talking at high speed about abusing women, using drugs and shooting strangers. Sarge looked at Hannibal, who nodded. Yes, this one was occupied.

Again Sarge stepped inside, his bat held at high port. Hannibal thrust his head forward, just far enough to see the bald man with the crinkly beard snap his fingers and continue working on a VCR. A wave of deja vu hit him as a roaring growl came from the next room.

Fully prepared, Hannibal still barely took action in time. The gigantic pit bull moved like a long brown streak across the floor, jaws dripping. By the time Hannibal pumped his weapon the beast was airborne, targeting his throat. The blast was a deafening thunderclap, the recoil surprisingly light. Barely a meter away, the dog's head all but disappeared, its body flung the length of the room.

Only after the fact did Hannibal's stomach clench at the thought of what he had just done. The dog, he knew, was an innocent, turned by men into a dangerous killer beast. Even in self-defense he hated to destroy an innocent animal.

The dog owner's howl echoed the pit bull's as he leaped over his worktable. Sarge's body pivoted, with his right fist around the bottom of his bat's handle and his left against its center. With a small, economical movement, he swung its head into the bald man's gut. When his target doubled over, Sarge grabbed his shoulder and thrust him through the door. Timothy shoved him toward the stairs, shouting "Get your ass out of here, man."

With the shotgun's blast, the building burst into activity like a slapped hornet's nest. But inside that top flat, all was still. Hannibal stepped slowly forward, resenting the hairs standing erect on the back of his neck. He and Sarge moved through the rooms one at a time. A glance over his shoulder confirmed that Virgil and Quaker stayed at the door they had entered, watching their backs. Ray and Timothy waited outside the door, watching the doors across the hall and the stairway.

Hannibal and Sarge swept the apartment quickly, making sure that no one remained inside. At the other end Sarge opened the last door into the hall. He looked back toward the others and raised a palm, their prearranged signal indicating that all was clear. Hannibal stepped out behind Sarge, his gun now aimed at the floor. Ray and Timothy walked confidently down the hall to join them. Hannibal could hear the commotion below them as people fled the building.

"You know," Ray said, "I was a little worried about our only gun going inside the apartment. But now I see how these people are, it's no big deal, eh?"

Sarge nodded without really showing agreement. "That's just one down and five to go. Let's remember we don't know what's behind door number two."

As if to drive his words home, Sarge opened the door to the apartment across the hall very cautiously. Hannibal followed, leading with the shotgun's muzzle. Their technique for clearing the room was identical, but this time no one met them.

Sarge went to the edge of the second room's entrance and looked through to the end.

"Don't you smell that?" Hannibal asked from the other side of the entrance. "Nobody could stay in here."

"Maybe," Sarge said. "Can't see all of the kitchen though." The two men edged down the walls opposite each other. A streak of movement and Hannibal shouted, "Shit!" and whipped his shotgun down. He barely avoided squeezing the trigger as a huge rat bolted past him. Sarge laughed his deep, staccato laugh.

Finally, Sarge opened the kitchen door into the hall. Over his shoulder, Hannibal saw five skinny, ragged young men coming up the stairs. Timothy and Ray met them, their batons held the way Sarge had taught them, at high port arms.

"You going the wrong way, my boys." Timothy showed brilliant white teeth. The youngsters stopped. Two of them, Puerto Ricans Hannibal thought, took a few more tentative steps. Ray rattled off a high-speed burst of Spanish, ending with "Vamanos!" The Hispanic boys turned and the others followed them down.

"Looks like he sure told them," Sarge said.

Hannibal's team moved down to the second floor with more confidence. Ray and Timothy were getting good at prodding people down the steps and no one had been hurt yet. The first door on the right was locked. Sarge kicked it open and stepped aside. A pudgy woman, much younger than her face revealed, whipped up a knife.

"You leave us alone," she yelled. Hannibal pumped the shotgun and stepped forward. She dropped her knife and ran into the flat. They heard her slam the door at the far end, but still proceeded carefully. In the middle room another woman lay motionless on a bare, stained mattress. Hannibal feared the worst but when Sarge bent to nudge her, she turned over.

"Too drugged to know," Sarge said. "Or care." After checking the rest of the apartment, Sarge lifted the girl to her feet and guided her to the stairs.

At the door of the second flat on the second floor, Hannibal stopped to gulp some extra air. He knew this was the center of the crack house. When he nodded to Sarge they burst in just as before. The first room was empty, but the sliding doors to the next room were nearly closed and they heard ragged breathing from the other side.

Sarge dashed across the room, stopped at the other end, and eased toward the dividing doors. Hannibal stayed even with him. He hated the sweat on his brow and started to wish he had given someone else the gun, despite the law. Sarge reached out and pulled one side of the sliding doors open. As the glass and wooden wall slid into place he found himself staring into the muzzle of a big revolver held by a shaking teenager.

"Get the fuck out of here, man," the boy said. "I swear to God I'll blow your fucking head off. I swear to God I will." His eyes held a vacant desperation, as if he knew this time these men would uproot him from his cocaine rich soil for good.

"You don't want to do that." Hannibal stepped into full view, his barrel pointed at the kid's face. "What you want to do is put that little gun away and walk out of here. You can't win this."

"You some kind of right wing fanatic or something?" the boy shouted. "All I want..." Hannibal hated hearing hysterics coming from behind a gun, especially since he, not Sarge, was now the target.

"All you want is your crack. I know. And frankly, I don't give a rat's ass if you want to drug yourself to death. I ain't no cop. Like I said before, I don't care if you use drugs. You just can't do it here."

The younger man took one hand off his pistol to run greasy fingers through flat-topped hair. Hannibal knew he should fire now. Waiting risked Sarge's life as well as his own. But the killing was not in him.

During the next minute Hannibal's lungs seemed frozen. The boy seemed to forget what he was doing there. He looked at his own gun as if he had never seen it before. Finally he bent down, placed it on the floor, turned, and fled for the far door.

"You can breathe now," Sarge said. He waved Hannibal on, and they went through the remaining empty rooms. In the hall, the group gathered for the final descent.

"How's everybody doing?" Hannibal asked on their way downstairs.

"Nobody dead yet," Timothy said. The hall was surprisingly quiet. Hannibal guessed everyone who got the message had already left. This time the rear guard men held the base of the stairs while Sarge and Hannibal prepared to enter the right hand flat. At the door, they watched one woman, dull eyed and empty stared, slip out of the flat across the hall and out the front door without closing it.

Sarge and Hannibal entered the right side apartment and took a quick look around. It was much the way Hannibal found it the first day. The winos had returned to their familiar sleeping space.

"You have any trouble in here before?" Sarge asked.

"No, it was just as you see it," Hannibal said. "I guess we just need to nudge them into action."

Sarge shook his head. "Why don't you go on back out into the hall? I got this."

Hannibal joined Ray and the others, feeling out of place carrying a shotgun. Wondering about the woman he'd seen wander past a few minutes before, he craned his neck to see out the door. He didn't see her, but several other ousted squatters stood around the stoop, looking shaken and lost. Beyond them, people went on their way to work or wherever, pointedly ignoring the small knot of castaways clogging the sidewalk.

With a squeal like an old man's yawn, the far door out of the right apartment opened. Hannibal turned to watch a string of men wandered out. Black and white, dirty and of indeterminate age, they shuffled past Hannibal and his club holding team members, angry at being roused from a good, wine induced sleep. He watched six pairs of feet slide out the door, with not one decent pair of shoes between them.

Sarge came out last, shaking his head. The group reunited at the base of the stairs. Hannibal and Sarge made solid eye contact, but no words were necessary. Hannibal scanned the other four faces before turning to the final flat's front door.

When Sarge tried the knob, a frantic voice snapped "Get away." Sarge pointed at the others, getting them repositioned through hand signals. Now Timothy held the base of the stairway, while Ray went to the other end of the hall to stand with his back against the wall beside the last apartment's kitchen door. Quaker stood behind Sarge and Hannibal. Virgil crouched against the front door, leaving it half open.

"This is it," Sarge muttered. "All the cornered rats are in here. Ready?"

"As I'll ever be," Hannibal replied. This time Sarge took a deep breath. He kicked out, there came the crack of twisted wood, and the door bounced open.

Sarge had just moved into his usual position when a shot split the air. As if punched by a giant invisible fist, Sarge snapped backward into the hall. Hannibal stepped forward, and Quaker slid between his legs, tossing his billy club, sending it spinning across the floor. Hannibal recognized his bright eyed enemy from his previous visit and was about to blast his face apart when he and a man behind him suddenly dropped out of sight.

Quaker crawled over one man to reach his nightstick as Hannibal's foot landed hard on Wild Eyes' hand, which was clawing for his dropped gun.

"Nice trick, Quaker." Hannibal kicked the pistol into a corner.

"Yeah, neat ain't it?" he answered, running long fingers through his thinning, short cropped hair. Hannibal could see he was happy to get into the action. But his concern was not ahead, but behind him. No one else was in that front room, and he didn't think they would wait for him in the kitchen this time.

Hannibal stepped back into the hall just as the kitchen door flew open. A handful of Saturday night special poked out. Ray swung his club down with both hands, raising a loud crack when it hit the gunman's arm. The pistol flew down the hall. The gunman ran howling toward the front door, clutching his broken arm. Three others followed, scattering for escape from the kitchen. They ran past Hannibal without looking at him.

Hannibal never thought it would go this well. Sticking to the plan, he quickly wandered through the apartment looking for any kind of trap. When he reached the kitchen he went back out to the hall and waved Ray to join him.

Timothy had apparently gone into the apartment to back Quaker up. Quaker shoved Bright Eyes and his friend past Hannibal who was helping Sarge to his feet.

"You okay?" Hannibal asked.

"Oh, yeah," Sarge replied, slapping his heavy vest. "These things work. Don't know where you got them, but I'm sure as hell glad you did."

All heads spun as the sound of very close sirens filled the house. The last two junkies stalled at the door.

"Jesus, the cops are here," Bright Eyes rattled in panic, back pedaling.

"Sucks, don't it?" Quaker grinned. He and Virgil shoved hard with their sticks, and the two men trotted, against their will, down the outside steps.

Hannibal handed the shotgun to Sarge who would hide, and stepped outside. He saw the last two junkies sprint past four policemen standing in a semicircle at the base of the stoop, guns drawn. One of them Hannibal recognized.

"Kendall," he called, taking a tentative step downward. "Now you show up."

"Some lady down the block called in a disturbance up here," Kendall said, staring hard at Hannibal's protective vest. "Thought you might need a hand."

"Well, we handled it without you, thanks." Hannibal sat on a step. "All cleared out."

"Shots were reported," Kendall said, but he holstered his weapon.

"No casualties on either side," Hannibal reported, "except one attack dog. But it don't have to be a wasted trip, Bro. The drug crowd came back, and they brought all their bad news with them. You can come in and collect up whatever drugs and paraphernalia they left behind. You might even want to make an arrest or two."

"With you in there with the dope and all of them out here on the street? That might not be too smart."

"Hey, you won't find any of our prints on any of that stuff," Hannibal said. "And if necessary we can all pass a blood or urine test. Come on in."

Kendall accepted the invitation, and brought three other officers with him. He paid less attention to the contents of the apartment than its occupants.

"And these would be?"

Hannibal smiled. "Officer Kendall, these are the other new residents. I'd like you to meet Ray, Timothy, Sarge, Quaker and Virgil."

"I hope you guys got a good break on the rent," Kendall said, shaking hands with each of them. "But I see you came prepared. So Jones, do you want to tell me about the flak vests and batons?"

"Not really, no."

Kendall and his fellow officers explored the flat, bagging and labeling illegal items. Back in the front room, Hannibal hesitantly picked up the telephone sitting in a corner.

"Hot damn," he called to the others. "Dial tone!" He pushed seven buttons from memory and perched on the windowsill. He heard less than half a ring before a breathless "Santiago" filled his ear.

"You're not anxious or anything are you?" he asked.

"Hannibal, please," Cindy said. "Just tell me."

"Okay. We're in. Nobody hurt. Got a few cops here helping out. Are you ready to handle your end?"

"Think so," she answered. "Soon as you hang up I'm calling a cab and heading in to the office."

"A cab?" Hannibal asked. "Don't you have a car?"

"You mean you didn't even notice?" Cindy asked, sounding hurt. "I always take a taxi, unless I'm riding with someone. Well, I'll see you later."

"See you," Hannibal replied. As she hung up, Cindy blew him a kiss through the phone. Hannibal did not return it, but he regretted that oversight as soon as he cradled the receiver. He started to lift it again, but Sarge stepped up behind him.

"Cops just left, man, so the junkies might figure it's time to come home. I think you, me and Ray, we ought to do security while the other guys get to work."

"Getting ahead of ourselves," Hannibal said. "We're not quite secured. Where's the shotgun?"

"Behind the fridge."

"Grab it and check the basement. Thoroughly. Take one of the guys with you. Send Ray up here with me and put the other two dudes on rear security. I think we need to stay in pairs until we're sure the house is secure and there are no surprises in here waiting for us."

"Makes sense," Sarge said. As he left, Hannibal picked up the telephone again. As he reached for the buttons a roach skittered along the baseboard near his foot. He called information and asked for the listing of an exterminator's number. First things first.

"Que Pasa, Paco?" Ray asked from behind as Hannibal hung up.

"What do you think, Ray?"

"I think everything is everything for a while." Ray swished his billy club through the air. "If we want it to stay that way, I think we ought to get our stuff and get settled in. Su casa, mi casa, at least for a while."

"Yeah, guess so. Want to check the kitchen first, then we'll go." Hannibal led the way down the long tunnel to his kitchen. He found Timothy perched on the sink's sideboard. The door to the hall stood open, so Timothy could see Virgil in the apartment across the hall.

"Hey, pretty smart," Hannibal said. "Your idea?"

"Uh-huh," Timothy responded. "You checking up?"

"Actually, I came back to see if the junkies left my coffeepot. Since it's still in one piece, I want to get it going."

"I'm with that," Timothy grinned. "You bring some coffee?"

"We just going to get it now," Ray said, pulling Hannibal's sleeve. They returned to the front of the house, but opened the door slowly. Hannibal glanced up and down the street before they went out.

Heat was already rising off the sidewalk, making Hannibal aware of their flak jackets' weight. Those same starlings were cursing him out about something. Squinting against the glare of bright sun off his white car, Hannibal opened the trunk. Between them, he and Ray pulled out six small suitcases.

"Oh wow, man, check it out. You dudes a SWAT team or something?" Monty skidded to a stop and flipped his skateboard up into his hands.

"Morning, Monty," Hannibal said. "Ray and me and a couple friends just moved in. Seen anything of the previous tenants?"

"Hey, they all, like, split, you know?" Monty looked down, then over at the house. "The man, he'll be back, you know."

"Good," Ray spat. "We got something for his ass when he does."

"Got lots to do today, little guy," Hannibal said. "Check with you later."

The men started inside. When they were halfway up the steps the door opened and Sarge leaned out, shotgun first.

"Get in here," he said. "You nuts going out like that with nobody covering you?"

Ray opened his mouth to snap back, but Hannibal preempted him, saying simply "Didn't think, Sarge." Once they hustled the bags into Hannibal's living room, he told Sarge to get everybody together. Sarge nodded and walked away. Within two minutes, they were assembled, each man picking up his suitcase.

"Okay, here's how I see it," Hannibal said. "Everybody ought to pick a spot to crash. Once we're settled in, we'll start fixing this joint up. I'm flopping right here. "

"Three outside doors," Sarge observed. "Three can watch, three can work."

"My nose telling me the plumbing situation is critical," Timothy said in his Jamaican lilt. "I need to get to work on it."

"So what's stopping you?" Virgil asked.

"Hey, man, I'm a genius with the pipes, but I can't do nothing without the tools." In answer to Hannibal's unspoken question, he added "Had to hock my own for food."

“Right.” Hannibal made a quick decision, and pulled out his wallet. “Ray, take Timothy and get whatever tools and stuff he needs to do the job. While you’re out, get new locks for all three of the doors.”

“Defense,” Sarge said quietly.

“I know,” Hannibal replied. “In fact, Sarge, I think you just became the front door guard. Take the shotgun. Virgil and I’ll take the back doors for now. When the delivery arrives we’ll refigure it all, okay? Right now I got more important stuff on my mind. Like coffee.”

-26-

In the following hours Hannibal brewed and drank a lot of coffee, watching his new, overgrown backyard. He had planned precisely for taking the house, but now realized how vague his thoughts were on keeping it. He thought forty-eight hours would be enough to keep the squatters from returning, and one failed attempt at reclaiming it would be enough for young Sal the pusher. He had not really thought about the prospect of several hours staring out a window, literally looking for trouble. It could be a long, lonely couple of days.

At twenty after twelve, a truck horn sounded four harsh notes in front of number twenty-three thirteen. He had seen no sign of trouble since his team cleared the house out, so he did not worry much about deserting his post. He found Sarge at the front door, checking the perimeter. Outside, Cindy hopped down from a furniture delivery truck's cab, cradling two cardboard buckets of chicken. She had found a black tee shirt and jeans, the unofficial team uniform, but somehow she did more for them than any of Hannibal's fellow house sitters.

"Told you I'd handle it," Cindy said, sprinting up the outside steps. "When I gave Dan the report, he authorized me to talk to his manager Denton. Through him I arranged to have the big ticket items delivered. The icebox, the desk, beds, chairs and so on."

"Didn't you think they could find the place?" Hannibal asked, stepping back into the hall and welcoming the girl's warm form into his arms.

"Just wanted to see you, so I took the day off, and..."

"Come here a minute." Hannibal led Cindy through his flat until they were two rooms away from the others. "Now, tell me, just what the hell were you thinking coming here?"

"I was excited," Cindy said, all but bouncing free of his grip on her upper arms. "I just think what you're doing here is so special, and it's so very cool kicking the bad guys' ass and you know, I could just.. just..." Her eyes were flashing as she covered his mouth with her own. The frantic kiss quickly became warmer and tenderer. Paradoxically, Hannibal felt himself calming down while at the same time he was becoming excited. He was swimming in his own emotions for only a moment, before he gently separated himself from her.

"Look," he said with some effort, "you can hang here for a little while, but you shouldn't stay her long. I'm expecting some nasty people to come by today and I don't want you here when they arrive."

"Aw, how nasty can they be with all the help you got?" Cindy joked, fingers playing in his short hair.

"This nasty," Hannibal said seriously, pointing at his own face. "The guys that did this don't care I got friends."

From two rooms away Sarge called, "Hey Hannibal. You need to be talking to these people out here." Hannibal dropped his hands, returned her smile for just a second, then took her hand and led her to the front of the building. He found a very large, very black uniformed delivery man staring down at Sarge. Hannibal couldn't decide if he thought the man looked like Biff or Sully, but he was certainly reminiscent of one of the Sesame Street construction workers.

"Is there a problem?" Hannibal asked.

"You Jones? Suppose I could see some ID? I've delivered to lots of buildings that have a doorman, but they usually ain't sitting on the inside steps cradling a pump scatter-gun. Makes me nervous."

"We've had a little trouble with local gangs," Hannibal said, presenting his driver's license. "I think you can put that away now, Sarge. I don't anticipate much trouble while we have delivery guys running in and out of here."

"Maybe, but I still want somebody watching those back doors," Sarge said, dourly moving to toward the back of the building.

While Sarge focused on security, Hannibal inventoried the incoming equipment on a clipboard pad Cindy had brought with her. He stayed by the front door while Cindy flitted around like an interior decorator on acid, pointing out where each item should land. The delivery men made no comment as they wheeled in the refrigerator, six beds, electric fans, and folding chairs. They only grimaced slightly when Cindy pointed out where the twenty cheap light fixtures and fifteen lamps were to be used.

But then came the odd stuff. When two men entered with the narrow desk, Hannibal had them position it in front of the stairway, making passage difficult. Then the team leader set bags full of supplies on the desk and raised an eyebrow.

"Brother, either you people are seriously paranoid, or you're expecting some serious problems," he said.

"We're just safety minded," Hannibal said. "Just read it off will you, and I'll check them off the list."

"Okay, here we go," the deliveryman said, emptying the bags one at a time. "Six each flashlights, fire extinguishers, smoke alarms, and walkie-talkies. One bag of cement. Sixteen sets of window bars, including two short enough for the narrow basement windows. This stuff ought to keep you safe enough so you don't need to walk around the house with a shotgun."

*   *   *

Five hours later, Hannibal sat against a wall in his kitchen listening to a cricket chorus. He was looking out a broken window at a sharp enough angle to see anyone approaching either back door. He carried his gun in a side draw holster over his tee shirt, waiting for the assault he knew must come. His back hurt a little. The light purple twilight sky stole his attention for a moment, reminding him that he was pushing the limits of his focus. He sipped hot black coffee and stirred his mind into activity.

The afternoon and evening had been a blur of activity that he had sat out. While he guarded the back and Sarge watched the front door, the other men moved feverishly to reverse the ravages of neglect the building had endured. Cindy helped when she could, cleaning or just being an extra pair of hands. Ray made three trips out in the Volvo for needed equipment. Cindy joined him on the last trip out. Hannibal was just wondering if they had run into trouble when he heard Sarge welcome them back in. Seconds later they staggered into the kitchen, overloaded with plastic bags of various sizes.

"What's all this stuff?" Hannibal asked as Cindy shoved two bags onto the counter beside the sink.

"Just what you and the macho men forgot," she said with a mischievous smile. "That's enough groceries to fill your new refrigerator. Over there, six sets of sheets, blankets, pillows and pillowcases. And here, a takeout Chinese dinner. I pretty much know what room everybody's working in. Want me to distribute the food?"

Hannibal watched her putting away food and realized how worn out he was from sitting still, and from the odd loneliness that comes from guard duty. Too much solitary work could create the same feeling.

"I don't think so," he said. "I think the gain from eating together exceeds any risk from leaving the doors unmanned. Nobody's come anywhere near the building all day. Of course, that's at least partially because of those deliverymen running in and out. But still, it's a good sign."

Ten minutes later, a fan meant for a table hummed contentedly on the floor, blowing the aroma of stir-fry out a front window. Seven paper plates shouldered each other around the edge of Hannibal's card table. Cindy and the six men sat on chairs placed at various distances from that table. Each in turn stood up long enough to gather food from the assorted white cartons. As they took their plates, Cindy handed each a cold lemonade. Without saying so, Sarge positioned himself so he could see out the back window at the far end of the flat. Seeing that, Hannibal made sure he had a clear view through his front window.

"You guys look like you been working in a sewer all day," Cindy said, through a mouthful of egg fu yung.

"You not far wrong for some of us, girl," Timothy said between bites from an egg roll.

"Making any progress?"

"Well, I got two more of the johns working now, so we won't be having to stand in line. I got two more of the bathtubs in order, and I managed to rig up showerheads, for those who don't feel like soaking themselves. Got another sink going upstairs, too. God, you wouldn't believe the shit people been putting down those sinks, child."

"That's great, man." Hannibal could feel the fan drying perspiration on his back. "How about you, Virgil?"

"Got about half the lights up," Virgil answered, frowning into his plate. It crossed Hannibal's mind he might not like Chinese food, but he decided Virgil just did not smile much. "Tried to light up where Timothy needed to work, so there's three bathrooms and three kitchens done, and two in the basement. And two up in the first floor hall. And know what? There was lights outside the front door, and the back doors. Just needed bulbs, so I put them in."

"Solid," Hannibal told him. "How about you, Quaker? You're doing security, right?"

"Roger that." The gangly white man leaned back against the wall, his chair balanced on two legs. "We been busting, ain't we Ray? Me and Ray, we got the bars up to all the first floor windows. Fire alarms are hung in all the flats. And I got good dead bolt locks on both back doors, so we don't need to be nailed in no more, do we? Got enough locks for every door in this frigging place, at least the ones that ain't nailed and painted shut."

"Poor old Dan," Cindy said. "He's going to have a cow when he sees the money you spent."

"If he was going to rent this firetrap he would've had to do it anyway, sooner or later," Sarge said. "And he was going to pay us to be here doing security work, so actually we saved him a pile of cash." Then to Hannibal he said, "While I been sitting out there at the desk, I worked us up a duty roster."

"Duty roster?" Ray said. "Now there's some bad memories."

"You mean for tonight, right?" Hannibal asked.

"Three shifts, three hours each." Sarge replied. "Always have two guys up."

"You really think it's that dangerous?" Cindy put her now empty plate on the table.

"No doubt," Hannibal said, standing, "which is why I'm fixing to call you a cab. Sun be down soon, and that's when all the slimy things crawl out from under their rocks."

* * *

Minutes before the sun finally hid below the horizon, Sal Ronzini walked with his two bodyguards through newborn shadows up number twenty-three thirteen's front steps. A storm was brewing on his face and his heels clicked indignantly on the sandstone steps.

"Boy missed a second appointment," he muttered to Ox. "Wasted my time, and time is money. If something was wrong, idiot should have shown up to tell me so."

Sal stopped just short of the door, letting Ox turn the knob and push it open. He had advanced one foot before he really saw the big black man with the Marine tattoo, seated behind a desk at the base of the staircase. Deep shadows, cast by an overhead light, pooled on the desk below the man's head like spilled ink. His expression was stern, his eyes narrowed to slits. But it was the shotgun pointing out across the desktop that really caught Sal's attention.

"What the fuck is this?" Sal snapped. "And who the fuck are you?"

"You better dig yourself, talking to folks like that," Sarge snarled, "unless you want to see my magic trick of sawing a man in half." Then his left hand keyed the walkie-talkie beside him. "Three down front."

"You don't know who you're screwing around with here, boy." Sal's face reddened.

"I know," Hannibal said, stalking up the hallway.

"No." Sal shook his head, as if that might make it all go away. "Not you again. You about a slow learner, shithead."

"I think it's you ain't getting the message." Hannibal stood beside Sarge with arms folded. "Your buyers are all long gone down the road. There ain't nothing for you here, no reason to mess with us. Go set them up wherever they split to. Why fight over this rat trap?"

"Cause it's my rat trap," Sal shouted. "I don't care about the dope, I can sell dope anywhere. But nobody takes nothing from me." As if to punctuate those words, something hit a back door hard enough to make the vibrations reach those standing in the front. Sal showed his teeth in something halfway between a snarl and a smile.

-27-

Frustrated by the back door's new lock, the fullback type reached up to climb in the open window beside it. His hand hit the new bars as if he had not noticed they were there. Just as he got a firm grip on them, Quaker swung his nightstick. The crack sound was not just wood on metal.

"Christ! You broke it!" the thug screamed, yanking his hand back outside.

"Yeah. Sucks, don't it."

*　　*　　*

One room to Quaker's right, a face pressed against another set of window bars in surprise. Confusion became shock when Ray shoved his billy club between those bars, point first into the invader's mouth. His outcry was muffled. However, the gun barrel he thrust toward Ray seconds later spoke quite clearly.

*　　*　　*

When he heard the shot, Hannibal drew his pistol so quickly it made Sal blink. After only a second's hesitation, Hannibal raced down the hall.

“Sarge!” Hannibal shouted over his shoulder. “If any of them gets any closer, or goes for a weapon, shoot the white boy.”

Seconds later Hannibal stood against the wall on the left side of the basement door. Looking around it, he saw Ray on the floor, crawling slowly toward the hall. A second and third shot blasted over Ray’s body and into the floor.

“Back off, man!” Hannibal shouted. “Can’t...can’t we talk about this? It ain’t worth getting shot.” In answer, the shooter turned the gun as far in Hannibal’s direction as he could and fired again. This time his bullet split the doorjamb leading to the hall.

“Shit!” Hannibal spat. It was never easy or fun to fire a gun at another human being. For Hannibal, it required an extra effort to drop certain built in safeguards, as if a version of the gun’s safety catch existed inside his mind. Still, he knew that once the decision was made, hesitation could be deadly. He extended his left arm to its full length and squeezed off one round. The blast rocked his ears. A curse came through the kitchen window, and the gun dropped into the sink. From where he stood, Hannibal could have only hit the man’s forearm. Leaning back against the wall, he slid to the floor, considering what one of his one hundred eighty grain, forty millimeter hollowpoints would do on its way through an arm.

“That’s one asshole won’t be back.” It was Ray’s voice, jubilant.

“Cat started in on this side ain’t likely to stop by again either.” That was Quaker, sounding like he had won something.

Taking a minute to dredge up a smile of his own, Hannibal holstered his pistol, pushed himself to his feet and trotted to the front door. He found Sarge standing behind his desk, holding the shotgun at waist level, barrel forward. Virgil stood on his right, Timothy on his left, both holding their sticks at the ready.

“Hit the bricks,” Hannibal said, standing even with his team. “I brought an army with me this time and we mean to stay. Go tend your wounded and get on with your life, idiot.”

Sal pointed a fist at Hannibal's face, his index finger stabbing forward. "This ain't over, stud. Before it is, it's going to be me and you."

"Then let's get it on right now," Timothy said, jumping forward with his baton raised overhead. Hannibal was too surprised to react in time but Sarge's left hand snapped out, catching the back of Timothy's shirt. Timothy was jerked backward, and Sal's head snapped back just quickly enough to let the club's tip whistle by. Before it was quite past Sal's head, his two bodyguards had their revolvers out.

Hannibal had drawn a tenth of a second faster than either of them but instead of firing, he stopped with finger tense on the trigger and his muzzle pointed at the bridge of Sal's nose.

"Hold it," Hannibal barked, his eyes on Sal's. "Everybody freeze. We don't want a fight nobody can win." Both guns on Sal's side faced Hannibal at first. Then Hannibal saw realization dawn on Ox's face, and the bodyguard shifted his point of aim to Sarge's face. Sarge's barrel was already pointed at Ox.

From there, no one moved. The four men could have been mistaken for a museum diorama, except that museum exhibits don't sweat. A car passing in front of the house sounded like a freight train in Hannibal's ears. His heartbeat was out of control but his breathing had not yet caught up. He saw the ghost of terror behind Sal's eyes, but the two bodyguards showed no hint of fear. He had no doubt that they were quite ready to go down if they could take the opposition with them. Hate blazed from Timothy's eyes, but Virgil and Sarge looked less anxious to press the battle. Hannibal licked dry lips and considered the mess that would result if all four guns went off at once.

"This isn't the time or place for a showdown," Hannibal said through a ragged breath. Maintaining eye contact with Sal, he slowly lowered his automatic. Sal glanced at his two companions, who put their guns away just as slowly. Sal looked at Hannibal with renewed malice and no evident respect.

"Not the time now, maybe," Sal said in a low, even tone, "but that time's coming." As if making a point, he turned his back on Hannibal and walked down the steps. A beat or two behind him, Ox and Petey backed away three or four steps before they too turned and left. When they reached the sidewalk the house seemed to breathe a sigh of relief. Sarge finally moved around the desk to push the door shut.

"Lot of mouth on that boy," Sarge said, "And this one too," indicating Timothy.

"We had a chance to do it right now." Timothy swung his stick down sharply, as if he could see a head falling under it. "We should have killed the mother while we had the chance."

"You almost got us all killed," Hannibal said, slamming his gun into its holster for emphasis. "Didn't you see those guys? That kind of muscle, they're bred for loyalty, trained to die protecting their principal. Believe me, I know. We just barely avoided a blood bath with no winners because of your hot West Indian head. Go cool off in the back. And you better get your shit together if you're going to stay in here with us."

Sarge watched Timothy stamp off down the hall like a spoiled child. "Don't mind saying that had me scared."

"May be, but you weren't alone," Hannibal said. "And, whether he'd admit it or not, I think Sal got the message this time."

"Yeah, the only way that kind ever does," Ray said, joining the others at the door. "Face it, Paco, we kicked their ass." Their tension broke into laughter, but no one really felt like celebrating.

-28-

TUESDAY

At five minutes before one Sarge and Quaker stepped out of the right hand flat. Quaker was stretching and yawning as they approached the desk in front of the stairs.

"Hey fellows," Hannibal said, shoving a bookmark into his paperback. "It is good to see your ugly faces. I'd like to say I'm sorry that you drew the tough one to four shift on the first night, but…"

"But that would be a bald faced lie," Sarge said with a grin. "Now you go on to bed. I know how you young bloods need your rest."

"So you taking the front?" Hannibal asked, standing and handing Sarge the shotgun.

"Quaker's down the back relieving Ray now," Sarge said, dropping down onto the stairs behind he desk. "You leave my copy of FHM in the drawer?"

"Hey, I wouldn't touch a man's educational reading," Hannibal said. "Listen, I'm leaving the kitchen door unlocked so you can get to coffee and snacks."

"Okay, buddy. Don't worry about us. Just go get some sleep."

Hannibal nodded good night to Sarge and went back to his new flat. He hung in his front room door long enough to wave a tired arm at Ray who was on his way upstairs. From the way he was dragging his feet, Ray was as ready for some sack time as Hannibal felt. He pushed his door open and turned to go.

"Hey Hannibal."

"Yeah Sarge," he replied, pausing again at the threshold.

"This is a really good gig."

Hannibal blew out a puff of air in self-derision. "Oh yeah. I got you a chance to live in a shit hole."

"Hey, it's three hots and a cot," Sarge replied.

"So was the shelter," Hannibal said. "And a safe cot at that."

"Yeah," Sarge said, "but that was a handout. I earned my place in this shit hole."

"You sure as hell did, Sarge," Hannibal said, shaking his head, but smiling.

"So, um," Sarge allowed a couple of seconds to pass. An embarrassed pause. "Thanks."

Hannibal looked up, smiled and gave Sarge a thumbs up before stepping into his apartment and closing the door behind himself. Like the others, he had found his own space there. Ray, Timothy and Virgil had all settled into the top left apartment, the one whose toilet had worked all along. Hannibal, for reasons unknown, had gotten comfortable in the ground floor left side flat. Without thinking, he had directed the deliverymen to put the refrigerator there. Sarge and Quaker had set up camp across the hall from him because Sarge thought both bottom flats should be occupied.

Like anything you fight for, Hannibal figured, he was really getting to like the place. A coat of paint, some new flooring, and it could become pretty comfortable. After pulling off his tennis shoes he made his bed in the middle room, the one with a fake mantelpiece. Then he went into the kitchen, got a final cup of coffee, and took it back to his bedroom.

While sipping from a Styrofoam cup he opened his suitcase on the card table, which he had also moved into his new bedroom. A small lamp beside the suitcase cut out sharp shadow silhouettes and tossed them around the room like art deco paste-on decorations. Even with the doors closed at both ends of the room, Hannibal could hear footsteps occasionally wandering into his kitchen. His kitchen? He was feeling a little too much at home in Balor's building.

From his suitcase he picked up his treasured photograph, the one photo he displayed, the one which made him feel at home. He stood the small frame on the mantelpiece, kissed a fingertip, touched it to the woman's face as usual, and moved on.

Wearing only a pair of shorts, he left his gun in the belt holster on the card table. Then he used the bathroom, brushed his teeth and washed at the working sink in the kitchen. When he returned to his bed, he was determined to go directly to sleep. With no headboard, sitting up did not appeal to him anyway. Lying back, he thought about the woman who had remembered to bring pillows. It would be nice to be with her, but Sal might try one more trick. Besides, Hannibal moved slowly in matters of love, which could explain why he spent so many nights alone. Romances usually lasted a while for him, but when they ended the fallow period stretched on.

Unfortunately, his brain would not sit still. He wondered if Sal would send night visitors, and if his mobster father really would get involved. Another part of his mind considered whether he should pursue Cindy. He wondered how long it would take Balor to start filling the building with legitimate tenants. And what would become of his homeless friends? All these questions revolving in his brain explained why Hannibal did not immediately fall asleep.

He was on the very edge of unconsciousness when the shattering window jolted him upright. He turned his head to find light dancing through the crack under the door and it put his teeth on edge. One second later, the screaming smoke alarm jolted him into action.

Flinging the opposite door open, Hannibal dashed for the fire extinguisher he had put in the kitchen. He could hear Sarge calling behind him, but was too far away to catch the words. Hannibal raced back to his bedroom, his bare feet slapping cracked tiles. As he passed his bed he pulled the extinguisher's pin. He yanked his front-facing bedroom door aside and crossed the last room before the front.

"Watch it!" shouted Sarge standing at the door to the hall. "There's glass!" Flames splashed the floor and the wall on Hannibal's right. Almost in the center of the room curved glass shards and charred rag fragments told an old story. Molotov cocktail. Hannibal's extinguisher sprayed in a slow arc from left to right, covering the empty room with white, choking foam.

Hannibal raised his angry green eyes, looking for and finding the shattered pane. It was the upper part of his left front window. Nothing prevented a bottle full of gasoline from sailing through above the bars.

Welcome as a Christmas present, and just as big a surprise, Hannibal saw a lone man standing across the street, mesmerized by the dancing flames. No one could have seen the fire from outside unless they were looking for them.

"I got this," Hannibal hollered over the extinguisher's hissing. "You get him." Sarge's dark face disappeared from the doorway, as Hannibal continued spraying as far as he could without stepping too far into the room. He was about to risk cutting his feet when Quaker poked his own extinguisher into the room and let fly.

Hannibal's own extinguisher was soon spent, but the fire had already lost its battle with the white foam. He went back into his apartment and dropped onto his bed, pulled on his sneakers and the belt with his holster, and scrambled through the smoldering room for the front door. Sirens screamed from his right.

"Stay here and watch the crib," Hannibal called, handing Quaker the shotgun Sarge had left on the desk. He did not wait for Quaker's nod as he ran down the front steps three at a time.

Something about the bluish street lamps drained the color from the night, leaving the world in an almost black and white state. Against the strong shadows, a revolving beacon threw a red wash over the scene periodically. The siren was fading out as Hannibal approached the end of the block, lungs straining after his hard sprint. He had expected to see a fire truck, but very quickly saw differently. He slowed to a walk, allowing his eyes time to decipher the scene.

Two uniformed policemen stood straddle legged, guns drawn, aiming down with the two-handed FBI grip. Beneath the cold eyes of those two revolver muzzles, the man Hannibal had seen outside his house lay face down on the concrete. Sarge knelt on his back, holding the man's arm twisted behind him. Hannibal was close enough to smell the sweat of the chase before he spoke.

"Whoa, chill fellows," Hannibal said. He smiled, hoping to defuse the situation. One gun snapped up toward him, and he saw nothing but anger in its owner's colorless face. Too late he realized his wearing a gun had only raised the anxiety level on an already tense situation. A third perpetrator entering a two officer scene created a problem. He realized right then how easy a problem he would be to solve.

The five men formed a frozen tableau in the dark. The lights continued to revolve on the patrol car's roof long after the siren died away to nothing, leaving a pained silence. After his own years of police work, Hannibal knew well what an officer would feel in this kind of situation. He remembered the combination of emotions that could lead to a reaction like that of the policemen who captured Rodney King. His stomach clenched and he tasted bile rising into his throat. It could happen all at once unless everyone involved did the right thing.

"Officers, my name is Hannibal Jones." No apparent recognition. "I'm a private investigator."

"ID?" A policeman asked.

"Not on me," Hannibal said. His face showed frustration with himself. "Look, this is an awkward situation. I'd like to put my gun on the ground now, okay?"

Four long beats of silence, then, "Put it down," from one of them. Hannibal pulled his automatic very slowly with two fingers and placed it on the ground behind him. He looked around again as he stood up. Sarge and the arsonist were still frozen and silent. Good.

"The man on top is in my employ, helping me with a security assignment. The man underneath him just threw a Molotov cocktail through my window, just up the street here."

"How do we know that? We got here, the bigger spook was pounding the shit out of the little one." This was the shorter cop, whose ears hung like gull wings beneath his hat. He must be the senior man. Hannibal spoke directly to him.

"I'll tell you what. How about my man gets up, and you smell the other guy's hands, huh?"

"Put your hands on your head," Big Ears told Sarge, as if inspiration had suddenly struck him. Then to Hannibal, "You too." Both men obeyed, and Sarge slowly stood up.

"You too," the policeman ordered. The arsonist got up quickly, rubbing his arm. Big ears grabbed the injured arm, flung the man against his car, and lifted one hand, then the other, to his face.

"Gasoline," The policeman said in a softer tone. "Into the car." The junior man got their prisoner handcuffed and into the back seat. Big Ears waved his pistol downward, and Hannibal and Sarge dropped their hands.

"Will you come back to the building?" Hannibal asked, smiling now. "I can show you the damage, and I'd like to press charges."

"Go. We'll follow in the car."

"May I?" Hannibal pointed toward his pistol. The cop shook his head, then motioned Hannibal aside and picked up the gun.

"I'll give this back to you when we get to your place and your show me your credentials," the cop said. "Just procedure."

"Perfectly reasonable, under the circumstances," Hannibal said. He slapped Sarge on the shoulder, and the two of them started walking toward their temporary home.

"Good job," Hannibal said quietly to Sarge. "Didn't really think you could catch that little bitch. You must've been hauling ass."

Sarge nodded, and chuckled to himself. Hannibal looked over, his forehead furrowed. In answer to his unvoiced question, Sarge said “You sure talk different when you talking to white folks.”

-29-

"So, you're moving down to the second floor?" Hannibal asked. He was on the third floor, standing in the front room of the apartment Ray shared with Virgil and Timothy. Hannibal stood in just shorts and tennis shoes. With no curtains in place, morning sunshine flooded the room, glinting on Hannibal's still-wet hair and warming his bare chest nicely.

"Got to," Ray said. "These railroad flats are okay, but I got too many people to get past to get to the bathroom."

Hannibal nodded understanding, turning toward the window as movement caught his eye. Two men were walking toward the house. The closer man was blonde, very thin, and wearing a loose linen suit. He walked very quickly, as if anxious to get inside. The other, by contrast, moved in no great hurry. Dressed in green work clothes, his hair was quite short, his tan face round, his expression bored. Hannibal waited for the first man to reach the door. He looked both ways and grabbed the doorknob just before Hannibal sprinted down the hall.

Hannibal stopped at the head of the stairway on the second floor. The thin blonde slowly pushed his way in. Bright outdoor sunshine gave way to the hall's cave-like gloom. The young man looked toward the door on his left, apparently waiting for his eyes to adjust. His mouth dropped open when they did and he found himself facing a very large man behind a rather small desk.

"Something I can do for you?" Sarge asked with a smile his shotgun belied. The younger man stuttered out a few random syllables, found the doorknob behind himself, and left.

"Who was that?" Hannibal asked, coming down the stairs behind Sarge.

"Just another druggie," Sarge said with a yawn. "Between us we've turned eight of them away since about three this morning. About half of them were like that young fellow, just in from the suburbs to score some dope. Didn't realize our little pusher had such an upscale audience."

Hannibal walked around to sit on the desk. "Yeah, well, the yuppies don't want dealers in their neighborhood, but they still want the products. Anyway, they won't come twice. I think we got it licked, bro. After we got the cops into it, and one of Sal's in the joint, he won't want to get into it again."

At that Sarge grunted. "Get your shower?"

"Yeah buddy, and I sure needed it."

"I'm hep," Sarge grinned.

"Yeah, but I wish I'd remembered to bring towels."

"That's why God created tee shirts," Sarge countered.

Shoes scuffing on the stoop snapped Hannibal to his feet and Sarge's hand to the shotgun. A man opened the door and stopped cold, harshly backlit, his hand never leaving the knob.

"What's this shit?"

"Something I can do for you?" Sarge asked again.

"Don't know," the man in working clothes said. "I'm the exterminator, but it looks like I got the wrong address."

"No no." Hannibal pulled the man's arm. "Come in. Please. We just moved in, and we had some trouble with the neighbors. But man, are we glad to see you."

"Yeah, well, this is my first stop of the day and I'm not used to having shotguns pointed at me," the newcomer said.

"Look, just do what you do, okay?" Hannibal urged him. "Start at the top and work your way down to the cellar. This whole place is..." A woman walking in behind the exterminator drew Hannibal's attention.

"Mother Washington," Hannibal said, breaking into a broad grin and grasping her hand. "This is a pleasant surprise. Yo, little bro," he added to Monty, standing behind her.

"Gabriel told me you had actually moved in here, but I just couldn't believe it," Mrs. Washington said, as Hannibal guided her toward his front room door. "Well, at least the hallway looks clean." He followed her eyes down to the floor, certain that she registered the faint but still recognizable trail of blood leading from the basement door to the front. Then their eyes met. She smiled, and he gratefully accepted her decision not to mention the stain.

"We're making a little progress," Hannibal said, opening the door to his apartment. His guests walked in, but stopped just inside.

"Lord today," Mother Washington moaned, looking at the shapeless black splotch on the floor, following it up the wall.

"Had a little problem last night," Hannibal said lightly.

"Y'all got water? Electricity?"

"All the comforts." Hannibal eased a folding chair up behind her. The woman sat stiffly, nodding her thanks.

"Just you and your friend with the gun to fix up this big old house?"

"No, ma'am," Hannibal said. "There are four other fellows helping out."

"Six of you, huh?" she asked, looking around. "All men?"

"Yes ma'am."

"What you eating?" Mother Washington asked.

"Whatever." Hannibal was feeling a little pressured. "We got food, but none of us is much for cooking."

"Had breakfast?" she asked, standing. Hannibal stammered a negative answer, following her to his kitchen. Mother Washington explored the refrigerator and every cabinet, muttering "Lord, Lord, Lord" and "have more mercy, Jesus." Finally she began piling food on the sink's sideboard, talking intermittently to herself, or to Monty.

"Got eggs. Got bacon. I need my big iron skillet, boy. And a cookie sheet for the biscuits. Have mercy, there ain't no flour. Bring the flour, child. Bring two skillets. They got potatoes at least. And bring my apron, the yellow one. Oh, and a spatula. Boys living alone. Lord have mercy."

*   *   *

An hour and a half later, Hannibal found himself washing dishes, gazing vacantly into his overgrown backyard while his hands moved automatically over borrowed pans and utensils. A drying rack found under the sink had been pressed into service. The water was as hot as his hands could stand, and he used a real scouring pad. Mother Washington apparently didn't believe in Teflon or any other kind of nonstick coating. Staring out idly, he started thinking about how the yard might look with its weeds mowed down and a grill sitting out there. Shaking his head, Hannibal reminded himself how being in that building was strictly business, but the image of a backyard barbecue would not go away. His reverie was interrupted by a welcome voice echoing through the length of the apartment.

"Anybody out there?" Cindy called from the front. She quickly moved the length of the apartment, slipped up behind him and settled her head onto his left shoulder as if it were the most natural motion in the world.

"All clear," Hannibal smiled. "Another day off? You're going to get fired."

"Worked real late last night." Cindy eased away, reaching for a chair. "Anyway, thought you could use some help. Looks like you had a little problem in your front room."

"Yeah, some clown tossed a firebomb in," Hannibal said, turning off the water. "He's in the joint now and I think I can keep him there. Think he was the drug boy's last play."

"So you're saying it's safe around here now, right?" Cindy asked, staring around. "Listen, I'll dry if you'll show me the..."

"Sorry, no towels," Hannibal said. With a laugh he turned and started shaking out his hands, prompting Cindy to raise her hands to try to fend off the flying droplets. She wore yet another barely legal pair of shorts, and another black tee shirt, this one emblazoned with "Jack Daniels" across the front.

"Sound to me like we need to go shopping," Cindy said, as if she were inviting him to a ball game. "You need towels, some paint and maybe a piece of carpet, eh?"

"What's this we stuff?" Hannibal asked, leaving the kitchen. "I got to stay here."

"I thought you said it was safe now."

"Well, I guess," Hannibal said. "Actually, I was going to call Balor tomorrow if nothing changes and tell him to get the place painted, get flooring put in and order the rest of the appliances. I figure I'll keep the team here until he's renting the flats out. Then I can phase them out one at a time until all six places are rented out. After that, no `vacuum' like you said, so no more druggies or vagrants wandering in."

Hannibal had talked all the way to the front room, but Cindy stayed behind momentarily at the middle room, the one with his bed in it. The small photograph held her gaze. It was a portrait of a white woman, neither ugly nor really pretty, a rather plain blonde but with an unmistakable sparkle in her eyes.

When she followed, Hannibal pretended not to notice her brief stop. By the time she stepped into the front room Hannibal was standing with hands on hips, looking up at the charred wall.

"You know, I'm thinking maybe you're right," he said absently. "I'll probably be here a couple weeks. Guess some paint might be in order."

-30-

Hannibal did not notice the shadow at the edge of the wall until he hit it with his paint roller. He silently cursed himself for getting so much on the baseboard. Sunlight and his energy, he realized, were both running out. He dropped wearily onto a folding chair, looking up at Cindy on the ladder using a small brush on the molding. Hopefully, the brown she was using would cover the crème color meant for the walls. The colors weren't bad but, Lord he hated the smell of fresh paint.

"Why didn't I just make Balor pay a professional to do this?" Hannibal muttered. "Take a break," Cindy called down, "I spent a couple hours on my ass this afternoon."

"And a lovely ass it is." Hannibal smiled wearily at his own lame humor. This girl was something else. He had driven her to the stores, but she picked out the towels. She selected colors off a chart and even pointlessly asked his opinion of them. She knew how many gallons of each color paint they needed, and chose brushes and rollers. She had picked a beige carpet that would come within an inch or two of his living room walls on all sides when they unrolled it. At her insistence they picked up a boom box, at Balor's expense, and the vintage George Benson CD they listened to while they worked. The disc was the first step toward replacing Hannibal's extensive music collection, which now lay buried under the pile of charred masonry that used to be his old apartment.

Back at the house, she had made sandwiches for everyone's lunch, unasked. Before anyone was really sure what she was doing, she had gathered up all their laundry, piled it into his car, and gotten her father to drop her off at a Laundromat for a couple of hours. This was the time she referred to as "sitting on her ass." And, while she had merely delivered the clean clothes to the men she had just met, she folded her father's clothes, and Hannibal's.

"I could get used to this," Hannibal muttered absently.

"You mean living in this place?"

"Er, yeah." Hannibal said, clutching at the vine she offered, although he was thinking something entirely different. "It ain't a bad place, you know. And this neighborhood, it ain't as bad as I figured either. You know, this morning, this old lady down the block, she wanders in here, bops down to the kitchen, and cooks breakfast for all of us. Just like that." Hannibal leaned forward, shaking his head in disbelief. "Nice old lady. Still got class, and self respect. Like this building. A nice old lady."

Hannibal's overtired brain repeated for him all the good things about staying in number twenty-three thirteen. He looked up at Cindy, who stepped up one rung on the ladder with one foot, drawing his attention to her nicely rounded bottom. She had also pointedly turning her back to him.

In a voice overloaded with casual unimportance, she asked, "Who's the girl?"

"Girl?" Her shift of subject caught Hannibal off guard.

"The Anglo," she asked. She appeared to be concentrating her entire being on the molding she was painting. "In the picture on the mantle."

"Oh. Mama."

Cindy chuckled. "Oh, your mama's white?" But then she stopped and turned. He could feel her eyes on him, looking at him as if for the first time. She scanned his hazel eyes, his golden skin, so close to her own Hispanic complexion, and his hair, neither straight nor kinky.

"Your mama's white," she said again, this time quite solemnly.

"Does it make a difference?" Hannibal asked, standing.

"But the picture's signed `to my honey'," Cindy said, dropping two rungs closer to him.

"Yeah, well when I was little she used to say my skin was the color of honey," Hannibal said through a faraway smile. "She called me her honey boy and it kind of stuck."

Cindy touched down. On the portable stereo, George Benson made the train sound with his guitar, a plaintive, mournful cry. "I'm really sorry," Cindy said. "I feel so stupid."

"Don't sweat it," Hannibal said. "Listen, why don't we quit for the night."

While Hannibal cleaned brushes and rollers, Cindy headed for the kitchen. Involved with his own activity, Hannibal didn't notice her return until the living room light went out. The lamp in his bedroom was on, but a huge full moon actually threw more light on him. He turned, to see Cindy seated at the card table. She had put out a bag of tortilla chips, a bowl of salsa, a bottle of white wine and two Styrofoam cups.

"Come eat something," she said, beckoning him, "and tell me about your mama."

Hannibal left everything as it was and joined her in his room. He kicked off his shoes, got comfortable on his bed and gathered his thoughts to tell a story.

"Well, my dad was in the Army, stationed in Germany when he met her," Hannibal said, picking up a cup. "It wasn't too common then, but they got married and had me. I don't remember him too well. Ran out of luck in Vietnam when I was six." That prompted a big swallow of wine. Halfway down it burned, but by the time it reached his stomach it had become a soft, warm glow.

"God, I seem to be hitting all the wrong nerves tonight." Cindy looked everywhere but into his eyes.

"No, it's too old to hurt. Besides, it's kind of different to have anybody ask me about me. I mean, in my line of work I ask all the questions."

"Well, in my work too," Cindy said with a smile. "You grew up in Germany, I take it. That's why you spoke German before, after those animals beat you up. By the way, what's, um, scheiskopf I think you said."

"Very good," Hannibal said, impressed by her pronunciation of the foreign word. "Did I say that? It's German for `shithead' I guess. This drug pusher, he kept calling me that while his friends were pounding my skull in."

"Guess that explains all that babbling about wanting to get to the base, too," Cindy said, almost to herself.

"A nightmare left over from when I was small." Hannibal sipped, then refilled their glasses. "There was an army hospital in Berlin, but one of my great fears as a kid was getting hurt and ending up in a hospital where they didn't speak English."

"So your mama raised you," Cindy said around a mouthful of chips and salsa. "Funny, my papa pretty much raised me after mama decided she didn't want a family after all."

"You mean she just took off?" Hannibal asked.

"Met a new guy," Cindy said simply, staring again at the photograph Hannibal clearly cherished. "Your mother was a bit more of a mother I guess. So is that the kind of woman you looking for? They say most men are looking for their mothers."

"Not me." Hannibal grinned and gulped more wine. Because he drank seldom, he had little alcohol tolerance. He already felt a respectable buzz under his skull. He leaned back for a better look at all of his guest. "I'll tell you. I'm really attracted to brown-eyed girls with high IQs. You know, the helpful type, with a nice smile, long hair, long legs, slim waist, and, er... nice big tits."

Cindy almost fell from her chair laughing, but she managed to right herself and gain her feet. None too subtly, she reached behind herself, pushing the door closed. "Well, my eyes are brown." She walked around the bed to close the door at the other end of the room. "My hair is fairly long, and they tell me I'm pretty intelligent." Now she was standing directly in front of Hannibal who leaned back on his elbows on the bed.

"So far, so good," he said.

"And..." Cindy crossed her arms, gripped her tee shirt's bottom edge, and pulled it up, turning it inside out as it slid over her head in one smooth motion and fell to the floor. Her bra barely contained her.

"Oh, yeah," Hannibal said, smiling broadly as he got to his feet. "I'd say you're a hundred percent." She stepped into his arms and he quickly released the hooks behind her, his fingertips trailing sparks down her back until he could cup the globes of firm flesh at the lower end of their journey.

Cindy's sucked in a sharp breath between full but parted lips as Hannibal trailed kisses down her chest, tonguing the increasing roundness until he finally drew a hardened nipple into his mouth. Cindy rewarded him with a low moan and her nails gently raked across his back as she fell backward onto the mattress.

"So, how'd you ever end up with a name like Hannibal?" Cindy asked an hour later. Her head now floated with the rise and fall of Hannibal's chest as she clung to his lean form in the darkness. He savored the citrus scent of her hair and tried to hold onto the warmth of afterglow.

"Not a typical Afro-American name, is it?" Hannibal said. "Well, Mama told me my dad was looking for the name of a great military leader, a conqueror. Alexander was too common. Being German, Mama wouldn't even consider Napoleon, thank God. Somehow, they settled on Hannibal."

"That name must have made school a drag," Cindy said while her fingertips lightly drew figure eights on his belly. "Kids can be so cruel when you have a name that's a little different. So, what was it like, growing up in Europe?" He knew she wanted an exciting story, but he did not have one to tell her.

"What was it like? Well, home was cool. School was kind of Shitty. What was it like? Kind of like being in the ring six hours a day. After school I got to go back to my corner, but it sure wore me out."

"But you went to an American school, right?" Cindy pressed. "I mean, you said you lived in Berlin and I know the Army's been there since World War Two."

"Yeah, and I was an Army brat," Hannibal said. "Somehow Mama managed to stay in American quarters after Papa died, to make sure I was raised like an American, not a German."

"So if it wasn't Germans making school tough."

"What, you think Americans leave their prejudice at home when they go overseas?" Hannibal asked. "Mama did her best to convince me I was right and everybody else was wrong, but it didn't help all that much. No, babe, it was pure hell, right up to high school."

Cindy craned her neck to kiss his. "What happened then?"

"Well, there was this cracker, first week of my freshman year." Hannibal sank into the past, protected by the darkness, inhaling the sweet mix of Cindy's perfume and her own natural scent. "He said something about me being an Oreo, or a zebra, or one of the usual remarks. So I told him to kiss my ass. It was a Friday. After school we walked across the street and he kicked my ass. No great surprise. He had me by a good twenty pounds."

Cindy gently rubbed his face, as if she could soothe those long ago injuries. "God. What did you do?"

"Well, something snapped in my head, and I kind of just said, that's enough. Monday rolled around and I went after him. So he beat my ass again. I fought him again Tuesday. And Wednesday. And Thursday. Finally Friday came around and by then the audience was getting thin. I guess it got boring just watching me fall down. When I caught up to him after school he asked me what my problem was. What MY problem was."

After waiting through a long enough silence, Cindy asked "What did you tell him?"

"I told him he was going to have to fight me every day until I won. If he won that day, I'd be at his house the next day. Well, he slapped me around a little more, then we just kind of stood there looking at each other for a while. I'll never forget it. There was blood running out of my nose, blood running out of my mouth, I had this cut over my right eye. You know what he said to me?" Hannibal chuckled at the memory. "He goes `I quit. You got more balls than any nigger I ever seen' he says. And then I said `Don't ever call me that again'. And after a minute, he goes `I won't, and neither will anybody else in this school'."

Cindy hugged herself to Hannibal then, throwing her leg over both of his. "So you won."

"Not really," Hannibal replied, putting his fingers into her thick hair, absorbing her warmth. "I just didn't lose, because I didn't give up. A lot of times, the guy that looks like he won, he's just the guy who was the last to quit."

"That's why this happened, I think," Cindy said, patting the mattress. "You're a cowboy, and I guess I got a thing for cowboys."

"A cowboy? Me?"

"Not like a country music fan, but like the old movies. You know, the mysterious stranger who rides in from the west and solves everybody's problems. Like what you're doing in this house, chasing the drug crowd out. That's really noble. And what you did for my papa."

"What? You mean hiring him?" Hannibal asked.

"You know what I mean. Dealing with the loan shark. He thinks I don't know, but he couldn't keep a thing like that from me. I could have given him the money, but what you did was so much better. You preserved his pride. I think I started loving you that first day you came to my house."

Silence settled on them like a comforter as Hannibal reacted first to Cindy's knowledge of his secret charity, then to her first use of the "L" word. He was in no way ready to deal with that concept. Cindy tensed, and too late he realized she must have felt his stomach tighten.

Stillness held the room so tightly that they both jumped when the telephone rang. Then they laughed, tension draining from them as Hannibal reached for the lamp. Cindy shielded her eyes, glancing around between her fingers.

"Okay, so where is it?"

Hannibal's arm snapped out, pointing across the room toward the front of the building. "The phone's waaaaay out there."

"Well, since you did all the work this time..." Cindy rolled to her feet, pulled on her shorts and tee shirt, and scampered across the floor into the front room.

At first Hannibal lay back, basking in the warmth of recent sex. He loved that partial dream state, when the body and mind are immersed in the joy that comes when everything works just right in bed. But as the seconds slipped by, time began to erode the afterglow. Cindy was too quiet to be on the phone, and who could it be anyway. He glanced at his watch. It was after eleven, and almost no one had that telephone number.

When Cindy returned, her face drawn and eyes wide, Hannibal was sitting up on the edge of the bed.

"It's Dan." She said simpy, wrapping her arms around Hannibal as he stood up. "He's at Bethesda. Oh, Hannibal, he's been hurt. Hurt bad. They found this number in his wallet and he's been asking for you."

-31-

WEDNESDAY

Not long after midnight, Daniel Balor's eyes flickered open. They scanned across his wife, then Cindy. Finally they settled on Hannibal, farthest away, leaning against the door. When Balor spoke, it was to him.

"Get the women out of here," he whispered. Hannibal moved in closer, not sure he understood. "Get them out," Balor repeated, his eyes pleading. Swallowing hard, Hannibal gently took both women's arms and led them out the door, closing it behind them.

When he turned, he saw Balor again as if for the first time. The top sheet made his broad form appear to melt into the bed. His thick hair was an unruly gray mop on the pillow. Dark brown eyes were sunk deep in caves beneath excessive eyebrows. Tubes were everywhere, running into his arms, his mouth, his nose. In a corner, some sort of monitor beeped periodically. Despite the odor of alcohol Hannibal could smell dried blood.

Nothing makes a man look as insignificant as lying in a hospital bed, Hannibal thought. Not wearing ballet shoes, not being driven someplace by his woman, not even sitting on the toilet. Cindy must have thought he was being cruel sending his wife away at a time like this, but Hannibal understood. He was embarrassed.

"Took three of those punks to do this." Balor began, but coughed hard before he could say more.

"Don't talk." Hannibal picked up Balor's chart, hanging at the foot of his bed. "Doc says they cracked a couple ribs." They had broken no limbs, but they had worked his body over pretty well. He was a mass of bruises, his lip split, his right eye blackened. His nose would need straightening. Overall, he looked a lot like Hannibal had the day he woke up in Cindy's guestroom.

"God, I'm sorry." Hannibal hated the room's alcohol stench, its smell of death. "Look, we better not take this any further. These guys don't play by any rules. I'll move my people out and..."

"Bullshit," Balor whispered. He seemed to be fading into the white sheets, white pillowcase, white walls, white ceiling. "Nobody's going to run me away from something that belongs to me. Understand? You said you wouldn't quit until the job was done. You can't walk out on me now, damn it."

"All right, all right." Hannibal moved closer, squeezing the older man's arm. "Look, this is one time you're glad you're a Navy vet. I happen to know this hospital's got pretty good security. I came here a couple of times with, a man I was protecting on my last job. If you'll just relax, I'll get the police to watch your wife. Then I'll go find the guys responsible for this and send them in to keep you company. Okay?"

Balor smiled. "They better look worse than me when they get here."

* * *

Somehow Hannibal swallowed his rage when he left Balor's private room. Two people waited in the hall, but only one was expected. Mrs. Balor stood facing her husband's room, wringing her hands. The other person sat slouched in a chair, but pulled himself up to stare into Hannibal's eyes arrogantly. "So you're this Jones guy?"

"Maybe," Hannibal said, matching the stranger's stare. "And you are?"

"Denton, Mick Denton." He was Hannibal's height, but soft around the middle with thick, stubby legs. He had clearly come here straight from bed. He was unshaven and his breath smelled of leftover beer.

"So you're the building manager," Hannibal said conversationally.

"Yeah, and I do my job," Denton sneered. "I thought you were supposed to help people out of tight spots. I got a look at Balor. Did you help him out of a jam?"

"Well I tried to," Hannibal said after a deep breath, "but I guess I used a little too much force."

Then he turned to Mrs. Balor. There was no shortage of steel in her spine. Hannibal guessed she would handle this okay.

"Ma'am, I'm truly sorry."

"I understand, young man," she said softly. She took his hand in both of hers and stared up into his eyes. "My husband still thinks he's the young crusading lawyer. And he doesn't want me to see him as anything but tough and strong. He just doesn't understand, that's the only way I can see him. That's what he is."

"He's very lucky to have you," Hannibal said in the hushed tones people so often use in a hospital. "Now, ma'am, did you see where..."

"Your young lady went down to the chapel. I think she needs you."

* * *

After the brightness of the halls, it took his eyes a moment to adjust to the dim, somber lighting in the chapel. The silent room held the slightest scent of some incense he could not name. He felt ill at ease in church settings, as if he were always on the verge of doing something wrong in the eyes of the Lord.

Several people were seated inside, spaced as far apart as possible it seemed. Hannibal walked down the aisle very slowly, hoping not to disturb anyone even as he checked every face. He finally located Cindy at the very right edge of a center pew. Her head was leaned forward, resting on her folded hands on the back of the next pew. Moving as quietly as possible, he walked in from the center to sit beside her. His arm started around her, but then he felt it would be inappropriate there. After a moment of feeling helpless, he rested a hand on her shoulder and leaned in close, almost resting his mouth against her ear.

"Are you all right?"

She turned her tear-streaked face toward him, the corners of her mouth pulled down so far that it distorted her features, so he barely recognized her. "I am so, so sorry," she said, on the verge of a sob. "Can either of you ever forgive me?"

"What are you talking about?" Hannibal asked. He found his handkerchief and held it to her face. "None of this is your fault. Balor had no way of knowing...."

"No. No. It was me." She blew her nose quietly, and dabbed at the seemingly endless flow of tears. "I thought I was so smart."

"Cindy, please tell me what this is all about," Hannibal said, almost pleading.

"Oh Hannibal, I could have gotten you both killed. I just wanted to do something." She squeezed his hand hard and he let her, waiting quietly, letting her work out whatever it was she wanted to tell him.

"I knew about that building in Anacostia," she went on after a moment. "At first, he said he'd fix it up and get nice people in there. I convinced him to do that. I thought it was a chance for him to do something positive, to make a difference. I just knew it would save that neighborhood if he did."

"Come on," Hannibal said. "That was a sound business decision that would have had a nice side effect."

"But he never really tried to get those drug dealers out of there," Cindy said, shaking her head. "He was ready to drop the project and take the loss. Then you came along."

She stopped to blow her nose again, giving Hannibal time to put it together. Still, he knew she wanted to say it all without interruption.

"That night, while I watched your apartment house burn, it all just seemed so right, like a gift from above. You were a hero, like the cowboy, you know?"

"Yeah." Hannibal could not help but smile. "I was the guy who rides into town looking for work the day the sheriff gets shot."

"I knew Dan's other properties were all about full," Cindy said, looking at her shoes, or her hands, or anything else that kept her eyes away from his face. "And here you were, a specialist in solving other people's problems. I knew if I took you up there to talk about an apartment..." she shoved her face into his chest and sobbed.

"You scheming, manipulative little minx," he said, but with a smile in his voice.

"Oh, Hannibal, I'm so sorry. I did manipulate you both, and now you've had to pay. And poor Dan, at his age, to get..."

"Now that's enough of that." Hannibal lifted her face and kissed away the two most recent tears. "I'm sure he didn't do anything he didn't want to do. You brought us together, but you didn't make me take the job. I snapped at it. This is no more dangerous than anything else I've done to make a living all my life. Now, I don't want to hear any more guilt tripping out of you. I'm really grateful to you for giving me the chance to do this."

"You...you mean it?"

"Of course," Hannibal said. He retrieved the handkerchief, trying hard to dry her face. "And Balor's beating's probably his own fault. He shouldn't have blabbed his good intentions all over town."

Cindy sat up, her eyes wide and her mouth forming a circle. "But he didn't. I think he was embarrassed by it. It's like all the charity work the firm does. "They do it all anonymously. I think he believes it's not charitable if anyone knows who did it. That's how I know this wasn't just a business decision to him. He swore us all to secrecy about what you were doing."

"Well I never mentioned his name in this," Hannibal said. Someone behind them shushed him, and he realized he had been a little too loud. More quietly he said, "Got to go," and kissed her softly on the mouth. He suddenly realized he had some arrangements to make before sunrise.

-32-

Mick Denton squinted against the early morning light as he pushed his office door open. He looked as if he had not slept much, his naturally unkempt hair spiking on all sides. His tread was heavy and his breathing labored. He was three steps into the small, darkened office before he froze, as if his legs were late getting the message something was wrong. Hannibal Jones was sitting in his chair, behind his desk. He wore black leather pants, jacket, and gloves. Very dark wraparound sunglasses only accented his light skin.

"Come on in, Mick," Hannibal said, slowly standing up. "We need to talk."

Hannibal doubted if Denton's fight or flight reflex ever knew confusion, considering how quickly the flight reaction took command. Denton turned before Hannibal's sentence was finished, just as Sarge slammed the door shut. Sarge had been standing behind the door with his Louisville Slugger.

" Pretty proud of yourself, aren't you Mick?" Hannibal asked, walking around the desk. "I'll bet it was worth it being up so late just to see the look on my face, wasn't it? Well that's okay. You got me good."

"What the hell are you talking about?" Mick stuttered out.

Hannibal sighed. "Look, we can do this the easy way if you like, Mick. Just tell me who ordered the stomping. I don't think it was Sal, but, who knows?"

"How would I know?" Denton howled. "I don't know nothing."

"I ain't got time to dance with you, Mick." Hannibal wrapped one gloved hand around Denton's chin, fingers pushing into the man's fleshy cheeks. Twisting Denton's face, Hannibal turned his back to the desk. "I'm betting it was your idea, wasn't it? Stop messing with servants, right? Go to the source. Yep, you're the finger man. I just need to know who you report to, dig? Now, easy or hard?"

Hannibal knew that fear could bring the fight out, even in the most dedicated coward. He watched Denton take three deep breaths to screw up his courage. Then, as expected, Denton swung his best right for Hannibal's jaw. Hannibal effortlessly caught the punch with his right hand, spun to clamp the arm under his own shoulder and slammed Denton face down onto the desk with his free arm outstretched along its surface.

"I never told anybody who I was working for, Mick," Hannibal said, looking over his shoulder at Denton. "Kept wondering how they fingered Balor. He didn't tell anybody, and neither did anyone else at his office. Then you walked right up to me last night and repeated word for word what I said to Balor in his office. You know, about how I help people out of tight spots. You left the speaker phone open, didn't you?"

"I didn't do nothing," Denton whined. "I swear it."

"Guess we'll do this the hard way." Hannibal nodded toward Sarge, who walked around the desk, making sure Denton could see him. At the far end, he raised his bat over his head. With a burst of energy, Denton struggled to free himself, but Hannibal leaned back, locking him in place.

Denton gave a gargled scream as the bat came down. A loud crack sound reverberated in the room as the bat crashed into the desk five inches from Denton's fingers. Hannibal could actually smell Denton's fear, and he was afraid he smelled something else the man had released. The only consolation was that he knew Denton smelled it too.

"Who'd you talk to, Mick?" Hannibal asked again.

"Oh, God, let me go," Denton whined. His mouth sounded as dry as sandpaper and his eyes bulged as he watched the bat rise again. He curled his right hand into a fist, trying to hide his fingers. Sarge grunted with the swing and this time the crashing impact was only two inches from Denton's hand.

"Last chance, Mick," Hannibal said through clenched teeth. "You talk to Sal Ronzini? Huh? Or one of his flunkies?" Sarge raised the bat again. Hannibal looked at his friend and said, "Okay, break something."

"No," Denton shouted, shaking his head and smearing the desk top with sweat. "It was the old man."

Hannibal was stunned enough to smile. "Well, what do you know. Sarge, I feel like I found a diamond in a Crackerjack box." He eased the pressure, and Denton pulled himself free.

"If you ain't lying, you might come out of this in one piece, slime ball," Hannibal told Denton who cowered at the other end of the room. "You just give me the phone number and we'll be on our way."

"But...but I don't have a number," Denton choked out. Sarge rushed toward him, ball bat upraised, but Hannibal put a hand on his chest.

"You meet him somewhere?" Hannibal asked.

"Yeah, that's right. There's this place he goes to have a drink. I just answer questions and he takes care of me. Lots of guys go there and tell him things."

"You report to him?" Hannibal asked.

"He just likes to know what's going on around town is all," Denton said.

Hannibal turned his smile on Sarge, who shared it. "I think Mick here will ride with us today, just so he doesn't get himself in any trouble. And tonight, maybe we can get to meet the big guy."

Denton was docile when Sarge took his arm. They all went outside, and Hannibal made sure the office was locked behind them. Ray had been waiting for them in Hannibal's car with the engine running. Hannibal slid in beside him, but neither man spoke. Sarge pushed Denton into the back seat and sat beside him. Denton jumped when Ray pushed the button that locked all the doors.

Denton continued to sweat despite the air conditioner's breeze. Ray constantly checked the rearview mirrors as he moved the Volvo through cross-town traffic toward the Capitol. Hannibal sensed his nervousness, but purposely said nothing. He did not want to get into a conversation about the relative morality of what was undeniably a kidnapping. Projecting as much calm as possible, he pushed buttons on his telephone. When it stopped ringing he asked for Ms. Santiago, and then waited patiently for her to answer.

"Hannibal?" Cindy asked when she picked up the receiver. "Do I want to know where you are or what you're doing?"

"You?" Hannibal said. "An attorney? An officer of the court? Probably not."

"I was afraid of that," she said. "So I guess this isn't a pleasure call. I'm sorry, but with Mister Balor out I really had to come to work. But if you need me..."

"I appreciate that. More than you can guess." Hannibal said seriously. He heard the concern in her voice, and stronger emotions as well. "I do need your help, but you won't need to leave the office. Do you think anybody would mind some of your resources being used to help Balor's case?"

"Are you kidding?"

"Okay, look," Hannibal said. "I need you to find out everything you can about an Anthony Ronzini."

"Ronzini," Cindy repeated, rolling the name around her tongue with a Spanish slant. "Didn't he used to be a mob boss or something?"

"Probably," Hannibal replied. "Anyway, put together what you can and buzz me at the crib." Hannibal thought it would be a long day, sitting at twenty-three thirteen with one eye on Denton until late afternoon when he would release him. In that time he would make plans with his team, assuming his team was ready to stick with him through what would come next.

* * *

The moment Hannibal hated to face arrived a couple of hours later. Standing with his back to his big front windows, Hannibal scanned the faces I the room and saw anticipation in every one of them. Sarge sat on his right hand with his beefy arms crossed. Quaker sat beside his best friend with is wild hair sticking up and long legs stretched out in front of him ending in a pair of Timberlands. He made it easy to sometimes forget he was white. Virgil, both the tallest and darkest, stood leaning against the wall looking grim. He always looked grim. Ray, in a chair to Hannibal's left, smiled as if anxious for whatever came next. Beside him stood Timothy, a fiery ball of West Indian nervous energy. Hannibal gathered his thoughts, not wanting to leave Denton locked in a room alone upstairs for long.

"I just wanted to get everyone together to tell you that things are about to get a bit hairier," Hannibal said. "It could get more dangerous and on top of that, we may come into some conflict with the law. From here on out we might be walking the line pretty damned close."

"You mean the line between legal actions and not so legal," Virgil said in his deep, gravelly voice. It was not really a question, but he clearly was looking for confirmation.

"Right," Hannibal said. "So before I tell you what I have in mind, including some things that could get you in trouble later if you're questioned, I thought I should give you a chance to move on. No one will think less of you if you want to call it a day here."

"Wrong," Virgil said, and all eyes turned to him. "I'd think less of me. You took a chance on me, Hannibal. I know you're a good man, so I guess I'll have to take a chance on you."

When Sarge spoke, he addressed Hannibal but everyone knew he meant his words for the entire group. "You're not stupid, and you're as honest as they come. I know you're not going to put anybody at unnecessary risk an you're on the side of right. I'll back your play as far as you want to go, brother."

"Thanks, Sarge," Hannibal said. "Quaker?"

"I follow the Sarge," Quaker said with perfect calm. "If he says it's all good then it's all good. I'm down for whatever."

"Just so we hit these bastards where it hurts," Timothy said. His frantic motions, barely controlled, reminded Hannibal of a puppy desperate to start his morning walk. "But you got to be ready to go all out, mon. These people are dangerous, and they got a lot of friends. We might have to hit a lot harder than we did when they tried to break in before."

Hannibal's brow furrowed. "You know something I don't?" he asked. "Got history with Sal?"

"I just know the type," Timothy said, dropping into a chair. His eyes would not settle on one object.

"Whatever the deal, we'll handle it together," Ray said. "We've all got your back, Paco. Besides, Cindy would shoot me if I backed out now."

"Okay, I guess you're all in this with me," Hannibal said. "So you need to know how I see the next play. Step one is to question Denton and pin down the place where a certain business man likes to go for dinner and drinks. The good news is, if all goes well, we might be able to end this case for good in the next twenty-four hours."

-33-

The long black Continental limousine rocked down the scarred street all alone. Most of Georgetown had excellent roads, but Anthony Ronzini's favorite restaurant was a bit out of the way. His driver, now retired from professional wrestling, had found an approach almost empty of traffic. Ronzini thought the bumps well worth avoiding the gridlock.

His suit was cut full and comfortable, but for fifteen hundred dollars his tailor managed to make it look well fitted. He sat in the center of the back seat, his legs apart to allow for his ample belly, sipping a before dinner scotch. Freddy, his bodyguard, was crowded into the seat on his left.

Ronzini's unwieldy vehicle turned down the final narrow street on its way to the restaurant's shadowed back entrance. He did not like attention when he went to dinner. As they made their final approach, he handed his glass to his seatmate, who opened the bar and put it away.

Ronzini reacted with bored annoyance when he saw a car stopped in the street in front of him. It was an old, wide, Chevy with its blinkers flashing. In years past, he may have assumed that this was a ploy by one of his enemies to get at him, but it had been a long time since anyone had dared to give him any trouble.

"Can you get around that thing, Rick?" Ronzini asked his driver.

"On the sidewalk maybe," Rick said, "but not without risking scraping up the paint, boss."

Another car pulled up behind them, and for a moment Ronzini's old alarms went off. Then the other car's horn sounded three long blasts. Just another impatient driver, Ronzini thought. Like me. The driver behind Ronzini decided to put on his high beams, which prompted a curse from Rick.

"I ought to go back and punch that guy's lights out," Rick said. He dropped the column lever down into low gear, and powered his window down to see around the stopped car better. "Now which way around is less likely to scratch up the car? Damn. Some days I hate this job."

"Really?" Ronzini said, watching Rick's eyes in the rear view mirror. "Seems to me it has its advantages over being tossed around in the ring for a living."

"Aw, boss, you know I don't mean nothing."

Exactly, Ronzini thought.

Bored, his eyes wandered out the window. A shadow caught his eye. Was someone there, crouched beside the car?

He froze when a big black man rose to his full height beside the door. Rick had time to turn and open his mouth to speak before the business end of a Louisville Slugger swung through the window, smacking across his jaw. He fell to the side limply, his eyes glassy before his head hit the seat. The man with the bat didn't speak, but someone else did.

"If you sit still for a minute, we can do this without any more violence."

Pulling his attention from his driver, Ronzini turned toward the voice on his right. He was staring into the muzzle of an automatic pistol. The man holding it was dark, and wore sunglasses.

"Bullet proof is a bit of an exaggeration for this kind of glass," the gunman said, keeping his face straight. "Trust me, it won't resist twelve of these forty caliber rounds. Now I want you out of this car and into the one behind you."

"You're not serious," Ronzini replied, showing no more emotion than the gunman. "Do you know who I am?"

"Of course," the gunman said. "That's why I'm here. I'm Hannibal Jones."

"Hannibal?" Ronzini said, his brow wrinkling. "I may have heard of you."

"We need to talk," Hannibal said. "I've chosen the time and place. Get out now, and the other two don't get hurt. Otherwise..." As if to punctuate Hannibal's words, the bigger man opened the driver's door and leaned in on one knee. Ronzini assumed he had a gun, in which case, his bodyguard could never free a weapon without being killed.

The man outside the car seemed more in control of himself than the man in the front seat was. When in doubt, Ronzini would always choose to deal with the most reasonable person. He patted his seatmate's shoulder, opened his door and stepped out.

"Okay, Sarge," Hannibal said. Sarge nodded and slid out of the limo, taking the keys with him. Hannibal rested a hand on Ronzini's shoulder and walked him back to the white Volvo.

"I'm sorry, but you'll have to assume the position," Hannibal said, grim but polite. With a smile, Ronzini rested his hands on the car's roof.

"I haven't done this in a long time, stud," he said as Hannibal expertly frisked him. "You a cop? You can't be a Metro cop, but you sure act like a cop."

"Not a cop." Hannibal opened his car's back door. "Slide in."

Ronzini sat in the middle, against Sarge's bulky frame. Hannibal got in behind him, holstering his gun before closing the door. Up front, Ray shifted into reverse and pulled out of the street. In seconds they were back on Route 395 heading east toward Anacostia.

Hannibal felt like an actor in a bad play. In this play, the writer did not understand characterization and motivation, so he and his fellow performers could not put enough depth into their parts. They were trapped in this plot, going through the unavoidable motions that grew from their last irrational acts. His own behavior startled him at times. Ronzini was the most recent addition to the cast, and Hannibal wished he could figure out the man's motivation. He rode in silence, wrapped in his thoughts for several minutes, until Ronzini interrupted him.

"You're in charge," he said, stating the obvious like an ice breaker at a party.

"Yep."

"I take it this isn't a one way trip to the morgue," Ronzini went on, "So? What? Money?"

"Not money, Mister...not money, Tony." Hannibal watched Washington flow past for a moment before shifting his focus to look deep into Ronzini's face. "This is about your son, and selling drugs, and beating up a noncombatant."

At first Ronzini did not react, but Hannibal saw the wheels turning behind his eyes. It took him no more than a minute to make the connection.

"Balor," he said in a low voice. "Salvatore had Balor roughed up. Guess I should have seen that coming." He shook his head in regret, or perhaps in frustration at his son. "So what, you beat me up in revenge? I think in this case I'm a noncombatant like you said."

"Don't want to hurt you, Tony," Hannibal said, sounding weary. "You're here to make the boy listen to reason. When he gives me what I want, I let you go."

"What happens to my people back there?" Ronzini asked next. "They done nothing to you."

"And I've done nothing to them." Hannibal stared out the back window. Ronzini turned to join him looking through menacing dark clouds at the great orange ball hanging low in the sky, on its way to bed. Periodically he glanced at Hannibal's face, reading his expression, Hannibal guessed, the way good card players do.

"Something surprised you," Ronzini said.

Hannibal nodded. "I'm surprised by your interest. About what happens to your flunkies, I mean."

"I get bad press," Ronzini said. To Hannibal's surprise Ronzini actually smiled. He must have just really accepted that he was in no danger. "You're with people every day, you come to care about them. I'm not a monster, I'm a business man."

Hannibal nodded, but offered no more conversation.

When the car stopped in front of number twenty-three thirteen, it was Hannibal's turn to smile. Ronzini's eyes became silver dollars when Sarge opened the door. He stared around at the street, the teenagers wandering in hip hop shorts and tank tops, the rundown row houses. He was now surrounded by blackness.

"Wonder how many of these people know you make your money selling them numbers and women," Hannibal said as Ronzini stood. He left his gun in its holster, figuring Sarge's bat was enough to convince Ronzini he could not escape. Even if he ran, where would he go? This neighborhood itself was an effective prison for him.

With Ray on Ronzini's left, Hannibal on his right, and Sarge behind him, they climbed the sandstone steps toward the door. It opened as they reached it. Quaker waved the shotgun and said "All quiet. Pulled it off, didn't you?"

Any hope Ronzini had that a white face might make a difference should have died as soon as he got a good look at Quaker's eyes. He had no way of knowing this man was homeless, but anyone could see he was another member of some minority. Ronzini took another wide look around. While several people wandered or loitered outdoors, they all seemed determined not to see him. Then Sarge prodded him in the kidney, and they stepped forward into the hallway. The door closed behind them, followed by the loud click of a dead bolt lock.

Hannibal's stomach was playing host to a butterfly convention, so he was in no state for surprises. At first he jumped away when Cindy leaped into his arms and locked him in a deep kiss. After a couple of seconds of reflexively returning her kiss, he broke her embrace and pushed her back into his front room.

"Aren't you glad to see me?" she asked

"Cindy what the hell are you doing here?"

His words stopped her for a moment, but her resolve quickly returned. “Well, for one thing, Chico, I’m making dinner for this big boy’s club. I wanted to be with you. I thought you...”

“It could get dangerous here,” Hannibal muttered. He pointed Ronzini into a chair, heaved a giant sigh and turned to Sarge.

“Stay with him every second. Cindy, let’s go talk in the kitchen for a minute.” Gently yet firmly, he took Cindy’s arm and led her to the other end of his flat. There he dropped her, not quite as gently, into a chair. His eyes, changing from green to blue, slid over two large pans on the stove. The room was warm and steamy, its spicy aromas reminding him how hungry he was. The atmosphere transformed what was to be a lecture into an appeal. He dropped to his haunches in front of her.

“Cindy, sweetheart do you understand what’s happening here?”

“What is happening here, Chico, is my...” during her thoughtful pause, Hannibal noticed how Cindy’s lips curled back when she got angry, exposing her small, very white teeth, “...someone I care about is so focused on his job, he’s ignoring everything else, including his friends. And his new neighbors are worried about him. And my paella is burning.” At that she stood up and went to the stove.

Helplessness converted his anger to frustration, and Hannibal found himself standing behind Cindy, his hands on her waist, watching her stir a big pot of rice.

“Cindy, just by being here, you’ve made yourself an accessory to a crime.”

“I don’t know that?” Cindy snapped sarcastically, suddenly sounding far more Latin, much less educated than he knew she was. “You forgot I’m a lawyer? I thought I should be here. Don’t make a federal case out of it.”

“Damn it, Cindy, it is a federal case. No matter how you cut it, what I just did is kidn...”

“Don’t you say that word.” Cindy spun in Hannibal’s arms, jabbing a finger in his face. “Now you listen to me mister I-can-handle-it. You got you a delicate legal situation here. Yes, you got him by the cojones, but he got you too. If you do this right, you can kind of trade what you got and you both get away with your balls. But it's going to be tricky. You need me. Let me help." When she turned back to the food, Hannibal could feel the energy flow out of her, making her feel smaller between his hands. "Everybody's hungry now," she said more quietly. "Let me do this."

A lifetime as a loner had left Hannibal ill prepared for anyone being this determined to help him. As tenderly as his rough history allowed, he pushed her hair away and kissed the back of her neck.

"Let the girl cook for Christ's sake," said Sarge, walking in behind them. "Like in the old Sinatra song, man, I get too hungry for dinner at eight."

-34-

On the top floor, Virgil washed his hands in the kitchen sink. Behind him, Timothy paced back and forth. Virgil remembered seeing a movie about rodeo cowboys a long time ago. Timothy reminded him of the bull, fidgeting in the chute, anxious for a chance to get loose and gore some fool cowboy trying to ride him. As he dried his hands on a dishtowel, Virgil smelled a pungent, surprising but familiar odor.

"Hey, man, I wish you wouldn't smoke that shit in here."

Thin smoke leaked from Timothy's mouth as he answered. "You know, you smoke the ganja it keep you sharp. Keep a man ready for what he got to do. That Jones, he could use some of this."

"I think Hannibal's handling things just fine," Virgil said with the slightest edge in his voice.

"He afraid to take care of the business," Timothy said, putting extra emphasis on the last word. He took another deep toke from his ragged joint, dragging extra air in through his teeth. Then he began gesturing wildly. "We got the man right here, the man his self. Ought to just walk up to him and badow, take his head off." Unexpectedly, he pulled a Saturday night special from inside his shirt.

"Where the hell you get that?" Virgil's head snapped back in surprise.

"One of them junkies shot Sarge with this, first day we came in," Timothy said, twirled the small revolver in his hand.

"Damn," Virgil said, clenching his eyes shut. "I though the police picked that thing up when they cleared the apartment."

"I got there first," Timothy said, miming taking a shot out the window. "I don't like to leave guns laying around, man."

"You going to leave that one," Virgil said. When he straightened his form in front of Timothy he towered above him. "You going to leave it right up here. You one hothead, crazy Rasta nigger, and you ain't going down there with no piece. We trying to end a war here, not start one."

Genuinely startled, Timothy backed into his bedroom. "I don't get you, Virgil. This man bring the shit almost killed you when you stuck it in your arm. You don't want to kill him, you the one crazy."

But in the face of Virgil's stony silence, Timothy shoved the revolver under his pillow. Virgil had more to say, but Hannibal's voice called from the walkie-talkie he had left in the kitchen.

"Hello upstairs? You guys going to eat with the rest of us, or what?"

By the time Virgil and Timothy walked in, everything was set for dinner and all the other men were assembled. Among other little amenities, Cindy had brought a second card table with her this time. After moving both into Hannibal's front room, she had set places for the six men and herself. Ronzini sat alone in a front corner. Hannibal saw Timothy staring at him as he joined Ray and Quaker at the table. It was not a long stare, but Ronzini reacted, almost as if he recognized Timothy. Hannibal was already chilled by the smile on Timothy's face, when the man pointed an index finger at Ronzini, and winked his right eye while making a "tsk" sound out the side of his mouth. Timothy had mimed shooting the man.

As soon as the last two men arrived, Cindy carried the largest pan out and started ladling rice and chicken onto tripled paper plates. No one had chosen the chair at the end. Whether by design or accident, Hannibal was left with the head of the table. He draped his jacket over the back of his chair, sat down with Sarge on his right. Cindy's purse was in the chair on his left. He concluded that the seating was no accident.

"Excuse me, Jones," Ronzini called from his place in a corner. "You snatched me on my way to dinner. Do I get to eat?"

"Of course, pimp," Cindy answered, without looking up. "You're our guest. I just don't want you at the table with me." When her man and his friends were served, Cindy filled a plate for Ronzini and handed it to him.

After Cindy sat, everyone mumbled thanks to her and launched into the food. The paella was not as spicy as Hannibal would have liked, but it was still delicious with the flavors of garlic and saffron fighting for dominance. The atmosphere seemed a little strained. Hannibal hoped for some pleasant dinner conversation. As if she had read his thoughts, Cindy kicked it off.

"I don't know about anyone else, but I've had quite a busy day," she said. "As you may have noticed, I've taken care of all the kitchen equipment you'll need, if any of you ever get up the heart to cook something. I got you a new cordless phone, Hannibal, after yours was slagged in the apartment fire. And for all you animals, towels and shower curtains for all the bathrooms."

"And they all work now," Timothy said with pride. "Every sink in every bathroom and kitchen, every bathtub, and most importantly, every toilet in the building. All working perfectly now."

"How about you, Quaker?" Hannibal asked around a mouthful of chicken. "How's our security?"

"Solid," Quaker said, one eye on Ronzini. "Every first floor window's got bars now, and all the doors got dead bolt locks."

Not to be overshadowed, Virgil said, "Wiring work's done too. Not only do all the building's lights work, but I've brought the entire structure up to code."

Hannibal said "Really? That's more than I could have hoped for. That means the client won't have to bring in an electrical contractor after all, and the city won't give us any trouble about renting the place out." He could not help but notice the evident pride on those three men's faces. This job, he reflected, was presenting an unexpected bumper crop of pleasant side effects. Then he realized not everyone had gotten his chance to crow.

"I don't want anyone to think Sarge has been sitting this one out," Hannibal said. "He's kept an eye on security so everybody else could work in peace."

"Yeah, but I might be out of a job soon," Sarge said. "In case nobody noticed, we just got through our first completely uneventful night and day. Twenty-four hours without any uninvited guests trying to get in or any kind of assault on the building. Hannibal told us what happened to your boss, Cindy, and I don't want to minimize that, but maybe it means something. Maybe making that move on Balor means the little pusher finally gave up on threatening us."

"Say, Jones." Ronzini set his bone laden plate aside. "Can we talk a minute?"

Hannibal turned his chair toward his captive, but remained silent. With dinner finished, he pulled his black gloves back on and slid his shades around his face. Somehow, it made him feel more centered. Ronzini seemed unruffled by recent events. He was too calm for his liking, too much in control.

When he had Hannibal's attention, Ronzini turned his own to Cindy. "You're a good cook, miss. Do you mind if I smoke?"

With all the irony she could muster, Cindy turned a stern look on Ronzini. "Smoke? I don't care if you burn. In fact, if the justice system ever gets hold of you..."

"That's enough, Cindy." Hannibal did not want to appear less in control than his prisoner. "As you said, this man is our guest." Then he turned to Ronzini. "So, you got something to say?"

Moving slowly, Ronzini pulled a cigar from inside his suit coat and lit it. "Seems to me you figure I know all about what's going on here. I don't. I think it'd be fair for me to know why you snatched me. Once I know the whole story, maybe I can give you what you want and we can all go about our business."

He ventured an easy smile, and Hannibal could not help but return it.

"You know, you're not at all what I expected," Hannibal said.

"What did you expect, Al Capone?" Cindy asked, standing. "This ain't the roaring twenties, babe. His kind keep a legal front these days. They get all refined, maybe get into politics. It's all bullshit."

"Jocinta Yelina!" Ray snapped, and all heads turned toward his florid face. He launched a spate of rapid fire Spanish only one person present could follow. Although her breathing rate doubled, Cindy made no response. When her father finished, she piled the dirty utensils into the pan and carried it off into the kitchen, stomping like a chastised child. Everyone in the room seemed embarrassed during the long silence that followed.

"She's a lawyer," Hannibal told Ronzini, as if that explained everything. "As for why you're here, I want your son to leave me and my friends alone, and I figure you're the perfect bargaining chip to accomplish that."

"Just what is the conflict between yourself and Salvatore?" Ronzini asked, leaning back in the folding chair.

"Conflict is, two weeks ago this here was a crack house and a shooting gallery your son supplied," Ray said.

"Ain't no more," Sarge added.

Ronzini considered all this before asking, "How did Dan Balor get involved in this?"

"You know him?" Hannibal asked.

"Know of him," Ronzini answered. "He's a lawyer too, bit of a crusader. He put you up to trying to take over this dump?"

"He owns the place," Quaker put in. "Man tries to take back what he paid good dollars for and gets beat up for it. Sucks, don't it?"

"So let's see if I get this," Ronzini said. "You moved in, expecting whoever the pusher was to just go away, only he puts up a fight. You boys resist, maybe hurt one of his flunkies. And he goes after the owner?"

"That's about the size of it," Hannibal said. "I figured since he plays by his own rules, I'd just go out and get myself some bargaining power."

"So all you want is, he moves his operation somewhere else?" Ronzini asked, as if he was a diplomat just wanting to be sure about all negotiating points. "You ain't trying to bring him in or nothing?"

"I'm getting tired of telling people I ain't a cop," Hannibal said behind an exasperated sigh. "I just want some people to be able to rent in this place without fear of any repercussions."

"Maybe this thing's no big deal," Virgil told Hannibal. "Maybe the old man, he just tells the boy to go away."

Ronzini was apparently considering just such an option when the telephone bell's raucous jangle drew everyone's attention. When Hannibal stood to answer it, Sarge headed for the front desk, while Quaker and Timothy moved toward the back. After working with professional security personnel for half a dozen years, Hannibal appreciated these men's dedication and rapidly developed professionalism. He was thinking of them when he put the telephone receiver to his ear.

"You got my papa in there, spook?"

Hannibal's eyelids vanished and his breath froze in his throat when he heard Sal Ronzini's voice.

"How'd you get this number?" Hannibal asked in a low, menacing voice. He did not want to think about any more pain being visited on Dan Balor.

"You got my Papa in there?"

"How'd you get this number?" Hannibal repeated, a bit louder.

"You cock sucker, you got my father in there?" Sal shouted.

"How'd you get this number, you little bitch?" This time Hannibal's rage met with silence. Mumbling filtered through, as if Sal had covered the phone to talk to somebody else. When he returned, he sounded calmer.

"All right," Sal said through clenched teeth. "Papa's muscle, they seen you and the Rican guy. They gave me descriptions and I figured it had to be you. Nobody could forget a name like yours, so I just called information and got the number. Now.

Enough bullshit. Is my father in there or not? Come on, he ain't got nothing to do with this."

"He's here," Hannibal said. "And he don't look like Balor, either."

"Who? I don't know what you're talking about."

"Don't shit me, man," Hannibal said. "I know it was you. But this is between you and me, dig?"

"Yeah. Yeah, I dig," Sal said. There was another pause, but this time Hannibal knew that Sal was just thinking, planning. Finally he said, "Can I talk to him?"

Progress, Hannibal thought. He was asking. Hannibal handed the older man the receiver, watching his face as he talked with his son.

"I'm fine Salvatore," Ronzini said, "but I don't like getting mixed up in your little business, eh? You know, these six guys have done a lot of work in this slum building. Yeah, and the Spanish girl cooked us something. No, they're not waving guns at me. Only the leader, Jones, has a..."

Feeling stupidly slow, Hannibal snatched the phone from Ronzini's hand. It had taken him a few seconds to realize that the older Ronzini was more of a poker player than his son.

"That's enough, Sally," Hannibal said. "Now we deal. You're going to have to give this place up, and leave my people be."

"I ain't got to do shit, spook," Sal screamed. "What you got to do is let my papa go, or you're a dead man." Hannibal heard a sudden click, and imagined Sal had slammed the phone down. He stood staring out a front window, holding the dead phone. Darkness was settling at last, lights coming on in the windows facing him.

He was prepared for any response, any answer except total refusal. Ronzini, rather than trying to talk sense to his son, had tried to give him as much information as he could. Hannibal had to face the fact that he had misread the situation, and was not really sure what he should do next. He needed to control his hostage and maybe get some information from him. But Ronzini would never talk on his own, and Hannibal did not think he could beat or torture anyone.

"Put your foot in a bear trap," Ronzini said. "Now, there's no nice way out. Why don't you just let me go? I'll tell Salvatore to leave you alone long enough for you to blow town, and I don't think he cares about these other guys."

Hannibal dropped back into his chair and spun toward Ronzini, leaning forward.

"You are too smart, too reasonable to be in this. I can't see you as a bent nose. How'd you get into this business anyway?"

Ronzini crossed his legs and puffed his cigar, adding to the thick cloud of smoke hanging just above his head. "You know, son, when I was a kid back in Brooklyn I started stealing to help my mother feed my little brothers. When I got a little older, I found out I could make more money helping girls find dates."

"Yeah? Lots of brothers get lazy and get a string of hookers, just like you did." Virgil said. "I known a lot of them in that trade. Some got a lot of flash, fancy cars, clothes, jewelry and that kind of stuff, but I don't know even one that's getting rich."

"It was a different time," Ronzini said. "Cops didn't really care, and I was part of my community. Later, I found several profitable enterprises I could become involved in that didn't require no high school diploma, if you know what I mean. Later on, I found out there's legal things like that too. All you need is the drive."

"Well if you done so good, how come you didn't get your boy in college?" Ray asked, looking over Hannibal's shoulder. "I mean, I ain't nobody, and I ain't got nothing, but I got my little girl through law school."

Ronzini's eyes receded into the past. For a moment, Hannibal thought he could see the real man. "I sent Salvatore to Harvard," Ronzini said. "He just couldn't...he's a little wild. Wanted to follow in his father's footsteps. Do you blame a boy for that? I set him up, got him going, but I don't really know nothing about his operations."

"I know you were into whores and gambling at one time," Hannibal said, "but your boy Sally's pushing poison to a pretty young clientele that don't know no better."

"Every one of them knows better," Ronzini said. He sat forward, waving his short cigar for emphasis. "When I was a kid people wanted to gamble, and they wanted to have whores, and I took care of it. I filled a need. I never did the drug thing, but people want them and that's the need Salvatore decided to fill. Nobody ever gets his arm twisted to smoke a pipe or stick a needle in his arm. There's two kinds of people in this world. There's weak people and there's strong people. You know that Jones. Weak people like to gamble. They like to buy women. And they like drugs."

"So you just figure all the weak people's Latino, or black, is that it?" Ray asked, stepping close enough to be all Ronzini saw.

"I don't know," Ronzini slowly stood up. "You tell me why most of Salvatore's customers ain't white."

Ray and Ronzini looked like boys in a schoolyard to Hannibal. He thought they were about to get physical when he heard an authoritative knock at the door. A stern, aggressive voice spoke the one word he was not prepared to hear.

"Police."

-35-

In the hall, Sarge looked to Hannibal for guidance. Hannibal held up his palm, instructing his friend to wait. Then he handed Ray his gun, pointed at Ronzini, and pulled on his jacket to cover his holster. Ray sat five feet from Ronzini, pointing the gun at his gut. Virgil sat on the front windowsill, his billy club poised.

"Virgil, if he makes a sound, cave in his teeth." Hannibal ran into the hallway, pulling the door closed behind him.

Sarge held the shotgun under the desk, but still pointed forward, as Hannibal leaned against the door.

"Who's there?" Hannibal called.

"Officers Johnson, Webster and D'Angelo, Metro Police," the voice said. With a deep breath, Hannibal flipped the bolt off and opened the door a crack. He saw three uniformed white men. Behind them, a police car stood parked behind his own. Their faces were serious but carried that bored, tired look police so often have when sent on missions they consider pointless.

"How can I help you gentlemen?" Hannibal asked, opening the door another foot or so.

"Got a report of a kidnapping, Mister..."

"Jones," Hannibal said. His eyes shifted left and right, checking the street for other watchers. "Can we exchange identification?"

"Why don't we do that inside?" Officer Johnson asked sharply. "I think what you really want to see is this search warrant." Johnson handed Hannibal a folded court document and stepped past him. "Save yourself some problems, boy. You got a Mister Anthony Ronzini in here?"

Hannibal waved his three visitors in, reflexively locked the door behind them before rushing to get ahead of them, cracking the door to his front room.

"Pocket that," he told Ray, then turned around. "I want it understood that my disagreement with Mr. Ronzini is personal. I'm in this alone."

"That's lawyer business," Johnson said. "My job is to make sure this Mister Ronzini is safe."

Hannibal stood, stunned, as the three men filed past him. He never suspected that Sal might try the simple expedient of calling in the authorities. Yes, Hannibal could be charged with kidnapping. But during a long, messy trial, he would bring up the illegal activities both Ronzinis were involved in, and could summon a long line of witnesses. A huge spotlight would focus on them, certainly crippling their crooked businesses. It was hard to believe the boy might love his father so much that he would use the safest means to assure his safe return.

Ray and Virgil stood back, as startled as Hannibal, while two of the officers helped Ronzini to his feet.

"You are Anthony Ronzini?" Officer Johnson asked.

"I am."

"And are you all right, sir?" the cop asked.

"I'm fine, officer," Ronzini said, but he would not make eye contact with them. Hannibal thought that maybe he felt embarrassed to be saved by the police.

No. Ronzini had not avoided anyone's eyes since Hannibal picked him up at gun point. But he must have had some real reason for not facing these simple patrolmen.

It was all happening so quickly that Hannibal might not have questioned it all if not for that. Now he wondered why no detectives accompanied them. For that matter, why no FBI personnel? Kidnapping is their business, after all.

A closer look at Johnson, now facing Hannibal standing in the doorway, revealed nothing unusual. His uniform was absolutely regulation, his haircut within regulations, his shoes the cheap ones policemen can afford. He carried all the usual tools of the trade: mace, a nightstick, handcuffs and an automatic. A stainless steel automatic, in fact.

D'Angelo held Ronzini's left arm. His holster was police issue, but it held a blued automatic. Webster carried a revolver.

"Tell me, Officer Johnson," Hannibal began, putting a hand in the other man's chest, "just what is the standard issue firearm in this city?"

Johnson's right hand moved toward his holster but Hannibal jarred him with a right cross before he could reach it. Webster managed to get his gun pointed at Hannibal, just before Virgil's nightstick arced down on his wrist. The sound of the pistol hitting the floor was drowned out by Webster's cry of pain.

Ray got his arms around D'Angelo's neck but the phony cop jammed an elbow into Ray's midsection. After a third elbow smash, Ray dropped away. Still, Ray held him long enough for Hannibal to swing his right foot into D'Angelo's stomach, dropping him onto the tile floor.

Johnson, clearly this rescue team's best fighter, managed a foot sweep that put Hannibal down hard on his left hip. In the hall, Sarge was bringing the shotgun on line. Charging low, Johnson got under the gun's barrel to smash a shoulder into Sarge's gut. Both men flew backward over the desk, dropping hard on the other side of it.

From his low vantage point, Hannibal watched as D'Angelo whipped a side kick up into Virgil's face and quickly tried to hustle Ronzini out of the room. Hannibal managed to capture D'Angelo's ankle with his own. A sharp twist, and the false policeman fell forward fast, his chin meeting the desk with a stomach wrenching crack.

On the far side of the hall, Johnson knelt up and sent two hard rights down into Sarge's face. With Sarge dazed he was able to scoop up the scatter gun, turning on his knees to cover the hallway.

Ronzini had stumbled when D'Angelo fell, but he was up now, reaching for the door to the outside. Using the desk for cover, Johnson controlled the front hall. It wouldn't last forever, but it didn't need to. His objective was clearly to cover the area long enough for Ronzini to escape.

On the front room floor, Hannibal could see Ronzini was having trouble getting the dead bolt lock off. With a roaring shout Hannibal thrust his body forward, slamming the desk into Johnson and driving it forward until he smashed Johnson against the wall. He felt the desk slam to a stop, and heard Johnson's cry of pain.

Ronzini had just about released the bolt lock when Hannibal slid across the desktop, grabbing up the shotgun as his shoulder stopped him, thumping against Johnson's face. He turned his muzzle on the Italian trying to escape.

"You open that door," Hannibal growled out breathlessly, "And I'll blow your fucking face off, I swear to God."

The hallway became a stop action scene and, for a moment, Hannibal thought Ronzini might go for it.

On the front room floor, Webster whined pitifully, cradling a fractured arm. Under that sound, Virgil breathed through clenched teeth, testing his tender jaw. Ray lurched to his hands and knees and vomited noisily. On the hallway floor, Sarge rolled onto his stomach, moaning softly as he gathered his consciousness.

For a moment, Hannibal hoped Ronzini might go for it.

Somehow, Ronzini must have sensed everything going through Hannibal's mind. He slowly, carefully turned the knob that slid the bolt back into place. When he turned to face Hannibal, he looked like a man who had just decided to try a marathon after not running three steps in a year. Slowly his famous control returned and he managed a smile.

"Shall I just return to my seat?" Ronzini asked.

Running footsteps arrested Hannibal's attention. He swung the shotgun toward the sound to find himself aiming at Cindy, who was racing down the hall from the kitchen. She stopped short, staring at the muzzle pointed her way. Hannibal very quickly swung the barrel back to cover Ronzini. Timothy ran into the hall from Hannibal's front room, glaring at Ronzini who did not react. Quaker raced down the hall, stopping to help Hannibal to his feet. Hannibal didn't feel much like talking right then, but waving a shotgun barrel proved an effective form of communication. Signaling with the muzzle he managed to get everyone into one room, and got the necessary frisking and securing done. Everyone, his own team and the Ronzini's, behaved like professionals, clearly mindful of Hannibal's twelve-gage prompting tool. He didn't realize he had been dealing with shock until he felt it wearing off. When his mind was working normally again it was jammed with questions.

"How in hell could he have put it together so fast?" Hannibal asked the room, rubbing his left shoulder, which had been his contact point with the desk.

"Yeah, they were mighty convincing bulls," Virgil said. Others shook their heads in agreement.

"I heard it all from the kitchen," Cindy said. "I figure these guys are probably full time police impersonators. Mighty handy, you got to admit. A cop can go a lot of places nobody else can." She held a cold cloth on her father's forehead. Ray sat in the chair Ronzini had occupied.

"Sorry, man." Sarge stood in the doorway between Hannibal's front room and the hall. "That son of a bitch caught me with my drawers down. I feel like a real asshole."

"Don't Sarge," Hannibal answered. "He fooled all of us. And these guys were good. I mean, smooth, fast, and good with their hands." Hannibal looked at Johnson, who offered an ironic smile and nodded. The three men in blue sat on the floor, handcuffed together in a circle with their backs facing each other.

"Sorry I wasted your Paella," Ray told his daughter quietly. Then he turned to Hannibal. "Well, jefe, what do we do with these fakes, eh?"

"Ought to bury them in the backyard, in one hole, with their boss here," Timothy said. His heated comment drew a stern look from everyone but Ronzini, who refused to look at him at all.

"They brought some nice stuff with them, anyway," Quaker said, waving at the pile in a corner, consisting of the three pistols, mace, nightsticks, and extra ammunition the uniforms had yielded. "Neat, ain't it?"

"Yeah." Hannibal smiled. "As for the three stooges here, I think our only choice is to cut them loose." He knelt to face Johnson. "You take a message back to Sally for me. Tell him we're not amateurs in here. Tell him we're ready to deal, and that's the only way he's going to get his old man back." Then he turned to Ray. "When Sal sees them, like this, he'll know he can't just bust in here and take him."

More roughly than necessary, Virgil and Sarge dragged the fake policemen to their feet and hustled them outside. They looked to Hannibal like cops out of an old Mack Sennett movie, moving haltingly sideways down the stairs, arms outstretched to maximize their freedom of movement. He stood in the doorway holding one of the big flashlights until the three actors managed to get into their patrol car and drive away. Hannibal watched the car until it was out of sight, then returned to his front room. His confident smile had faded as soon as the counterfeit cops were gone.

"Only an idiot doesn't learn from his experiences," Hannibal said. "That little visit kind of changes my view of proper defense. Not saying anyone screwed up, we just misjudged the enemy, and we need to adjust. Step one is to deal with our guest better. Virgil, can you handle getting Ronzini up to the third floor?"

"Not a problem," Virgil said, taking Ronzini by an arm.

"He'll be a lot harder to get at up there," Sarge said. "Should have thought of that sooner." Hannibal nodded. He would also be under fewer watchful eyes. That thought moved Hannibal to a more difficult decision.

"Hey Quaker," Hannibal said. "Toss me one of those guns. I'll give this piece to Virgil in a minute, because I want him to stay upstairs and watch our guest. The other two stay with the back door guards from now on. Ray and you, Quaker. Sarge and Timothy each get a can of mace, and I think Cindy better hold the other one."

The team moved to their assigned places like well-drilled troops. As Hannibal handed Cindy her mace he pulled her into a long, firm hug. He released his tension silently in that hug, and could feel her doing the same. When the tremors stopped Hannibal headed for the stairs, still holding Cindy's hand. The long walk up gave him time to realize how much tenser the situation had become with more guns in the house. Instinctively, he had maneuvered to keep one of them out of Timothy's hands.

He wanted to keep his conflict with Sal from becoming a war, but he was beginning to wonder if that was possible. He certainly didn't favor banning guns, but he knew that firearms sometimes seemed to create a self-fulfilling prophecy. Given enough armed people, sooner or later somebody would shoot. Then somebody would shoot back, and the powder keg he was sitting on would violently explode.

Ronzini was sitting on the bed in the front room puffing another cigar when Hannibal and Cindy walked in. The gangster turned toward them, his poker face back in place.

"Out there kind of reminds me of the old neighborhood," Ronzini said, pointing out the window. The moon was still fat and full, hanging low. "Kids are hanging out under those street lights down there, except instead of singing do-wop like we did, it's that damned rap shit. So, what kind of revenge are you going to take for that little attempted rescue?"

Hannibal found a chair and fell into it. He moved a few feet away from his captive, reducing the impact of the strong, sweet cigar smoke. "I don't think you get it. That was a pretty good shot Sal just took, but it was a fair ball. I still want to deal with him. I figure if we keep bumping heads, he'll figure out we can deal."

"The Balor thing was different somehow?" Ronzini asked. Bed springs squealed as he sat forward, watching Hannibal closely.

"Sally's problem is with me," Hannibal said firmly.

"If I understand the setup, that ain't quite right," Ronzini said. "It's Balor who's paying you to get his building back."

"I'm the man that confronted Sally," Hannibal snapped, feeling his face flush.

"Okay, so let's say Balor's the king and you're his knight errant. Apparently Salvatore decided, instead of working to capture the knight, metaphorically speaking, he'd just go around him and take the king out of play. Think about it. In a war, the general doesn't usually shoot anybody, but he's not a noncombatant, is he? Now me, I didn't even know this whole war was going on. I got some information and passed it on to my boy, but nobody bothered to tell me what it was all about. Way I see it, I'm the only non-player on the board."

Leaning back against the wall, Ronzini blew a long, thick stream of smoke toward Hannibal's head. Cindy stood behind her man as he turned toward the window, trying to avoid the smoke screen Ronzini was sending out, clouding his reasoning.

"Nice try, pimp, but it won't wash," Cindy said. "Your boy's a rogue, not even playing by your own rules. You know this little crack house isn't worth beating up a prominent member of the bar, of this society. That only makes enemies, and you got where you are by making friends. Besides, in case you didn't know, a lot of what he sells here gets cut and sold again to bored students and housewives who come in from the 'burbs to score. Eventually, that's going to make more influential enemies. He's out of control and you know it. And right now, the only way Hannibal could stop him was to block him. You're part of the game, all right, but in this case, to extend your own metaphor, you're just a pawn. A pawn from his side used to block him."

Cindy tossed her hair triumphantly, and Ronzini gave her a nod.

"You must be very good in court," Ronzini said. He leaned back against the wall and lowered his eyes.

Hannibal got up and moved to stand at one of the front windows. Beneath him, young men in knit caps and baggy, low slung jeans stood together in a cone of light almost like a theater spotlight. He could just catch their voices on the slight summer breeze. They were not rapping. They were in fact singing do-wop, a low sweet love song, a cappella, the base voice anchoring the rich harmonies playing above it.

"When you were part of your old neighborhood, it was different," Hannibal said, still facing away from Ronzini. "So, you hooked some lonely boy up with some whore. Or you showed him where he could shoot craps or play some poker. Okay. But the next day, he was the same boy. When Sally convinces some kid to start smoking crack, or shooting up, that kid ain't never the same."

"Let's not get moralistic," Ronzini said, never opening his eyes. "We both know you're not doing this to save the youth of our nation. You're just a mercenary on a mission."

Watching the singers just down the block, Hannibal did not feel that way. He had come to care about this little community, this tiny city within a city. If he was a troubleshooter, then this was where he needed to be. Balor's trouble had really been a symptom of the trouble with this neighborhood.

He had brought a lot of trouble to this block himself in the last few days, by simply disrupting the status quo. But somehow, while disturbing the smooth water on the surface, he had made a place for himself. He remembered Cindy's words about nature's feelings toward a vacuum. If he finally forced Sal Ronzini out, who or what would rush in to fill the void?

The singers stood off to his left. At the right of his field of vision, another young black man seemed to be looking up at him. As Hannibal watched, this man's eyes slid from Hannibal's window to one in the building directly across the street. Odd, he thought. That room was darkened. Why would anyone be looking into a window where there was nothing to be seen?

Focused on that black square across from him, he thought he saw a glint of reflected light. It could be nothing. Or, it could be a stray moonbeam dancing off a pair of binoculars. It occurred to him that Sal might be keeping good surveillance on them.

No, that couldn't be right. He saw only one glint of light. His skin suddenly seemed too small and the tiny hairs on the backs of his hands stood up when he realized what that fact implied. A single lens. A telescopic sight.

-36-

The crack sound came from the sniper's bullet breaking the sound barrier on its way across the street.

Hannibal's elbow cracked painfully on the tiles. He heard Cindy scream and the impact of three bodies hitting the floor. Bile tried to rush up his throat when he realized how narrowly he had 5escaped death, saved by his own reflexes. So many years of waiting for someone else's bullet to find him had driven him to the floor before he consciously made such a decision.

His hands shook, the aftermath of the sudden adrenaline rush. Hannibal grabbed that tension, forced it through his anger and converted it to action. Crouched low, he managed to sprint over the other bodies on the floor.

"Virgil! Stay low, and watch him," he shouted back through the door. He was already dropping down the stairs at top speed, hitting every third step. One irrational idea consumed his entire mind. Nobody would ever take a shot at him twice.

"Sarge," Hannibal shouted when he hit the second floor. "Open that Goddamn door!" Sarge looked up and, seeing Hannibal was not slowing, jumped from behind the desk. He just managed to unlock the door and pull it open before Hannibal bolted through it.

Listening to the tap of his own shoes, Hannibal darted across the street and into the facing building. It was set up exactly like

Balor's, but with only a single dim bulb for hallway light. He pocketed his Oakley's as he hit the stairs. He was up one flight of steps before his rational mind took hold. This building was occupied. He could not start a firefight in here. The shooter might not be in a vacant apartment. He could have hostages inside. If he got scared, he might just start firing wildly.

Leaning against the banister on the second floor, he pulled the gun from his holster. Only when its brightly polished slide glinted in the dim light did he realize it was not his. He handed Ray his pistol when he went to answer the door. That was when the fake police came in, and Ray still had his pistol. He had intended to give Virgil the one he was carrying. He held a stainless steel, nine millimeter Beretta 92F, the Army's standard sidearm. Dropping the magazine he saw that it was fully loaded. That was predictable. Of course, its sights were set for someone else's preference. He hoped he would not have to use it anyway.

Shoes on the steps above him arrested his attention. He pushed himself against the wall, ears ringing from straining to analyze those footsteps. It was a man, not in a hurry, but stepping carefully. Maybe just a resident, trying to get out of the line of trouble. Maybe.

A giant invisible hand compressed Hannibal's chest. He held the gun low, aimed at the base of the stairs but hopefully in his shadow. The tall man rounded the corner of the staircase and stopped dead. He was white, with flyaway hair and a quirky smile. He was dressed, like Hannibal, entirely in black. His reason for being there hung from his right hand. It was a bolt action rifle attached to a wide scope. A light gathering type, Hannibal assumed, unnecessary in this case since Hannibal had been nicely back-lighted for his convenience.

"Freeze, you son of a bitch," Hannibal whispered, thrusting his pistol out in front of himself. "Who the hell you think you shooting at, huh?"

He could have put the rifle down and gone with Hannibal to the police. A sane option. He could have tried to fire, and fallen under a hail of nine millimeter shells. A courageous alternative.

Neither very smart nor very brave, the shooter turned and rushed up the stairs.

Carrying less, Hannibal figured he could catch this fool before he reached the top. But amid that double clatter of racing feet, fear gave the shooter an extra push. He stayed just far enough ahead of Hannibal to reach the third floor and get through the kitchen door. He swung the door back into Hannibal's face. Since the door had no lock, Hannibal was only seconds behind him.

Hannibal burst into an empty kitchen. A lack of utensils and furniture told him it was a vacant flat. Moonlight flooded into each room as Hannibal scrambled down the length of the apartment. He had heard no doors open or close, yet the entire flat was empty, but for the sound of his own pounding heart.

Charging back to the kitchen, Hannibal coughed in the dust he had raised. The only other sound he detected was a squeak sound he could not readily identify. It was a scraping sound, like rusted metal on metal. He closed his eyes to get a directional fix, but the answer made no sense. The sound was not coming from anywhere inside the apartment. It was outside.

As absurd as it seemed, Hannibal leaned over the sink and stuck his head out the back window. A narrow steel ladder ran down the back of the building like a rusted spine. A fire escape ladder. The shooter moved slowly down it, seemingly held to the brick surface by his own thick shadow, fighting to hang on to his rifle. A prized possession, Hannibal thought, which could well get him caught.

Putting the automatic in his holster, Hannibal sat up on the sink, let his legs out, and started down the ladder behind the shooter. His motion, combined with his quarry's, made the ladder grind against the rusted bolts holding it in place, creating a bizarre, syncopated ratcheting noise. Competing with that noise was a raspy voice.

"Leave me alone, you crazy coon." That voice, heavy with fear, rushed up and slapped Hannibal's ears. When he looked down, Hannibal saw the shooter, only five or six feet from the ground. He had stopped and was trying to get a round into the rifle's chamber.

"Don't be stupid," Hannibal called down, but the shooter was not listening. He managed to pull the bolt back, and he had what looked like a pretty heavy round in his hand. Hannibal stopped, hanging on by his right hand while he pulled the pistol back out.

Detail was hard to see, even in the stark moonlight, but sound carried well. The click of a well oiled lockup told Hannibal the bolt was closed, the rifle ready to fire. The shooter leaned in to the ladder, locking the rifle's stock into his shoulder.

Hannibal kicked his left foot loose and swung out like a gate. While the shooter frantically tried to adjust his aim, Hannibal looked straight down his own three-dot sights, seeing the luminous front dot squarely between the two rear sight dots, and squeezed his trigger lightly. It was a good trigger, and the gun surprised him when it let off. There was the sharp clap of the shot, and a soft glass tinkle right behind it. The telescopic sight was shattered.

The shooter's hands relaxed, as if they had lost all sensation. He fell backward in slow motion, dropped through space for three seconds and landed with a thump on the well cut grass. Hannibal swallowed hard, snatched a couple of deep, slow breaths, and followed him down.

From the ladder, the killer had been just a spread-eagled figure. Up close, Hannibal could see his right eye was missing. The hole in back of his head would not be nearly as neat. Hannibal had no desire to see it.

Only then did he realize how careless errors and coincidence had conspired to make his life easier. He had killed a mob killer, but he had done it with a mob gun, and while wearing gloves. Unwilling to question the fates, he simply dropped the pistol beside the corpse and sprinted down the narrow tunnel between buildings.

At the front of the building he stopped in the shadows. Clinging to the brick wall he checked left, then right. He spotted three men who definitely did not belong there. Sal was having his building watched, and these men could not avoid standing out on the sidewalk. Thinking it was better to be safe than shot, Hannibal sprinted across the street and up his own front steps.

Sarge opened the door and stepped out with one foot, brandishing the shotgun, as if daring anybody to start something. Once Hannibal got inside he scanned the street one last time before closing and locking the door. A second later he was leaning forward on the desk, his chest heaving from the running, the tension, the thing he had just done.

"You get him?" Sarge asked.

"I got him."

"Uh-huh. How you feel?"

Hannibal took three more breaths. Then he looked up, finding Sarge's eyes. "Let you know tomorrow."

Hannibal sometimes ran wearing leg weights for training, so he recognized this feeling. He thought he had never seen two longer flights of stairs. He knew he had reached the top floor only because Cindy tried to crush his ribs when he came within reach. No words were needed, but he drew strength from her body, from her love being pressed into him. Her love? Yes, he could say it now, at least himself.

Ronzini had been moved back to the second room. He sat on the bed there now, with Virgil sitting just beyond his reach, holding his billy club as if at any moment he might decide to put it into Ronzini's teeth. Ronzini looked up with more curiosity than anything else showing on his face.

"Your friends are minus one shooter," Hannibal said, pacing to bleed off tension. "He's dead. And your boy the nut case has got people out there, watching this building. Are they going to try it again, or what?"

Ronzini nodded. "He won't give it up."

"That don't make no sense." Hannibal found a folding chair for himself. "What's to gain?"

"It ain't about what," Ronzini said patiently, as if lecturing a slow student. "It's who. It's just who the boy is, and who you are. See, the problem is, nobody knows who they are anymore."

"You mean we don't know our place, right?" Cindy asked sarcastically.

"It's this melting pot thing," Ronzini went on. "It's got you all confused. Cultural diversity. Civil rights. Bunch of crap. In the old days, I'd have called him a nigger, and you a spic." Flames arced from Cindy's eyes, but Ronzini was unsinged. "So? You'd call me a wop, or a dago, or a guinea. So we all knew who we were, I mean in relation to each other. We didn't get confused, know what I mean?" Hannibal thought Cindy was probably waiting for him to strike out, but he was really listening, really trying to understand this weird philosophy.

"You're saying Sal thinks he's naturally superior," Cindy said with a sneer.

"No," Hannibal said, "He's saying the boy don't know any other way."

"Not with you," Ronzini said grimly.

"If I was another Italian, he'd know how to deal with me," Hannibal said, standing. "Or at least, he'd know he could deal with me. Sure. Sally probably only sees black guys as servants. Or customers. Maybe competitors. But not as men."

"He knows who he is," Ronzini said. "He doesn't know who you are. I mean, he thinks you're a nigger, but you don't act like a nigger. And he's still acting like a dumb wop."

What the hell planet did these Ronzinis live on, Hannibal wondered. What century were they stuck in? He turned away from Ronzini, finding Virgil's intense black face. "I need a drink behind that shit."

"Ray's got some Bacardi in the kitchen, and some coke too," Virgil said. "I don't think dagos can swallow the stuff."

With a chuckle, Hannibal staggered into the kitchen, with Cindy behind him. There he found a bottle of rum. From it he poured two Styrofoam cups half full, filling them a second later with warm cola. He watched his woman's eyes as he took a couple of sips. She looked so beautiful to him, a single spot of loveliness in a world that was otherwise looking very ugly right now.

"I want you out of here," Hannibal said softly. "You don't belong in all this ugliness."

"You want me out, you put me out." Cindy watched his face closely. "That's the only way you'll get me out. You'll have to pick me up and carry me out. I belong with you." Again she sipped her drink. "You know, I've never seen a man with hazel eyes before."

Hannibal chuckled, wrapping his arms around her. "Me too."

"You know, you've got what they call a situation here," she said.

"Yeah, and the situation's getting away from me," Hannibal said. "I mean, we're handling each thing as it comes up, but if it all comes apart, I don't know if I can protect you and the guys."

"You know, you could always just call the police," Cindy said. In the dim light, as the rum warmed his belly, she became the voice of reason. "Explain your motives for grabbing Ronzini. Put me in a courtroom with them, and I'll at least bring the son down."

"Yeah, I could do that. It would get everybody out of here safe." He held her at arms length now. His mouth twisted as if he had swallowed something bitter.

"So?"

"Only thing is, it just feels so much like quitting," Hannibal said. They shared one last strong hug before heading back toward the front of the house. Almost there, they heard Sarge calling from the walkie-talkie they had left on the mantelpiece.

"Hey, Hannibal. Can you hear me?" Hannibal reached up to get the walkie-talkie, thumbing down the send button.

"I got you, Bro."

"Listen, something weird is happening out there," Sarge said. "Think you ought to come down."

-37-

Hannibal trotted downstairs grimly. He briefly considered Cindy's suggestion. By just calling the police and confessing, he could get his people safely out of the building. In a courtroom, he could still bring Sal Ronzini down.

Considered and rejected it, in the space of one flight of stairs.

Sarge met him on the second floor, leading him to the front room of an unoccupied apartment. It seemed unlikely any snipers had sighted this room in. There they sat on the cool tile floor scanning the darkened street. The singers were gone, replaced by an apparently random assortment of men, just loitering up and down the block.

Sarge pointed out one of the wanderers. "That big mother right there's got to be mob muscle. And this big head dude here."

"Yeah, and this one," Hannibal said, targeting another. "How many you think are out there?"

"Well, so far I seen six, I think," Sarge said. Hannibal could see worry lines forming on Sarge's face for the first time. Not liking what he saw, he turned back to the window.

"Wait a minute." Hannibal had seen a black man walk across the front of the building, carrying a baseball bat. "What about this guy? He can't be one of Sal's boys. Too small, for one thing."

"Nope, I think he's one of the neighbors," Sarge said. "That brother over there, he got a razor in his hand. Saw him jostle one of the mob types a while back. I know he lives here, cause I seen him on the street the last couple of days."

Hannibal put his back against the wall and slapped the heels of his palms against his forehead. Was Sally bracing for a final, all out assault on the building? Hannibal was psychologically prepared for that eventuality. He had considered it one of the possibilities.

But now the picture was changing. Local people occupied their street, acting as if they were bracing for a fight. One more eventuality he had not anticipated.

"Where's Ray?" Hannibal asked.

"Back door, left."

"Thanks." Hannibal stood up. "Keep watching the front door."

Hannibal moved to his own kitchen, where Ray sat on the sink sideboard. Hannibal remembered sitting in that exact spot watching for movement out the window. Ray had a pistol in his hand, but kept it pointed low. He looked up and smiled when Hannibal walked in.

"I think we've got them scared," Ray said. "Haven't seen a hint of movement out there since I got here."

"Good deal," Hannibal said. "I stopped back here to get my own gun back."

"Oh yeah," Ray said, pulling he weapon out of his waistband and handing it to Hannibal. "I was feeling a little heavy packing two."

Hannibal holstered his automatic and went as far as the door before turning.

"Listen Ray," Hannibal said, "I don't think Cindy should be here right now. Think you could talk to her?"

Ray grinned and shook his head. "Paco, I'm just her papa. If she won't listen to you, I'd be just wasting my breath. But for what it's worth, I'm glad you at least thought about it."

Hannibal walked toward the front of the building, feeling as if he had no control of anything. He nodded at Sarge but walked past him to unlock the door. Sarge stood up quickly, grabbing his arm.

"What the hell?"

"I got to go out, Bro," Hannibal said. "These people could get hurt messing in our problems."

"Yeah," Sarge said. "You could get hurt too. Wait for morning."

Hannibal shook his head. "People could die before morning." After a deep breath, he opened the door just enough to squeeze out.

Timothy filled his lungs with marijuana smoke, held it for five seconds, and let it slowly leak out his mouth and nose. He sat alone in the total darkness, hugging his small pistol to his stomach as if to keep warm.

That coward Jones would do anything to avoid a fight, Timothy just knew it. And in this case, anything meant cutting a deal with Ronzini and his bastard son. Jones would bargain away their advantage and everybody would walk away from this as if nothing had every happened.

Except for one thing. Ronzini had to die.

And he, Timothy, would do it. If Jones or one of the others didn't finish Ronzini off, he would be set free. He would walk out that door as if he owned the place. And then.

And then Timothy would come up out of the dark, and aim his little gun, which he stole from one of the junkies Ronzini created, and blow his head open.

* * *

It was eerie on the sidewalk, and it took Hannibal a moment to realize why. There were people on the street, all men, but it was quiet. This was the first night since he arrived on the block that he heard no music from anywhere, no loud laughter, no partying sounds.

Feeling a dozen eyes on him, he walked left toward the cross street. He recognized the black man coming around the corner carrying a golf club. Monty had called him Mister Lincoln. He was still limping, because of Hannibal.

"Where you headed, bro?" Hannibal asked, falling into step with the man.

"I don't want no trouble with you," Lincoln said.

"Won't be none," Hannibal said, trying a tentative smile. "I'm really sorry about what happened before. I don't want you to get hurt again."

Lincoln stopped. "Look-a-here, brother. Everybody knows what's going down on the block. You done what we all should have done. Now the man's out, we don't aim to see him get back in, dig?"

"Look, I hear what you're saying, but it could get dangerous out here," Hannibal said, walking with Lincoln as if they were having the most normal conversation. "People could get hurt."

"Hey," someone else called. Hannibal spun, to find a muscular young black man behind him, clutching a length of lead pipe. "You this Hannibal Jones?"

"Why?"

"Just want to tell you, we got your back," the newcomer said. "You right about one thing, bro. People could get hurt. Especially if they white, and pushing drugs, and they come up here in my hood and start messing with a brother who's trying to get the junkies out."

"Look, fellows, I appreciate all this, really," Hannibal said, backing away slowly, "but these boys don't play. Let's try to keep it cool, okay?"

"Relax, man," the pipe carrier said. "They don't start no S-H, won't be no I-T."

Hannibal headed in the other direction, not at all relaxed by the conversation he just had. It made him realize how inwardly his eyes had been focused since his arrival there. Looking out through defensive portals, looking for enemies the whole time, he had only actually met two true members of the community and one of them he had shot in the leg. He headed for the other now, thinking she might make a difference.

On his way up the block, he passed several sets of eyes, all aimed at him. Some watched him encouragingly. Most of them, a good majority, stared hatred at him. Those faces, many of them white, carried fear as well. Bravado aside, no one really wanted to take part in a nighttime street brawl.

Sal must carry a lot of weight to get them to do this, he thought. That thought frightened him most of all, since he saw Sal Ronzini as a rogue, dangerously out of control.

Figures stepped into, through and out of the street lamps' bright bubbles on both sides of the street. Almost at the far end of the block, Hannibal reached his destination. Surprisingly, the person he was looking for stood on her porch, watching him approach. Her hands were folded in what might be prayer.

"Mother Washington, what are you doing out here?" he called up from the sidewalk.

"I live here son," she replied, with the infuriating calm of a Buddha. By contrast, Monty was pacing the porch like a puppy, staring up the block, apparently aching to be part of the action.

"Ma'am, there's a lot of tension out here," Hannibal said, holding his own hands up as if in supplication. "There could be fighting any minute. Won't you please go inside?"

"Grandma's got me to protect her," Monty said.

"Why don't you come in, Mister Jones?" Mother Washington asked.

"Not a good idea." Hannibal was pacing in a circle, hands on his hips. "I'm a lightning rod for violence right now, and I don't want to bring it into your home."

"So what brought you all the way down here?" Mrs. Washington asked.

Hannibal hated the desperation he heard in his own voice when he answered. "Ma'am, please, please. Call your neighbors. I know you must have influence with the women here. Tell them to get their men off the street tonight."

The old woman's face was wrapped in shadow, but Hannibal could see her thinking it through. After a moment, her eyes like deep brown laser beams found his.

"Why?"

"Why?" He pointed up the block, unable to contain his frustration any longer. "Can't you see? They're badly outnumbered. They got kitchen knives and straight razors against switchblades and guns in the hands of people who do this for a living."

"Know what I see?" Her voice was soft but strong. The voice she used in church, her hymnal voice. "I see men who haven't stood up for anything in a long time, even themselves, standing up now. I see men, real men, standing together, working together, thank you Jesus. I see my fine black men getting together, my Lord, to push Satan out of our street. Hallelujah. Praise his name."

With one beefy hand raised high, she was no longer conversing. She was testifying. Hannibal suddenly realized how his single-minded quest had become contagious. He defied "The Man." Now everyone wanted to prove they could do it too. Only if it broke this time, it would not end with one man with bruises. It would be a blood bath.

"Would you at least just call the police?" Hannibal asked.

"Why? They'll come when they're ready. They're right there, just two blocks away."

He stared off to his right. He could barely see a tiny revolving red light.

For a moment he hesitated. He thought he could end this if he could talk to them, but could he risk getting that far away from his house?

The truth was, he could not risk not going. Besides, it was pure arrogance to think that his presence alone could hold back the rising tide of frustration and anger that was about to crest in a wave of violence. He started up the block at a slow trot, but his legs picked up speed of their own accord as desperation pushed him over the sidewalk. All the way he passed men moving slowly in the opposite direction, a tide of joking, laughing, yet grim black faces. They all wanted to be where it was happening, and that was in front of number twenty-three thirteen.

When the three parked police cars were half a block away, a uniformed man leaning on one of them laid his hand on his sidearm. Hannibal slowed his pace to a crawl and held his own hands away from his body. He was not sure what he planned to say to these men, but he had to get close enough to avoid shouting.

"Something I can do for you, sir?" the cop holding his gun asked. Hannibal thought he looked too young to be trusted with a gun. Just as Hannibal was about to speak, another man stepped out of the second car.

"That you Jones?" Kendall asked.

Hannibal felt tension slide off his shoulders. "Man am I glad to see you. What the hell are you doing out here anyway?"

"Watching," Kendall said.

"Well then, you can see what's going down. Come on up the block and break this thing up before it gets out of hand."

Kendall took a long last drag from his cigarette and flipped it into the gutter. "No can do, friend. Orders."

"Orders?" Hannibal asked, stepping closer to the policeman. The other cop slid his revolver out of his holster, but Hannibal didn't care. "Look, screw your orders. I got a hostage situation up there. A man's been kidnapped. Now come get him and take me in if you have to. It's about to blow up down there."

"I don't care if you got the mayor bent over a barrel, pal." Kendall's piercing eyes bored into Hannibal's as if trying to force a message home. "The bosses got long memories. They don't want another riot like they had here in the sixties after the assassination of Martin Luther King. I reported everything I saw and we, meaning every cop in the city, we have been forbidden to interfere. Seriously, if anything will set it all off in this neighborhood, it's a blue uniform." His eyes dropped to the ground then. "We'll come in when it's all over."

Kendall's words hit Hannibal like hailstones. He felt the ground sliding out from under him. Without another word, he turned and walked as quickly as he could without breaking into a run back toward his own building. This was not the situation he had bought. It was just too big for him. It was not fair that he should be responsible for all these men and their families.

When he reached the front steps at twenty-three thirteen, Hannibal hesitated at the bottom. Maybe he could say something, make an announcement, that would make these people disperse. He could see about thirty men or so on the street at this point. Probably two-thirds of them were Sal's flunkies. He might be able to make the local people see common sense and get to safety.

Before he could turn around, two black men slapped him gently on the back.

"Chill, brother," one man in undershirt and baggy pants said, grinning wide. "They ain't the only ones with guns, dig?"

"Oh, God!" Hannibal moaned, bolting up the stairs. Sarge opened the door in silence. Hannibal did not speak either, but maintained his pace, jogging up the stairs. This nonsense had to stop, and he only knew one person who might be able to make that happen.

-38-

On the top floor, Hannibal burst into the flat that had become his command post. Looking neither left nor right, he marched into the room he had left Ronzini in. Not speaking, he grabbed up Cindy's purse and pulled out her cordless telephone. While his right hand held the phone toward Ronzini like an olive branch, he drew his automatic and thrust it forward, pressing its muzzle against Ronzini's forehead.

"You call that asshole son of yours and tell him to call this shit off," Hannibal snapped. Somehow, maybe from experience with a dozen gangland attempts on his life, Ronzini managed to not react.

"He probably thinks I'm already dead," Ronzini replied blandly. "Now, if you can tell me what this is all about, I might be able to stop it."

"About?" Hannibal repeated, his gun still in the other man's face. "It's about getting the drugs out of this building. Right now, it's about no innocent bystanders getting hurt."

"Fine," Ronzini said in a maddeningly even tone. "Give yourself up." He looked deep into Hannibal's eyes, which were more green than brown right then.

"The hell I will!"

"Okay," Ronzini said, as if he had just made a point. "Now you see. It ain't about drugs and it ain't about innocent bystanders. It's about egos. Yours and Salvatore's. You won't give up. Neither will he. And now we both know your reason's no better than his."

Fearing the confusion now clouding his mind, Hannibal turned away from Ronzini, again resting his hands on his hips. Looking over at Cindy, he saw indecision in her eyes. He wanted badly to ask her what to do, but he would not, because she might tell him to quit. Would giving up save all those people outside, his new neighbors and Ronzini's men? No, there was another way. He spun back on the gangster lounging on the bed.

"It ain't just me and Sal no more," Hannibal said in a guttural street voice that apparently surprised Ronzini. "And you ain't the only outsider in it no more. People fixing to get hurt bad."

"So?"

"So? So?" Hannibal dropped the gun and the phone on the bed, fingers digging into the collar of Ronzini's expensive suit. Ronzini's eyes bulged as Hannibal lifted his bulk up from the bed. Heaving with all his weight, Hannibal hauled the gangster upright, spun, and flung him into the next room. Ronzini's knees cracked on the floor. Hannibal gripped the back of his collar, dragging his heavy body forward until his chest slapped onto the windowsill. Ronzini's hands pressed against the windowsill to keep him from being choked. His head was thrust half way out the open window.

"Look down there, you greasy slug," Hannibal said through clenched teeth. "Look! You see them. They ain't just pieces in some big game. They're living, breathing human beings. Not just my people. Some of your best boys too, I bet."

He knelt beside Ronzini, pushing their faces together, holding the older man still by a handful of thick graying hair. He thought he saw something new in Ronzini's face. He prayed it was the light of understanding beginning to dawn.

"Even you can see he's already lost this block," Hannibal said. "Even if he got the building back, those people down there would never let this place stay a crack house. They'd fight to the end, now. And you know if any shit starts down there, dudes will come running in from blocks away, just to be in on it. All of Anacostia, all of Southeast. Maybe down from Northeast too. You ready for this? You ready for a blood bath, right here in D.C.? A sure enough riot? Were you here when King got shot? Or maybe you saw it up close in New York in the sixties. These people are just as frustrated, just as mad. I could die here. You could die. Your son could die. A shitload of people who got no business in this could die. You want this?"

It was time to shut up. Hannibal locked eyes with Ronzini and would not let go. He watched Ronzini's gaze roam from shadowed face to shadowed face below them, sensing the mood, the tension, the hatred on the street. Those forces created an unbroken circuit of anger ready to flare up into a firestorm, engulfing this block and, maybe, several around it.

"I don't want this," Ronzini said quietly. His whisper reverberated in the otherwise silent room. Soft, slow footsteps approached from behind. A telephone hung close to his ear.

"Call your son," Cindy said. "Call this damned thing off before it's too late."

Ronzini sat on the floor. Hannibal knelt beside him. Between them, Cindy's hand held her telephone. Slowly, like a boy choosing his own whipping switch, Ronzini accepted the phone. He pushed six buttons, stopped and looked up.

"Salvatore is too proud," Ronzini said. "I think you are not as proud as you were an hour ago. You agree to settle this with him, one to one?"

"Me and him," Hannibal said. "That's what it's all about."

Ronzini nodded and pushed the last button. Holding the telephone an inch from his head, he made sure Hannibal and Cindy could hear the ringing at the other end. Over his shoulder, he noticed Virgil, in a chair. He had picked up Hannibal's pistol, and held it casually on Ronzini.

A soft burring buzz sounded four times before a voice said "What?"

"Salvatore. This is Papa," Ronzini said firmly. The only response was silence. "Salvatore."

"Papa, you okay?" Sal sounded too up, as if he was using his own products.

"Salvatore, pull your men out of the street," Ronzini said. "Jones will let me go, and he will come out. It's over."

"The hell it is," Sal answered. "He got a gun on you, Papa? I know he's making you say these things. Don't worry, Papa. I'll get in there and get you out. You tell him that."

"No, Salvatore, listen to me. Listen to me!" Ronzini was on his knees, yelling into a dead piece of plastic. Three seconds later, the dial tone returned, like an EKG hooked to a flat lined patient. Shock showed on Ronzini's face.

"He hung up on me." Ronzini swallowed, as if a bitter pill had gotten stuck in his throat. "My boy just hung up on me."

"Well, no sense putting up with you no more." That deep, scratchy voice made Hannibal look up, and he watched Virgil stepping forward, gun first.

-39-

Virgil's yellowed eyes bore down on Anthony Ronzini as he approached. "That shit your son pushes up and down the street come close to killing me."

He was a big man, wide as Ronzini. His arms looked thick and soft, like sausages. His two hands nearly hid the back half of the pistol, but the gun looked bigger four inches from Ronzini's nose. Virgil's breathing was deep and loud, as if he were working himself up for something. Everybody in the room knew what it was.

"You don't want to do that," Cindy said, trying desperately to conceal her panic.

"The hell I don't." Virgil stared down the automatic's sights into a spot between Ronzini's eyes. The gangster betrayed no emotion, but new beads of moisture erupted from his forehead.

"Of course you want to kill him." Hannibal slowly rose to his feet. "So do I. But you won't. You're more of a man than he is. You don't have to kill him."

Ronzini swallowed, but when he spoke, it was with a clear voice. "I've done a lot illegal things. Probably caused a lot of other people to do some crooked things. But I swear to you, I never in my life sold any dope. Never." Then, without ever losing eye contact, he stood up. With the appearance of total calm, he walked past Virgil who seemed frozen in place, and sat back down on the bed. Virgil did not resist Hannibal taking back his pistol.

Cindy was staring out the window now, and Hannibal went to stand behind her. Ronzini was staring at a point in space between himself and the wall.

*   *   *

For a brief moment, Virgil had stepped center stage and felt the spotlight on himself. Now the light had moved on, and he knew he was invisible for a time to the main players. Unnoticed, he walked out and down the stairs. When he reached the bottom, Sarge stepped out of the left apartment.

"Hi," Sarge said, shaking his head. "I was checking the view through a window. Getting ugly outside. What's the deal upstairs?"

"It's out of control, man." Virgil said, his hands thrust deep into his pockets. "Hannibal can't stop it. Ronzini can't stop it. I'm afraid the whole thing's going to blow."

Sarge glanced up into Virgil's yellowed eyes, then looked again more closely. Virgil pulled his face away, but he knew it was too late.

"So what else?" Sarge asked.

Loud voices outside the door nearly drowned out Virgil's deep scratchy voice. "I just come real close to doing something real stupid. I had a gun. I got frustrated. I come that close to killing Ronzini."

Sarge whistled a descending note. "Yeah, that would have done it all right. Gang war and a riot for sure. What the hell put that idea in your head?"

"I been thinking about that." Virgil sat on the guard desk. "I think it was something Timothy said, about the guys pushing the junk. You know I used to shoot up."

"Yeah, it kind of shows, long after you quit," Sarge said, as if stating a commonly known natural law.

"Anyway, Timothy was talking about how we ought to just put a bullet in the man's head. He'd have done it himself if he got the chance."

"Yeah. That guy scares me. Back in the Corps we'd have called him a loose cannon on deck."

Virgil's eyes suddenly widened, his mouth hanging slightly open. He was putting puzzle pieces together in his mind and getting a very ugly picture.

"When's the last time you seen Timothy?" Virgil asked.

"Don't know," Sarge said. "Why?"

"He's got a gun, you know."

Sarge barely missed a beat before pulling out his radio. "Quaker, you there?" he asked it.

"Yo," the radio said. "Hannibal's kitchen."

"Timothy with you?" Sarge asked.

"Ain't seen him, man," Quaker answered. "And I can see through to Ray on the other side, and he's all alone. What's up?"

"Nothing," Sarge told Quaker. Then he turned to Virgil. "This ain't good, man. If he gets a wild hair up his ass and fires out into the street he could trigger a firefight to match anything I saw in Nam."

"Better tell Hannibal," Virgil said, starting up the stairs.

"No," Sarge said, pulling the back of Virgil's shirt. "Ronzini's pretty safe as long as Hannibal's with him. Timothy can do the most damage if he hits somebody outside. Let's you and me check for him on the first floor. If he don't turn up, then we go upstairs and do a room by room sweep, just like when we first come in."

"Okay," Virgil said, picking up Sarge's bat. "Hold that shotgun up when you go, man. I don't think he'd shoot me. Anybody else, well, I don't know. I think the pressure got to him. No telling what he'd do."

* * *

Upstairs, Cindy stared down at the men doing their war dance under the streetlights. "Madre de Dios," she murmured, "now what do we do." Tension was squeezing miniature tears through her eyelids.

"I don't know," Hannibal said. "I really don't know. They think they're doing the right thing down there. Hell, maybe they are. I can't stop them."

As if he was sitting in a different room, Ronzini said, "He hung up on me."

Hannibal's mind, left without focus for a moment, attached itself to Ronzini's internal conversation. "You set him up in business, didn't you?"

"Yeah, I got him started," Ronzini admitted. "He's a man now, he needs to find himself."

"But now you can't control him," Hannibal said.

"He never learned he can't just do anything he pleases," Ronzini said. "I know sometimes he gets out of hand. That's my fault. I never taught him he ain't God. Never let anybody else teach him. I protected him."

Behind him, outside and three stories lower, Hannibal heard a bottle crash on the sidewalk. A slightly slurred voice said "Y'all need to get the fuck out of here before I fuck you up." It would start soon.

"I thought I could do it," Hannibal said quietly to Cindy. "I thought I could, but it's too big for me. Didn't think anything was, but this is. Ronzini was right. My ego could get a lot of good people hurt." That thought kicked him forward, driving him to clutch at the only straw he saw. He faced Ronzini, his head dropping like an under inflated child's punching toy. "I quit. Okay? I quit. Sally wins. He gets whatever he wants. Now call it off."

"Haven't you been listening?" Desperation showed in Ronzini's red rimmed eyes. "He won't even talk to me."

"So undercut him," Hannibal almost shouted. "I'll bet every one of them hoods out there knows you, or knows who you are. The pros do, anyway. Think they'll listen to him if you tell them to hit the road?"

The room became a frozen tableau. Hannibal, rooted in place, became aware of the wetness under his arms. He could smell himself, an acid stench he guessed came from fear and self-reproach. Outside, a voice clearly not bred in Washington's inner city said, "Back off, spade." Something passed between Hannibal's mostly brown eyes and Ronzini's. It was the only movement in the room.

When Hannibal's chest began to ache from not breathing, Ronzini's face slowly wound itself into a twisted smile. "He needs a lesson. We still got a deal?"

Hannibal let his breath out in a strangled hiss. "Whatever it takes. Stop the riot."

Sarge held the shotgun barrel ahead of himself as he worked his way through Hannibal's apartment. In contrast to what was going on outside, the apartment held the silence of a tomb. He felt just as he did the first day that he entered that building. At any minute, someone could well step out of a shadow and try to kill him.

Keeping his breathing slow and even, Sarge swung his barrel under Hannibal's bed. Treading lightly he yanked the bathroom door open and swept the area with his shotgun. Nothing.

He reached the kitchen without seeing any sign of Timothy. Frustrated, he went into the hall and met Virgil at the front door.

"He's nowhere in that apartment." Virgil's voice was more gravelly than usual. "Must be hiding upstairs somewhere."

"That nut case is going to do something stupid," Sarge said. "I can feel it. If we don't find him real soon, I think we better get Ray and Quaker in on the search. This is a big place with too many nice, dark hidey holes."

Sarge's head turned at the creak of a stair from above. Ronzini and Hannibal were striding down the stairs side by side. They moved slowly, but in step. Sarge imagined this was what it looked like when a guard marched his prisoner to the execution table. The question was, who was the guard and who the prisoner?

As the two approached from above, Sarge and Virgil stood aside. Hannibal unlocked the door and moved away. Ronzini grasped the knob, but before turning it he turned to Hannibal.

"However this goes, it ends here," Ronzini said. "No unfinished business after tonight, no matter how this goes." Under his gaze, Hannibal closed his eyes and nodded slowly.

As Ronzini stepped out the door, Sarge tapped Virgil's arm and said, "Upstairs, man. Quick."

* * *

Hannibal heard the clatter of feet on the stairs behind him, but he could not spare the attention to whatever was happening there. He joined Ronzini on the stoop.

Hannibal scanned the area as he and Ronzini walked slowly down the sandstone steps in front of the building. Black men of every size, shade and description lined the sidewalk he was about to step onto. They paced up and down, sometimes crossing paths, but not staying too near each other. A grim determination showed in their faces. Armed with improvised weapons, they were ready for a fight.

The other side of the street was thick with white faces. These men were cooler, because they fought for a living, not for fun. He spotted the telltale bulges from guns under waistbands and in pockets. These were the professionals, smugly confident that they were more than a match for any unruly mob of disorganized troublemakers. They were prepared to strike on cue, a light brigade facing the Zulu nation.

They hadn't a clue.

Three men sat in low chairs on the porch directly across the street now. A command post, Hannibal guessed. Salvatore's field commander would be there, but he could not see any faces. He hoped Ronzini could make eye contact. Surprisingly, Ronzini turned his attention on a man standing to the left of the porch across the street.

"Hey, Charlie!" Ronzini called, in a strong voice that turned all heads toward him. "Charlie, you know me?"

"Mister Ronzini," Charlie replied. "You okay?"

"Here I am," Ronzini said. "I'm fine. Nobody's holding me. It's over."

A stunned silence flowed over the street, as white men and black looked at each other in as much surprise as disappointment.

"You hear me Charlie?" Ronzini asked. Then he spotted another familiar face. "Dennis. Get me a ride home, would you?" That man turned and started up the block at a trot. "The rest of you just go home before we start something here."

Smart, Hannibal thought. Rather than challenge Sal's lieutenants, Ronzini had spoken directly to men he must know well. Men he knew would follow his instructions over anyone else's. Behind Ronzini, he saw a subtle transformation in the street. He was aware of the grins on his neighbors' faces as mob muscle started fading away. The smiles meant the tension was drained. The powder keg crisis had passed. He even had a few seconds to think about how powerful Ronzini was in his way. That was when the other man ran off the porch across the street.

"No!" Sal Ronzini shouted, momentum carrying him halfway across the street. "You guys grab that nigger right there. He's the one. Get him."

Petey and Ox trotted down the steps behind their boss. Hannibal reflexively dropped into a ready stance, and men with knives and pipes and baseball bats seemed to shrink in around him and Ronzini.

"No Salvatore," Ronzini said, not loud but strong. The gang fighters who had moved in hesitated. "This is not the place. No more of this in the street."

"No, Papa," Sal shouted. "You don't know. Me and this cock sucker, we got business."

"I do know," Ronzini said, a bit more sternly. "But these men you have with you, they do not." He turned his voice out toward the crowd. "You men, you go home now. You do not belong here." Then to Sal, "What is between you and this man is personal, Salvatore. It is not for all of these to settle."

"No, you come back here," Sal called behind him, to either side. Despite his urging, the men who had come at his command now faded slowly away. In less than a minute, the street's population thinned by more than half. Sal stood alone in the street for a moment, but for the two mismatched giants backing him. Then a long black Lincoln rolled slowly down the street, making them step back. The man Ronzini had called Dennis drove up to the curb, directly between Sal and Hannibal.

With a smile, Ronzini walked carefully around the front of the car, not toward his son but rather, his black bodyguard.

"I commend your loyalty, old friend," Ronzini told Ox. "It must have been difficult to protect my Salvatore under these circumstances."

"That's what you pay me for," Ox said.

"Yes. Now I want you and Petey to bring Salvatore to Dominic's. Take about ten minutes longer than you need to. And come in the back way."

Surprise stole Sal's voice when his father turned away. Ronzini faced Hannibal, but looked past him. Hannibal looked over his own shoulder as Cindy appeared on the stoop and started slowly down the steps. Ray and Quaker followed, blending in with the neighbors. A general air of celebration shot through the block. Men congratulated each other and slapped each other's backs, threatening to turn the evening's excitement into a spontaneous block party.

Timothy took in a deep breath, rose to his full height, and gently pushed the basement door open. He had listened a long time and he was sure the first floor was empty. Clutching his weapon to his chest with both hands, he crept down the hall toward the front door. Outside it seemed quieter than he thought it should be. He was willing to bet Jones had made a deal, some compromise to avoid a real fight. Ronzini, that fat son of a bitch, Ronzini would get away clean.

But not if Timothy could help it.

Crouching against the front door, Timothy could feel his moment at hand. He was the engine of Justice. In seconds he would be a hero. And he would have revenge for the beating he got at the hands of Ronzini's men in a darkened parking garage. With his left hand, he turned the doorknob and eased the door open an inch. Just enough for a snub nosed thirty-eight's barrel.

Outside, all eyes were on Jones and Ronzini, who stood beside a big black car, looking like best friends. Nobody was fighting, but a few of the brothers looked like they were still ready. Good.

Timothy's face was pressed against the door so he could see through the narrow space. He turned his revolver until it was pointing at Ronzini. At this distance, he could hardly miss his target, and when Ronzini fell, someone was sure to get his son too. Anticipating the sweet shock Ronzini would feel in death, Timothy wrapped his index finger around the gun's trigger.

A roar behind him froze Timothy for a brief instant. His head spun in time to see Sarge bursting from the left apartment's front door, rushing toward him. Then Sarge's bulk, led by the shotgun barrel he held in both hands, crashed into Timothy's ribs and he was swept forward, past the door and into the wall beyond. The long gun was crushed into his chest, his head pushed through the plaster and slats in the wall, and darkness gathered.

"I knew you had to be down here." Sarge grabbed the pistol and tossed it down the hall. "With that puny piece you couldn't hope to hit anybody from a window, even on the second floor. I sent Virgil upstairs to be sure but, hell, I knew it."

* * *

Sal's two bodyguards had hustled their charge into his car already. When they drove away it was as if someone had pulled the plug on the machine that had been generating megawatts of enmity in the streets. Unmoving in a sea of human activity, Hannibal waited. Ronzini walked imperiously around the Lincoln again, stopped at its side and opened the back door. When he looked at Hannibal, it was a look of invitation.

"What the hell is this?" a burly black man asked. He cocked back his car antenna, showing his willingness to fight. Ronzini spoke to him, but his eyes stayed on Hannibal the whole time.

"It's all right," Ronzini said, waving his hand like Obi-Wan Kenobi at a checkpoint. "Mister Jones has agreed to come with me. Isn't that right, Mister Jones?"

"No!" Cindy cried, running the last few steps and wrapping her arms around Hannibal's waist. He understood her fear, but he could also see how quickly the crowd's mood could turn around. The brothers could overwhelm Ronzini and his few followers still on the street. Seeing no good alternative, he mustered a smile and aimed it at Ronzini.

"Yes, that's right," Hannibal said. "Mister Ronzini's just giving me a ride. We have, um, some unfinished business." He gently pried Cindy's arms loose, feeling her shake. Leaning close, he lightly kissed her ear and whispered "If I don't go, this won't be over. It's got to end tonight. Besides, I made a deal." With his woman at arms' length, Hannibal finally released her. Some of the faces around him looked unsure, and he had to correct that. Looking up, he spotted Sarge in the door, his shotgun in plain sight. He lifted his right arm, waving a sloppy salute.

"Take care of the lady." He spoke to Sarge, but he made sure everyone heard him. "Don't worry. I'll be back before sunup." With that he stepped past Ronzini into the car. Once settled, he leaned back, rubbing sweat soaked hands down the length of his thighs. Ronzini boarded beside him, and Dennis pulled away from the curb.

-40-

THURSDAY

Nerve shattering in the stillness, a steeple bell tolled the stroke of midnight. With each peal, the bell seemed to be calling Hannibal down into hell. Right now he appeared to be in purgatory.

Actually, he was in an Italian restaurant Ronzini had called Dominic's. It was a fairly small, rectangular area, its long side running parallel to a dark, narrow street. The front wall was glass panels from the ceiling down to just four feet from the floor. Tables for four stood in carefully random order around the room. A long wooden bar spanned the back wall. Ronzini chose to stand behind the bar, while Dennis chose a chair at one of the tables.

In some ways, Hannibal had no idea where he was. He had paid no attention during the drive, so he could be almost anywhere in the Washington D.C. area. That church in the background could be any house of worship with a bell. His body vibrated sympathetically with its final tone.

He also did not know where he stood with Ronzini. He only knew he had a debt to pay. He had made a deal with the devil, after all, but he had not agreed to sell his soul. And this place could not be the devil's home base. Not hell, perhaps, but certainly not heaven. Purgatory, then.

"You are a man of honor, Hannibal Jones," Ronzini said from behind the bar. "My son, my Salvatore, he needs a lesson in honor. Perhaps you can deliver that lesson for me. And maybe some humility too."

Pleasant smells hung in the room. Garlic. Onions. Parmesan. Oregano. Smells of happy times. Hannibal slid onto a barstool and said, "I'm not sure I follow you, Tony." To his surprise, Dennis pulled a revolver from his back.

"You call me Mister Ronzini," the gangster said. "I'm prepared to end your business with me and my son right here, tonight."

For Hannibal it had been a long day. After being up late at the hospital with Balor the night before, he had gotten up early enough to beat Mick Denton to his office by an hour. On the move all day, he had been drained by the tension of a kidnapping, the fear of a riot and the emotional shock of having to kill a man. He wanted an end to it.

"I'm with that," he said, "but how?"

Ronzini poured himself a shot of scotch, its pungent scent stinging Hannibal's nose. "You settle it between you. One on one."

"Quit pushing on me you big ape," Sal said, his voice preceding him from the kitchen. He came around the end of the bar with Ox and Petey gently prodding him. As he sighted Hannibal, he stopped, building a slow smile. Ronzini turned to his son, as if no one else existed in the room.

"Salvatore, Salvatore, Salvatore," Ronzini moaned, shaking his head. "You almost caused a riot tonight with your stupidity and your drugs."

"Like you care about those people." Sal pulled out a chair. "You said the drug operation in that area belonged to me. Then you come in and undermine me with my own men. Why Papa?"

"First, you had the arrogance to tell me no," Ronzini said. "This I might have forgiven. But I cannot forgive bad business.

You make too many enemies, Salvatore. And you let business become personal."

"Okay, so it's personal," Sal said. He sat down with his massive guards towering above him, glaring at Hannibal. "So let me take care of it."

"I'm going to give you your wish," Ronzini said. He turned his eyes to Hannibal, but everyone understood he was still addressing his son. "You two will settle your differences now. After this it is over. Mister Jones is here to have an end to this bad blood." Then he tapped an index finger on the bar. Hannibal understood, and slid his left hand slowly under his jacket.

"I win, I walk?" Hannibal asked very quietly. Ronzini nodded. Hannibal slid his Sig Sauer 229 out of its holster and placed it on the dark hardwood beside Ronzini's hand. Then he stepped away from the bar, tugging at his gloves to tighten them.

"All right." Sal raised his clenched fists. "Come on boys. Let's get that dick head."

"No," Ronzini said sternly. "Ox, you stand over there by the door to the kitchen. Petey, that far corner." After a brief hesitation, both big men moved to the positions Ronzini indicated. Sal stopped half way to Hannibal, his face reddening as he turned.

"Hey! Come on," Sal Shouted. "Who you guys work for, huh?" Sal stared at his bodyguards in disbelief. Petey stared stonily ahead without reaction. Ox looked at Sal apologetically and rolled his massive shoulders in a shrug. But he did not move.

"This is between you and him." Ronzini pointed first at his son, then at Hannibal. "Now you will settle this. You beat him, you have your crack house back. Otherwise, you close the book on that enterprise and move on to another place."

"You don't make deals for me, Papa," Sal said, louder than necessary. He advanced toward his father menacingly. Ronzini looked up from pouring himself another drink and froze Sal with an icy stare.

"You take away the federal squatters and the Washington that's left is just a small town, Salvatore. I make deals for everybody in that town." Ronzini's eyes never even blinked. "You think you are bigger than everybody? You are not even bigger than me. You lack humility, a sense of your own place in this big machine. You need to learn. Your problem with this man is just your problem. This you will do yourself."

Hannibal watched Sal's self-esteem rising and falling in his father's eyes. He knew Sal saw it too and realized what he must do. When he turned, Hannibal faced him on the other side of a square table, his fists held loosely in front of him. Sal curled his hands into new, tighter fists and pulled himself into a martial arts attack stance.

"All right, boy," Sal hissed, closing in on Hannibal. "Guess it's time for your ass whipping. I been studying Tae kwon Do since I'm seven. You want to quit now?"

Hannibal walked in a slow ark to Sal's left. "You think you want some of this? Then come on. Bring it. Time for talk is past, boy."

"You got that shit right," Sal answered. Then he leaped forward quickly. One foot landed on a table. The other lashed out in a wide arc that caught the side of Hannibal's head. Spinning away from his enemy, Hannibal felt his ribs grate against the table's edge before he regained his balance. When he stood straight, blood dribbled from the corner of his mouth.

The light of victory shone prematurely in Sal's face. From a standing start on the table he leaped forward. His flying stamp kick tore across the forearms Hannibal raised to block it. Hannibal staggered back. Sal launched forward in a flying stamp kick into Hannibal's chest. Hannibal's feet left the ground momentarily and he crashed down in the center of a table, shattering it around him as he drove through to the floor.

Sal stopped to scan the impassive faces of his father and the other three men in the room, as if he expected these experts in violence to be impressed. Substituting viciousness for technique, he snapped a foot into Hannibal's ribs.

"Shouldn't have got in my way, you dumb nigger." Sal's words focused Hannibal past the pain. He rolled onto his side, curling up, and suddenly lashed out with a stamp kick into Sal's abdomen hard enough to shove him back against the bar.

Sal shouted, "You son of a bitch," springing forward from the bar. Hannibal barely got to his feet before Sal smashed a hard right into his jaw. He caught the follow up left cross on a forearm and counter punched, a snappy jab that caught Sal just over his right eye.

"It ain't free, boy," Hannibal rasped as they stood face to face, their fists hiding them from each other.

Except their eyes.

Sal's gave him away. Hannibal saw a reverse punch coming and accepted it against his cheek for a chance at Sal's ribs. His left hook rocked the Italian boy back. Sal responded with a wheel kick, but Hannibal leaned quickly enough to take it on his right shoulder. Sal took a step back, then forward with a front stamp kick. Hannibal blocked the heel on crossed forearms. It hurt him, but he stayed on his feet.

"That all you got, son?" Hannibal asked. "Better get hot. I'm almost warmed up." Sal practically roared his anger. Three rapid kicks followed from different angles. Hannibal managed to block the first two, but the third caught the side of his head. He rolled across a table, smashing a chair into kindling on his way to the floor.

Rage blazed from Sal's eyes as he kicked and tossed chairs out of his path on his way to Hannibal's landing site. When he got there, he stamped down on empty space.

"That's about enough," Hannibal said from the other side of a table he had rolled under. Quickly sidestepping, he slammed a left hook under Sal's guard and deep into his solar plexus. Air blew out of Sal, just before Hannibal's right cross snapped his head around. Sal tried to retaliate with a side stamp kick, but Hannibal hopped back out of reach.

Waving his enemy toward him with an upturned fist, Hannibal backpedaled into the clear area in front of the bar. Sal wiped the corner of his lip, noticed blood on his hand, and followed.

Hannibal started bobbing and weaving. Sal set himself for an assault, but misread the signals Hannibal was sending. Just as the younger Ronzini shifted his weight for another kick, Hannibal moved in, driving a hard right jab into the other man's stomach.

"That's all you get for a while," Hannibal said, leaning back. "School's in." His soft bluish eyes flicked to Ox, Petey, and Dennis on the other side of the room. All three men stood relaxed, watching with cold, professional attention. Sal watched Hannibal closely, but never caught his rhythm.

Three more times Sal tried to deliver a snap kick or a stamp. All three times Hannibal moved first, slamming a black gloved fist into Sal's midsection. Desperation and pain showed on Sal's face, but he stepped back and whipped a kick at Hannibal's head. This time Hannibal hooked Sal's leg in his arm and swept his other foot out from under him. When Sal rolled to his feet, he was no longer moving in.

"You got good training, kid." Hannibal stepped in a slow circle around Sal. "Good technique. But you ain't been in no fights, have you? I mean, not real fights. Didn't take too many trips to the ring to teach me not to kick too much too early. Tires you out."

Sal's breathing was fast and ragged, but he was in no way out of the action. He half turned, as if confused, but snapped up a side thrusting kick. It was so fast that the four spectators barely saw. The material of Sal's pants snapped with the speed of the kick.

Hannibal slapped the foot away with his left hand.

"Your stomach's too sore to get any power into your kicks, boy," Hannibal said, as if addressing a slow student. Then he feinted to Sal's head and drove forward, landing a hard three part combination: left-right to the stomach and a left uppercut that put Sal back four steps before he regained his balance.

Hannibal's arms felt like lead, but he knew his job was not over. Sal was hurt, but not beaten. Side stepping, Hannibal got his back to the bar. Sal's eyes were wary, but his arrogant confidence was shaken. Hannibal lowered his hands and, after a few false moves with his shoulders, leaped up. His left foot barely left the ground, but his right heel slapped Sal's blocking arm into his head so hard he was sure Ox heard it across the room.

Panting, Sal spun back quickly, bringing his right hand down like an ax toward his opponent's neck. Hannibal leaned back out of range and brought up a roundhouse kick, his right foot chopping up into Sal's gut.

This time Sal stayed partially doubled over. He looked up at Hannibal, holding his hands as if to block another attack. Sweat dripped from Sal's forehead, mingled with blood from a gash there. His panting gasps made him sound like a young boy about to cry.

Dirty sweat also dripped into Hannibal's eyes, making them sting, but he did not dare block his vision wiping it away. Sore and aching, he turned an inquiring gaze at Ronzini, who had watched this ordeal with no sign of reaction on his face. The older man lowered his eyes almost closed, and tilted his head forward an inch.

Continue.

Hannibal's anger was renewed, but he did not know why. Straightening himself, he again made eye contact with the younger Ronzini. His hesitation ended when he saw Sal's lips move, forming the words "fuck you". With a shout, Hannibal jumped and twisted, executing a textbook perfect spinning back kick.

Sal never had a chance. The blow's full force took him in the center of his chest. Sal's sternum flexed in, then out, and he flew across open space. His back took the full impact on a table and he rolled backward over it. He landed among a group of wooden chairs, making a noise much like the sound of bowling a strike.

Shifting his aching shoulders, Hannibal walked methodically forward to Sal, who had managed to get up on one knee.

"You done?" Hannibal asked.

"Fuck you," Sal spat, slurring through swollen lips. Hannibal's uppercut caught the point of his chin, lifting him unsteadily to his feet. Hannibal followed that with a series of minor jabs, tossing Sal's face to one side, then the other, until his resolve crumbled, and he made the transition from blocking to covering up. When next he gasped in pain, it sounded like a sob.

"Leave me alone," Sal whined through clenched, useless fists. Hannibal paused long enough to catch a breath, then drove a sharper, stinging jab between Sal's hands. A tooth tore his glove over his middle knuckle.

Sal lay flat on his back across a table, staring helplessly upward, arms at his sides. Trained for three-minute rounds, Hannibal could barely lift his own arms by this time. He managed to get his fingers into Sal's collar and lift the man's upper body. His right arm cocked back, readying a pounding blow he had been saving since the day Sal Ronzini kicked him from behind and left him lying in a pile of trash.

"Enough," Ronzini called from behind the bar. His voice sounded strained, but only a little, as if something he saw had unexpectedly bothered him. Hannibal turned toward him, pulling back his lips, showing his teeth in a death's head grimace. His arm cocked back one more inch. Ox stepped forward, one step. Hannibal turned his deadly grimace toward him. Ox's dispassionate face reminded Hannibal of his professional status. With a look of disgust, he opened his left hand, letting Sal's head thump back onto the table.

When Hannibal reached the bar, exhaustion suddenly wrapped around him like a wet sheet. Afraid to sit, he leaned one arm on the bar and put a foot up on the brass rail. Inches from Ronzini's face, he wondered what he could possibly do if his host decided one of his three flunkies should shoot him through the head.

"Satisfied?" Hannibal asked.

Ronzini nodded. "Yes. It is done." Hannibal reached for his gun, but Ronzini raised an index finger to stop him. "Your business with my son is over. You will not become involved in his affairs again."

Hannibal looked at Sal, raising a hand in his direction. "It's over. He stays out of my way." Again Ronzini nodded.

Hannibal placed his hand over his pistol's grip, laying his index finger on the trigger guard. Dennis and Petey reached under their jackets but Hannibal's focus stayed on Ronzini.

"And you and the boy both stay out my hood," Hannibal snarled, pushing his face forward, almost nose to nose with the other man. Ronzini's face showed he did not quite understand. Hannibal took a deep breath and tried to pretend he was dealing with a businessman, not a street hood. "I want you and Salvatore to stay away from my neighborhood. A five-block radius around that house I just moved into. Those people are my neighbors and are to be considered to be under my personal protection."

All eyes now shifted to Ronzini. Showing no emotion, he again nodded slightly forward. "We stay out of your...hood," he said. Hannibal smiled with the left side of his mouth, the side whose lip was not split, and pushed his automatic into its shoulder holster. Rolling along the bar, he got his back against it so both elbows could support him. Ahead of him, Sal lay unconscious on a table, unaware of the commitment he had just made. It did not matter. He was without honor. Hannibal assumed his father was not.

"Our business is concluded," Ronzini said. He poured himself one last drink. "Be gone when Salvatore wakes up."

Hannibal pushed himself away from the bar. "Dennis," he called. "I need a ride home. To Anacostia." Dennis looked at Ronzini, who nodded assent. Hannibal, meanwhile, had reached the restaurant's front door and tried the knob. It was locked with a dead bolt that had no handle.

"I don't do back doors," Hannibal said arrogantly. Ronzini smiled and tossed Dennis a set of keys. Hannibal stood wishing the man could move a bit faster as Dennis unlocked and opened the front door. They passed through, just as Ox and Petey picked Salvatore Ronzini up from the table.

As Hannibal approached the Continental, he heard a high, piercing whistle.

"Hey, Chico. I drive Mr. Jones."

It was Ray's voice. Hannibal looked to his left to see Ray standing behind the white Volvo's open driver's door. Sarge stood on the other side.

"Sorry, Dennis," Hannibal said. "I made a deal with this guy for the next four weeks."

Seeing how slowly Hannibal was walking, Sarge opened the back door for him. Swallowing pained noises, Hannibal slowly pushed himself into the Volvo's back seat and closed the door. He was pleasantly surprised to find Cindy in the back seat. As he settled into the seat she leaned her head into his chest, but stayed quiet. He wasn't sure how she knew this was not the time for questions. He was just happy to put his arm around her and enjoy the silence. Her head fell against his chest and her warmth seemed to breathe life back into him.

As Ray pulled the car away from the curb, Hannibal felt a sense of blessed closure. He hurt everywhere, but he felt good. He was happy this case was over and miserable about how it ended. He had managed to do what he was hired for, and had certainly earned his fee, but Dan Balor had paid too dearly for what he got.

At least Ray would be able to get his taxi business going. Hannibal would see to that. But what would become of his other new friends, Sarge, Quaker, and Virgil? And what about Timothy? He didn't really know, and maybe he shouldn't. He finally saw that their fates were not up to him to settle, but were in their own hands.

Would all the drug users find a new place to commit slow suicide? That he was sure of, and again, it was their own choice.

"You know, now I put so much work into it, I kind of like that building in Anacostia," Ray said from the front seat. "Hey, Hannibal, how much you think the rent will be there? Maybe I'll just rent one of those flats."

"Let's ask Balor tomorrow," Hannibal said. "We can be neighbors." He did not know he was going to say that until it came out. He did not know when he made the decision to stay in that run down, lousy apartment. He did not know how he would run his business from there, or even if the furnace in that building would keep his apartment warm in the winter.

But with a smile he realized that he did know who would help him decorate it.

THE END

Author's Bio

Austin S. Camacho is a public affairs specialist for the Department of Defense. America's military people overseas know him because for more than a decade his radio and television news reports were transmitted to them daily on the American Forces Network.

He was born in New York City but grew up in Saratoga Springs, New York. He majored in psychology at Union College in Schenectady, New York. Dwindling finances and escalating costs brought his college days to an end after three years. He enlisted in the Army as a weapons repairman but soon moved into a more appropriate field. The Army trained him to be a broadcast journalist. Disc jockey time alternated with news writing, video camera and editing work, public affairs assignments and news anchor duties.

During his years as a soldier, Austin lived in Missouri, California, Maryland, Georgia and Belgium. While enlisted he finished his Bachelor's Degree at night and started his Master's, and rose to the rank of Sergeant First Class. In his spare time, he began writing adventure and mystery novels set in some of the exotic places he'd visited.

After leaving the Army he continued to write military news for the Defense Department as a civilian. Today he handles media relations and writes articles for the DoD's Deployment Health Support Directorate. He has settled in northern Virginia with his wife Dee and son Phillip.

Austin is a voracious reader of just about any kind of nonfiction, plus mysteries, adventures and thrillers. When he isn't working or reading, he's writing.

Website: www.ascamacho.com
Email: ascamacho@hotmail.com

Other Hannibal Jones Mysteries by Austin S. Camacho

Blood and Bone

An eighteen-year-old boy lies dying of leukemia. Kyle's only hope is a bone marrow transplant, but no one in his family can supply it. His last chance lies in finding his father, who disappeared before he was born. Kyle's family has nowhere to turn until they learn of a certain troubleshooter - that self-styled knight errant in dark glasses, Hannibal Jones. But his search for the missing man turns up much more: A woman who might be Kyle's illegitimate sister, the woman who could be her mother, and a man who may have killed Kyle's father. Hannibal follows a twisting path of deception, conspiracy and greed, from Washington to Mexico, but with each step the danger grows.

Collateral Damage

Bea Collins was troubled when she went to Hannibal Jones' office. Her fiancé Dean had disappeared. Hannibal Jones, the troubleshooter, agreed to help her, even though he feared that his quarry had simply run off with another woman after taking most of Bea's money.

Little did Hannibal suspect that he would find Dean just before the man was accused of the bloody murder of a co-worker. Suddenly, Hannibal had a new client. Not only did the murder weapon and other evidence point to Dean, but Dean couldn't seem to remember what happened. Police believed that Dean might be following in the footsteps of his own mother, who had been convicted of killing Dean's father. Or was Dean covering for his mother, now out of prison and considered a possible serial killer.

The trail leads from Washington DC to Las Vegas and even to Germany, where Hannibal stumbles upon a third murder which seems linked to Dean's life. The web of murder also ties Dean to Joan, his sexy female boss, as well as the man Dean is accused of murdering. The killings have destroyed the lives connected to them, friends and family who represent the murder's collateral damage. It soon becomes clear that Hannibal will have to solve all three cases in order to clear Dean's name.